· JESSA ·
IS
BACK

· JESSA ·
IS
BACK

Stacia Moffett

ISBN: 978-1-59849-368-9
Library of Congress Control Number: 2024905706

BISAC Codes:
FIC074000 FICTION / Southern
FIC014000 FICTION / Historical / General
FIC066000 FICTION / Small Town & Rural

Printed in Korea

Editor: Danielle Harvey
Design: Soundview Design

www.lostandfoundintennessee.com

Requests for such permissions should be addressed to:

Classic Day Publishing
Seattle, Washington 98102
206-860-4900
www.classicdaypub.com

*The Lost and Found Books are dedicated to my parents,
who gave me so much to be thankful for, and to our two
granddaughters, Octavia and Marianne, as a way to tell
them about a history I was present for. I want to thank my
husband, David, for his early and continuing support of my
writing project, and I am grateful for the encouragement of
family and friends. My life has been enriched by many dogs,
and they could not help but get in the books!*

· ACKNOWLEDGMENTS ·

I am very grateful to all who read and commented on the manuscripts. They include Bob Babcock, Rolinda J. Bailey, Nikki Giovanni, Kelly Mcgee, Samantha McMahon, Patricia Perkins, Jon Rosenthal, Elizabeth Schuerman, Jerry Silvey, Jim Weddell, and David Wilma.

Also, I would like to credit the team at Classic Day Publishing for their help in bringing the books together: Elliott Wolf, Danielle Harvey, Ruthie Little, and Amy Vaughn.

When Jessa returns to Tennessee from Oregon, she has changed in an important way: she now has a best friend who is Negro. The Jim Crow practices in Tennessee come into sharp focus as she sees the many ways the laws and local customs are designed to keep the races apart. It turns out that Jessa is not the only one struggling with that issue, but white bigotry is deeply entrenched, and forces are mounting throughout the South to oppose *Brown v. Board of Education*. What Jessa is able to accomplish by pushing for a small change in the schools is secondary to her understanding that the problem could be solved if people of different races have a fair chance to get to know one another.

We must learn to live together as brothers
or perish together as fools.

– Martin Luther King, Jr.

· CHAPTER 1 ·

As the train sped along the tracks into Tennessee, Jessa rested her cheek against the cool window. Six months ago, she and Cassie had traveled west with her mother's cousin, admiring the deserts, mountains, rivers, and plains. In Oregon, everything had been new and exciting, but now, returning home, it was the Tennessee landscape that stirred her to tears. She hadn't realized how much she had missed her native countryside. The lazy brown rivers draped with grapevines and kudzu, the lush green cornfields and pastures, the red clay and stratified limestone in the road cuts, the familiar hardwood trees—they all welcomed her like family. She recalled family trips and the songs they used to sing. How they'd laughed and laughed as they made up new verses for "She'll Be Coming 'Round the Mountain."

That was before everything changed. Her throat tightened at the thought that her family, the core of her life in Tennessee, would not be here to greet her and say it was all a bad dream. Her vision blurred, and she let her dark hair curtain her face to hide her tears. After all, Jessa was twelve, too old to behave this way.

Jessa wiped her eyes and thought again about her goal for the summer. This plan had crystallized when she was hiding out on her grandfather's farm and the people in town thought she had been kidnapped. All through the months in Portland, whenever she thought of her dead parents, she had renewed her commitment to the plan she had dedicated to them. Now, she'd returned to Tennessee for her custody hearings, but her own focus was on fulfilling the dreams her father had had for the town's music program.

With a final hissing squeal, the train jolted to a stop inside the station. Her relatives, her wonderful new family, rose to join Jessa at the door. Together, the two adults, three children, and Jessa's dog stood waiting in anticipation. Thirteen-year-old April put down her suitcase to smooth the wrinkles in her skirt and reached up to spread her silky, brown ponytail. April's brother, eleven-year-old Michael, knelt to retie his shoelace. Jessa's dog nosed her hand, and she bent to reassure her, whispering, "We're home, Cassie! We're back in Tennessee!"

Finally, the door opened, and steps were placed beside the train. Cassie bounded onto the platform with Jessa just behind, followed by April, Michael, and their parents. The older Acrees were dressed stylishly in seersucker suits recommended for the heat. Ben had an athlete's build, and his wavy, sandy hair framed dark eyes and high cheekbones. Karen was petite and smiling, with dancing brown eyes and dark hair that circled her face in curls.

"Wow, is this hot, or what?" Michael wiped sweat across his newly acquired flat-top haircut as the sultry air hit them. They merged with the traffic moving toward the station and halted as a surge of travelers moving the opposite way temporarily blocked their path. Jessa's heart was beating fast, and she breathed in the air in big gasps. *We're home! I'm back in my world! Tennessee!*

Cassie's wet nose sought her hand, and Jessa touched and spoke encouragingly to the black poodle as they entered the cavernous interior of the L&N Station. Newspaper hawkers and shoeshine boys shouted to be heard over the hisses and squeals of brakes and the announcements reverberating throughout the lobby. " Read it, read all about it: Federal court rules Montgomery bus segregation unconstitutional." Another countered: "Get the *Tennessean*, read about Ike's operation," and another called out, "Massive earthquake in Afghanistan. Nineteen fifty-six will go down in history, 7.6 on the Richter scale. Get the story now!"

Jessa's happy smile evoked smiles from everyone. She hadn't known how much she'd missed the honeyed accents of home, the congenial faces. Michael pointed at the pigeons circling and landing near the train station's vaulted ceiling, oblivious of the crowds below. The once-jeweled stained-glass windows were coated with soot, so little light penetrated the colored glass. April's attention was drawn to the gleaming wood and marble at the ticket stations, where the hands and elbows of passengers had hollowed and polished the surfaces. The spell of the reverberating space engulfed them. Even in the late morning sunshine, spirits seemed to haunt the place, trapped there by arrivals and departures that had forever changed people's lives.

This family's previous trip had been an attempt to patch together the schism created by such a departure many years ago, although Karen was painfully aware that her father had not left Tennessee as a comfortable passenger. For her, riding the train had been a reminder of his stories of traveling as a hobo. For her, this trip offered the promise of finding people who had known her father as a boy, to explore the mystery of his early life.

Cassie stuck close to Jessa's side, looking for her to explain why they had come to this frightening place. In the confusion of announcements, wailing babies, and rushing travelers, they set out to locate restrooms. April pointed out the doors labeled White Only Gentlemen and White Only Ladies, but they were being cleaned, with the doors propped open. Michael studied the situation with wide, brown eyes.

He nudged April. "I wonder where you go if you aren't white?"

They joined the crowd milling outside the restrooms. One family, colored, skirted past them, and Michael saw the father question a shoeshine boy and get directions. Curious, Michael followed them down a dark corridor to doors labeled Colored Men and Colored Women. He was entering the Colored Men restroom when a station manager scolded him with "Don't *you* go in there! You want to get diseases, son?"

Back with his family, Michael exclaimed, "Boy, was that an insult!"

His father shushed him.

"The real insult is to the colored people," April whispered.

Distress transformed Jessa's face. Since leaving Tennessee, her life had been transformed by a new friendship. Her friend, Janie, her best friend in Portland, was Negro. Together, they'd ridden their bikes and taken the buses to the dime stores, and in that freedom she had forgotten that in Tennessee that would be impossible.

They filed out of the station into brilliant sunshine. Waves of heat reflected from every surface and penetrated their shoes as they headed toward the bus stop. Cassie's feet were clearly suffering, so Jessa found shade behind a streetlight post and pulled the black dog into it. As they scanned the oncoming traffic for a bus, a woman approached with a small girl and asked if the dog could be petted.

"Oh, yes, Cassie loves attention," Jessa replied.

The child timidly patted Cassie's nose and giggled as a pink tongue curled around her fingers. The little girl's black hair was divided into squares pulled into tiny braids tied with bows, and she tossed it back and giggled again as Jessa asked Cassie to sit up for her.

"Thank you, honey. She needs to meet good dogs. My brother's dogs jump and knock her over, and it's made her afraid of them."

As the woman and child moved back into the sidewalk traffic, April said, "Isn't it nice the way strangers call you *honey*!"

April's mother said, "Yes, and I must say Cassie *was* sweet. I wouldn't blame her if she were irritable in this heat! She must be doing better than I am, with my slip sticking to me and every breath an effort."

"I feel like I'm pushing through a brick wall!" Michael responded, punching the air.

"Mama, isn't this the humidity your teacher friends warned you about?" said April. "Remember how they laughed when you said you were taking your summer vacation in Tennessee?"

"Yes," said Karen. "They said Tennessee would be hard to take, and now I understand what they were talking about."

"I never paid any attention to humidity, growing up here, but now I'm spoiled by the Oregon climate," said Jessa. "There's a bus coming—you think they'll let us take Cassie on?"

Ben said, "Jessa, Karen and I decided to give it a try, and if a dog can't ride in the bus, we'll hail a cab." When the nearly empty bus pulled into the stop, Ben stepped on and asked the driver, "Can you get us near the Hermitage Hotel?"

"Right to the door," said the driver.

"Could a very well-behaved dog ride?"

Peering around Ben to see the dog, the driver smiled and nodded. "Just this once. Keep him out of the aisle."

They climbed on, dropped coins into the slot, and heaved their suitcases ahead of themselves as they followed Michael down to the long, empty seat that stretched across the back of the bus. Jessa scooted Cassie into the far-right corner where she would be mostly hidden.

The bus driver started to move into traffic but put on the brakes and craned his neck to address them, "You Northerners see that white line on the floor? Y'all belong in front of that white line."

Ben and Karen looked at each other. The driver had let Cassie on, but he could easily put them back off. They gathered their luggage and prepared to move, but cringed when

Michael called out, "Mr. Driver, we just liked being together back here."

Ben squelched him. "We'll move, sir—we didn't notice the line." He signaled for them all to push forward.

April shrugged and grabbed her suitcase, but Jessa's face was red, and her lips were pressed in a tight line as they settled into seats near the front. Her friendship with Janie had been a first for her, the first chance to be friends with a Negro girl. She imagined Janie having to stay at the back of the bus while she, her white friend, was forced to move up. Back in orchestra class on the last day, when saying good-byes, Jessa had so much wished that Janie could make the trip with them. Now, she reproached herself for forgetting what Tennessee was like for colored people.

Despite their curiosity about these Northerners and the dog that was allowed to ride in the bus, the few Negro passengers looked down and pretended to not notice what was happening. The family settled into their new seats in silence, enduring their discomfort as sweat trickled down their faces and the heat stuck their clothes to the seats. More passengers boarded at each stop, always assorting themselves according to the white line on the floor of the bus.

Aware of Jessa's distress, and wanting to avoid a scene, Ben pulled the cord for a stop as soon as he recognized the Hermitage Hotel up ahead. The driver turned and said, "I can get you one block closer."

Ben said, "Thank you, this will be fine. We can walk from here."

They began walking toward the hotel. The weight of their suitcases added to the heat to make the walk unpleasant, and Cassie's normally happy flag of a tail was carried at half-mast as she limped along on the hot pavement, but no one complained.

Suddenly, Jessa halted in the middle of the sidewalk and

stood there, tears running down her face. The family stopped and people had to walk around them.

"I just can't stand it. What if Janie had come with us? Back at the station, I realized that she would have had to use those different restrooms. And we couldn't even sit together on the bus!"

"Come on, Jessa. You grew up here, so you shouldn't be surprised," said Karen. "Act like the well-behaved young lady I know you are. Let's get our room and talk through it in private."

In the hotel lobby, the bell hops offered to take their luggage, but they clung stubbornly to their bags and politely refused. There was no way to be directed to their rooms without having one of the uniformed Negro men accompany them, and Ben tipped him generously.

Once the door clicked shut, Ben wiped his brow and said, "I'm not used to having people waiting on me when I'm perfectly capable of carrying my own bag. It makes me uncomfortable. It would be different if we really needed help, you know?"

"Yeah, I know," said Michael.

"I realize these people have to make a living, but we've been carrying our bags all this way, and it seemed artificial to have them taken from us just so someone could get a tip for handing them back. Don't you think people need work that has more meaning? Did I do the wrong thing?"

"Dear, I don't think you offended anyone. Many people need or appreciate the help. Maybe they can excuse us as ignorant Northerners."

"Well, I'm gonna keep toting my own bag," said Michael. "Northerners like us like to be self-reliant."

"I guess I'm still a Southerner, but in my family we always carried our luggage," said Jessa.

They filled and refilled the glasses they found next to the lavatory. The room's air was stuffy, but opening a window didn't seem like a solution, so they flopped down on the beds. April noticed the tears streaked along Jessa's face and brought her a tissue from the box in the bathroom.

"Thank you, April. I'm sorry I behaved like a child, everybody, but it seems so unfair when I think of Janie. I know it's been this way all my life," said Jessa. "Back in Portland, when I was getting to know Janie, I told her all about where I came from, all the good things, but I forgot it would be this way for her! How could I have been so stupid?"

"Jessa, the first time we came to Tennessee, we were shocked to see Negro men and women doing all the menial labor. In Oregon, you don't see that, because there wasn't the history of servitude like in the South," said Ben. "Oregon doesn't have the relatively large population of colored people that can be exploited to fill low-paying jobs."

"What you mean is, Oregon doesn't have a history of slavery," said Michael.

"Michael, you'd better be careful what you say in public," said Karen. "We were Northerners to that bus driver, and we have to recognize that we're visiting a different part of the nation. It's like *When in Rome, do as the Romans.*"

Michael squirmed. "When in Tennessee, do as the Tennesseans—that it?"

"No, I don't like that," said Jessa. "It's my home state. It isn't a foreign country, and it doesn't have to be this way! In Portland, my friend Janie can go to the same school we do—she even plays the flute! If she were here, she'd have to go into those colored restrooms and ride in the back of the bus. She'd have to go to a crummy school that doesn't have a music program!"

"Sorry, Jessa," said April.

"Jessa, I suspected it would hit you pretty hard when you came back, especially after you and Janie became best friends," said Ben. "But did you never discuss race relations with Janie?

I don't know what her family has experienced, but Portland isn't the wonderful place for colored people you might imagine. Certainly its history is pretty sordid."

"What do you mean?"

"There's a long history of the Ku Klux Klan's presence in Portland. The governor was in their pocket in the nineteen-twenties."

"And there were laws that kept Negroes from coming into the area, even before Oregon was a state," said Michael. "A sundown law said they had to be out of town before dark."

Karen added, "Jessa, if only you could have known my father and talked to him. Years ago, Dad led our Friends Meeting's response to the Klan. Negroes were in short supply to be targeted by the KKK in Oregon, so they took on other minorities, like Catholics, Jews, and Japanese."

"Oh, but I thought Oregon was different. Are things horrible everywhere? Why?"

"Jessa, people everywhere are trying to make things better," said Ben. "Even here in Tennessee. Remember the night we went to your welcome-back party at the Carlsons'? Your orchestra director must be on your side. At least he seemed pretty open-minded to me. He volunteered that he wanted to teach a beginners' class at the colored school."

"Daddy was disappointed he didn't get to do it," said Jessa, "but I heard Daddy talking about the strategy he was going to use, and it's what I'll do. I'll meet with the school board, and I've been rehearsing what to say. I figured it all out, back when I was hiding. I kept thinking about Daddy's dreams then. Now's the perfect time because Daddy said they make the curriculum decisions in the summer."

"You may be able to use your celebrity status as the missing kid to accomplish more than your father was able to do, but I recommend that you choose your battles," suggested Karen. "Just go along with the bus seating rules, the segregated restrooms, and the other local conventions and focus your energy on the school board. Just remember that we need to stay on the good side of these people to smooth the way for getting your custody papers signed."

"Jessa, Cassie looks *really* thirsty. Don't you have her water bowl in your suitcase?" asked April.

"Oh, poor Cassie! I forgot her when we were all hot, and I know the sidewalk burnt her feet—I'll get her water bowl."

Cassie lay on the cool tiles and lapped messily from the bowl. "At least Cassie got her nice, cool clip for the trip—thank you, everyone!"

Jessa knelt and hugged her dog. They had been inseparable through all the trials of trying to live in the forest. Together, she and Cassie had eluded the search efforts for weeks, while fear of kidnapping captured the minds of the Radford population and drove them to seize upon a Negro mechanic as the scapegoat.

"Cassie'd better go out for a walk now so she can stay here while we get something to eat," said Karen.

"Jessa, can you take her alone? I've *got* to change out of this dress—it's sticking to my body," said April.

"I'll go with Jessa and Cassie," said Michael. "I want to scout around for some place to eat besides that formal dining room." In the elevator, Michael confided, "Jessa, I'm with you. I don't go along with this *when in Rome* stuff!"

"Michael, I know things can be better. When we get to Radford, I'll meet with the school board. It's a small thing for them to add music to the colored school curriculum, but it's a start, and I promised Daddy in heaven I'd do it."

"I dunno, Jessa. My civics teacher told us all about how it is in the South. There's really bad stuff, especially in states like Mississippi. But now it's gotta change. Now, separate colored and white schools are outlawed."

Jessa, turned to him as the elevator door opened. "You really think so?"

"Yep. It's not supposed to be that way anymore, not since nineteen-fifty-four. Our civics teacher told us about the Supreme Court ruling—*Brown v. Board of Education*. He read it aloud, all the way through, and said the decision was unanimous. He talked about the evidence the justices considered, like how the colored girls chose white dolls in preference to brown ones. Society had brainwashed them into thinking brown was inferior!"

"I wonder what the school board in Radford thinks about the ruling," mused Jessa.

They led Cassie to the space set aside for dogs. Michael was on her side, and it gave Jessa confidence. Now, she could hardly wait to meet with the school board.

· CHAPTER 2 ·

Jessa wanted her new-found family to experience all the things about Tennessee that she was proud of. Her parents had run a music store and loved all kinds of music, but they had never been to the Grand Ole Opry in the few times they'd traveled to Nashville. It was always something that they would get around to doing someday. Now, it could never happen, but Jessa thought this would be a good opportunity for the Acrees to get to know Tennessee better, so she persuaded them to plan the train trip to arrive for the Saturday event.

They sat near the front of the bus for the ride downtown. The bus chugged its way up the hill, made a turn, and stopped in the traffic. April tapped Jessa's shoulder and pointed out the window where they had a view into an alley. Halfway down the alley, colored children were lined up by the fire-escape stairs.

Jessa grimaced as she recognized what was going on: Negro children and some teenagers were waiting in line to pay to see the matinee. The main line was in front of the theater, but they couldn't join that line or sit in the auditorium. Instead, they would pay to climb the fire-escape stairs and be hidden in the balcony, out of sight from the main auditorium. Jessa thought of Janie, and how much fun they had the last day of math class, beating out the boys in the teacher's version of a spelling bee for geometry. If Janie were here, she would see that line... Jessa began to count all the ways that Tennessee would separate Janie from her, just because Janie was Negro. She wondered whether Portland had laws that she didn't know about and decided to write Janie and ask.

They'd planned to eat a late lunch and then sight-see a bit before the Opry performance, which started in the evening, but when they saw the line already stretching down the sidewalk from the Ryman Auditorium, they realized they might not get in if they didn't join it right away. Ben headed for the Krystal Hamburger joint while the rest of the family held his place in line.

Unlike the mix of races on the downtown streets, the people waiting to get into the Opry were white. Colorful booths lined the steep sidewalk, selling postcards, souvenir pins, caps, cowboy hats, scarves printed with a map of Tennessee and MOTHER, and little flags with the stars and stripes and the Confederate stars and bars.

Ben hiked up the hill with dinner before the line moved, sweating from his exertion. The family hungrily consumed two of the little square Krystal hamburgers and a cold drink each. The heat barely diminished as the sun grew lower in the sky and the buildings cast long shadows. They talked with their neighbors in the line, exchanging genial comments about foreign-sounding accents. Some had traveled a long way to be there, but no one had come from as far away as Oregon. Before long, the line began to inch forward, and finally, Ben paid for their tickets and they got their souvenir programs. They entered the large, dimly-lit auditorium with the late evening's sunshine beaming through its church-like windows. Michael led the way to a stretch of empty spaces in the middle section, and they scooted in, surrounded by excited people of all ages.

The curtain went up, and the crowd hushed as the stage lights illuminated the impressive props. The performance was broadcast live on WSM, the "music channel," and announcements and musical ads were enthusiastically rendered before the first act commenced. April was intrigued by the square dancers, the men in chaps and shirtsleeves with glittering fringes, and the women in colorful skirts with flounces and layers of crinoline. After the dancing, a family group appeared and accompanied a little boy with a cowboy hat, chaps, and sequined vest. He played a small banjo quite competently, followed by huge applause. Then a pig was led on stage as part of a commercial for Purina feeds that claimed to produce the biggest weaner pigs for market.

Watching the performance, Jessa ached for her parents. How she wished they could be here now. Why did they have to die? Wouldn't it have been wonderful if they could have gotten to know their Oregon relatives and shared this visit to the Opry? The last time she had gone to Nashville with her father, the line of people had stretched down the street, and they had wanted to join it. Her father had promised her that one day they would all see it together, but now, that was impossible.

Jessa's eyes began to fill with tears, but she blinked them back, bit her lips and dug her fingernails into her fists. She focused on the violin played by the band member who'd moved downstage to the microphone and was shocked to see the thick white rosin dust on the violin's fingerboard. Her father had always instructed students who rented the shop's violins to wipe off the rosin before putting their violin away because rosin was bad for the violin's varnish. They even provided a little cloth with the rental violins for wiping the instruments. *I know he wouldn't have liked that*, she thought.

Another act was announced, and they apparently weren't ready, so Minnie Pearl—a well-known comedian at the Opry—sashayed out onto the stage, calling out "Howdeeeeeee!"

She received an answering call from the delighted audience, reset her big flouncy hat, and launched into her monologue, including a bit of dancing and interactions with the announcer. She then retreated to sit on a bale of straw and pretended to pick her teeth with a piece of straw. Jessa looked over at Ben and Karen, worried that they might not be enjoying the show, but they were clearly engaged. She so wanted this family to love Tennessee!

Bluegrass musicians from North Carolina were next, followed by an enthusiastic reception for Johnny Cash, with his hair in a smooth pompadour style and dressed in black, a contrast to the sequined cowboy outfits of the other performers. Among the selections he sang to the worshipful audience was "I Walk the Line," and Jessa noted that Karen seemed to approve the sentiments of the song.

The square dancers appeared once again, taking up the rakes that had been leaning against the barrels and straw bales, and raking the loose straw as they circled and danced across the floor two-by-two. Other acts featured a young boy, already overweight, who sang "He's Got the Whole World In His Hands" with ample gesturing while the crowd sang along with tears in their eyes. Then other members of his family joined in, playing harmonicas, violins, and mandolins. Finally, a pretty, young woman with a sad and lonesome voice took the microphone for several songs.

The stage lights went down, and the house lights came on. They merged with the pack of people, some carrying sleeping children. The family skirted around the lines forming to go backstage to get autographs on their programs and popcorn boxes. Outside, it was dark but still hot, and full buses were already pulling away, puffing a cloud of exhaust.

"Jessa, that was super!" said Michael.

"Yes, it was an evening to remember," said Karen.

"I'm so glad you liked it," said Jessa, searching everyone's faces. If only her parents could be here… She loved this family and knew how lucky she was that they had arrived just when she needed them and welcomed her into their family. Now, she would be depending on them to help her make things right in her hometown.

• CHAPTER 3 •

Early the next morning, they took a cab to the train station to pick up their rental car to drive to Jessa's hometown. Superimposed on the anticipation at going home was Jessa's recognition of the white-only constraints that she saw all around her. She began to worry that the school board would raise more objections than she had imagined when she plotted to fulfill her father's dream. She had assumed it was a technicality, a scheduling problem, that had limited the adoption of music education to the white schools, but now she could see it fit into a pattern. When she recalled her father's frustration over the condition of the colored school, a horrible thought began to take shape in Jessa's mind: *What if the neglect of music education in the colored school was intentional?*

They had been invited to stay with the Carlsons, the couple who had been Jessa's parents' closest friends for as long as she could remember. Jessa counted on Mr. Carlson, a lawyer, to help with her plan for the music program. She knew her father had described his frustrations with the school board to Mr. Carlson, so she felt he would sympathize with her plan. She stroked Cassie's head and settled back into an imaginary meeting with the school board.

Leaving the metropolis, they passed a stretch of used car lots, dead motels, gas stations, and abandoned farms with derelict buildings and peeling billboards that soon gave way to single-lane highways that wound through scrubby fields, forested stretches, and farmland to the northwest corner of the state. When the others exclaimed over the landscape, Jessa identified the crops, including sorghum that looked like corn, sturdy tobacco plants, and the cotton that was just starting to bloom. The small farms typically had a variety of animals and a home garden and orchard in addition to row crops and pastures.

"Tennessee can grow just about anything," she declared, proudly.

They passed a farm with a Negro family in the yard, including a girl Jessa's age who stared at the passing car. Jessa thought of Janie and the secret she'd kept from her Oregon relatives. In the six months she'd lived with them in Oregon, she'd corresponded with her school friends in Tennessee, and one friend, Barbara, had abruptly broken off the friendship, writing that her mother got angry about Jessa's description of her Negro friend and had called Jessa bad names. Barbara had been forbidden to have anything to do with Jessa when she visited. Jessa hadn't wanted her Oregon relatives to know that people in Tennessee were that way, and had tried to put it out of her mind.

Karen turned on the radio and dialed through a series of country music stations, finally settling on a clear rendition of "Cold, Cold Heart" by Hank Williams. When the song was over, the time and the weather forecast were given amid general commentary and commercial messages, but when a woman's voice took up a sad refrain, Karen turned it off. "I wish the local music didn't grate on my nerves," she commented. "I enjoyed the instrumental performances at the Opry last night, but the mournful, complaining, edgy sound of it, especially the women's voices, is too much!"

"It's the accents, don't you think, Mama?" asked April.

"Yes, but also the content of the songs, all about being heartbroken and cheating and loneliness. I get fed up with it," said Karen. "Would anyone like a piece of gum?"

Jessa thought about the country music and how her parents often tuned it out if anything else could be found on the dial. "Karen, I think my parents would have agreed with you. There's more to the Tennessee musical options than country music. On weekends you can get the Nashville Symphony performances on the radio at night."

"I'd like some gum, please," said April. "How about Elvis Presley, Mama? He comes from Tennessee."

"I think I could live without him, April," replied Karen.

"Maybe if he didn't have all the girls screaming over him, he wouldn't be so bad," said Michael.

"Karen, you and my mother would have gotten along really well," said Jessa.

"Yes, Jessa. It's a big hole in my life that I didn't grow up knowing my cousin and my aunt and uncle."

"I wish we'd had a chance to walk around in Nashville—there were so many things I wanted to show you. I love the Arcade. It's like a street with no traffic and has shops all along it on two levels. Daddy and I went to the music shop in the Arcade that's called Strobels. It's much finer than my family's music shop, with drawers and drawers of music and so many beautiful instruments, and a repair shop upstairs. And before you get there, walking down the Arcade, you pass by the store that always has a peanut man giving out a handful of warm, roasted peanuts."

"Really?" said Michael.

"For sure! And another place I visited once was the button shop on the second level of the Arcade—all the buttons were sorted by color, and I wanted all the green buttons."

"I'd have loved to see that," said April.

"There's another kind of music in downtown Nashville, too—if we'd been able to walk around by Harvey's and Cain Sloan—the block with the department stores, shoe stores, and ten-cent stores—you'd often see street musicians there. I remember an older colored man whose legs were just stumps. Another man pulled him along on a low platform to get him to a place where he could sing and play his guitar. The first time I heard him, I was little, and his voice and guitar were so loud that they frightened me, but Daddy held my hand, and we joined the men gathered around him and listened a while and put money in his hat. His singing was different from the Grand Ole Opry style. Daddy said it was the blues, and he wished he could get recordings of it."

Jessa fell silent, and Michael read the Burma-Shave jingles aloud and called out the roadside attractions and amusing place names. Soon, they began to look for a place to eat lunch, and settled on a diner Ben hoped would have good coffee. Jessa led Cassie to some grass to give her a chance to squat, then tied her under a tree. Through the window, they could see the neon lights of a juke box, and as they entered, "Your Cheatin' Heart" was starting up.

Karen almost turned around, but Ben, who was almost a foot taller than his wife, playfully grabbed her elbow and steered her in to a table saying, "Honey, just embrace the experience."

Michael, April, and Jessa, following behind, fell to giggling and had a hard time sobering up enough to look at the menus. The waitress sailed by the table carrying a slice of pie. When she noticed Michael's eyes riveted on the pie, she said, "Sonny, that's our specialty, coconut cream pie."

Ben raised his eyebrows at Karen, and she said, "I gather you want to *embrace the experience...*"

"Well, I don't see any of your soup on the menu, and I bet we can count on a well-balanced meal once we get to the Carlsons'."

The waitress poured two coffees without being asked, then turned to them with her pad ready. Karen nodded to Ben, and he ordered pie all-around and three glasses of milk. They washed up, and when they returned, the milk and frosted glasses of chemical-tasting ice water were waiting. Soon, tall slices of pie, its meringue dotted with tiny honey-colored drops of sweetness, arrived. They ate with relish, more coffee was served, and the glasses of milk were drained.

"Wow, that ought to hold us!" said Michael.

"I can't brag on the coffee, and the water was awful, but it would have been a shame to miss that pie," Karen agreed as they climbed in the car.

"Was it worth putting up with 'Your Cheatin' Heart,' honey?" Ben asked.

Karen gave him a rueful smile.

Jessa settled Cassie in and sank into the middle of the backseat. She closed her eyes and again pictured herself addressing the school board. She would first argue that the three-year trial with a music program should be continued, explaining how much her friends loved learning to play instruments. Then she would move to the necessity to expand the program to include all the students, as her father had wanted. In Portland, Jessa had been reminded of the fledgling music program in her hometown as she enjoyed the smoothly-run orchestra class. She knew that her father had worried that the trial adoption of music classes that he'd campaigned for would be revoked, unless the school board was favorably impressed. Her school friends had written her that they hadn't heard about any changes, but now that the school year was over, the school board might have dismissed Mr. Alton. Jessa knew that he was the best music director they could have hoped for.

Jessa recalled evenings when her father came home from a meeting with the school board so discouraged that he was ready to resign. They'd even insulted him, suggesting that his interest in getting instrumental music on the curriculum was only a way to drum up business for the family's music store. That argument made sense to the other school board members, but Jessa knew why he dreamed of music in the schools. Among his fragmented memories of his parents, his fondest were of his father playing a hammer dulcimer and his mother and father singing together. After his parents, sister, and brothers died of the Spanish flu, he'd lived in one foster home after another, and after that, he'd worked to support himself and put himself through school. He'd never gotten a chance to play an instrument, and it had been many years before he even learned the name of the instrument his father had played.

For years, the school board refused to consider his arguments, calling music a "frill." They joked that if he had his way, he'd replace sports with ballet. Finally, the woman who taught history and chorus retired and they reluctantly agreed to hire an orchestra director on a trial basis to teach beginning band and orchestra as well as chorus. Students had to buy or rent their instruments because the school couldn't afford them, but Jessa's family's shop had made the instruments available inexpensively for everyone. Jessa had studied flute with Mr. Alton, and she knew how popular he was with her classmates. She didn't want the program her father had worked so hard for to end.

As she reviewed the arguments she would make to the school board, Michael's question about the separate white and colored schools kept nagging her. She knew her father had been distressed when the school board agreed to fund the music program for only the white schools, but her father had accepted the partial victory. His strategy was to let them become accustomed to the idea of music in the curriculum first, and then use their own argument that they ran a "separate but equal" system to pressure them to add music to the colored school curriculum. Just before the accident killed her parents, Jessa and her classmates had been preparing a newsletter to promote attendance at the orchestra's first performance so the community would see how valuable the music program was.

Cassie stuck her head out the window, and her long ears blew back as she explored the odors of the countryside.

"Smells like home, Cassie?"

Shell-pink primroses and regal Queen Anne's lace blossoms waved from the roadside.

"It's really beautiful country," said Karen, gazing at the gentle hills. "Now that we can see it without the snow cover, I think I'm falling in love with Tennessee. I'm looking forward to seeing the farm where my father grew up."

"Jessa, what are you going to do first when we get to Radford?" asked Ben.

"I'm focusing on the school board, but I want to see my friends. We'll get together at the library, for old time's sake."

"Great!" said Michael. "Can you still check out books?"

"Sure, I can check out any books you want. Cherry, Jeff, and Alice will be there." Jessa thought of Barbara, but decided to not explain about the troubling letter. She recalled visiting Barbara's antebellum mansion, seeing the servants dressed in matching uniforms and the old slave quarters out by the tennis court.

She said, "You know, before I went to Portland, I never had a chance to know colored people like Janie. In Radford, I'd see colored people my age in stores and on the street, but we were always separated, and I never questioned why it was that way. It's different when you can make friends and share experiences. I think people around here have never questioned how things are. They just do what their parents did before them and never wonder why."

"Jessa, it's more complicated than you think," said Karen, "but keep it in mind that we have some serious legal business to settle to take you back with us to Portland, and we don't want to jeopardize that. Whatever your feelings about segregation, remember that nobody wants to have their way of life criticized by people from somewhere else. I'm glad Michael and April grew up knowing people of different races, but you'll encounter a lot of resistance if you start attacking the social structure around here. The people in Tennessee are proud and won't welcome criticism."

"Proud about what?" asked Michael. "Their corny battlefields with those cannons and piles of cannonballs that we saw advertised at the train station? Or their antebellum mansions? Do those mansions have slave quarters, too?"

"Michael, you are going to have to learn to hold your tongue!" Karen scolded.

"Yes, ma'am. I was just remembering that *Look Magazine* story about Mississippi—it's pretty awful!"

Jessa took a deep breath. She didn't think Tennessee was as bad as Mississippi, but Barbara's place *did* have slave quarters, and they didn't seem ashamed of them, either. It was hard to help her relatives understand what she was struggling with.

"What I think is, the people in Radford could start by changing just a little," said Jessa. "I know it's not major, this music thing, but it could make a difference in people's lives. I'm hoping that if the school board is convinced that music is valuable, they will keep it in the white schools and add it to the colored schools, too."

"Jessa, didn't we agree that this business about separate white and colored schools was silly?" asked Michael.

"Maybe Jessa's wise to try to work within the local culture," said Karen. "It sounds like that was what her father was trying to do."

"But it can't go on that way—it *has* to change, now," insisted Michael.

"Sometimes change takes time, and people have to want to change," said Karen.

"You make it sound like a twelve-step program, Mama," said April. "The addicts have to hit rock bottom before they swear off segregation for life."

"But if the Supreme Court hadn't thought segregation was bad, they wouldn't have abolished it. It'll force the South to change," said Michael. "That's what my civics teacher said!"

"I wonder how they'll do it," mused Jessa. "The white grade school was so full, we had to use the stage and the lunchroom for classes."

"Then they'll have to expand the schools," countered Michael. "That's cheaper than duplicating everything. If the colored kids attend school with white kids, they could be in the music classes that are already taught."

They slowed to drive through a small town. Several churches with spires offered options for worshipers. The red-brick courthouse stood out with its stately white columns. As they circled the town's square, they were closely observed by white men in overalls sitting under the magnolias, generating piles of wood shavings as they whittled, chewed, and spat. A Confederate war hero on horseback reared above a bed of red and white petunias. On the two flagpoles, the American and Confederate flags had equal prominence.

They drove out of the town in silence. Once they were again passing fields of corn and tobacco, Ben commented, "There's a lot that's going to have to change in addition to the schools."

· CHAPTER 4 ·

Ben drove down the wide, tree-lined avenue and parked in front of the Carlsons' beautifully landscaped home. The deep, shady lawn was bordered by flower beds and bushes constrained in a perfection that did not invite trespass. The family gathered their luggage and started up the walkway to the porch, where Jack was waiting for them. Fran, petite and as slim as her husband, burst out the front door, holding her arms open as if to gather them all into her embrace.

"How was the trip, folks? Radford's all abuzz over seeing you again!" Jack Carlson's amiable face broke into a grin as he held out his hand to Ben.

Fran's light-brown pixie curls almost bounced as she held out her arms. "Jessa, come give me a big hug," she said. "My, you're looking pretty—not so skinny, quite a fine young lady! And doesn't Cassie look svelte with her hair all trimmed!" She turned to Karen. "How were the roads?"

"It was a good trip! This weather is quite a contrast to last winter's snow, I must say!" replied Karen.

"Ben, I understand our local mechanics, Ray and Jacob, rounded up a car you can use while you're here," said Jack. "That'll let you drop that rental off in Landsdowne."

"That's great, Jack," said Ben.

"Come on in, April and Michael," said Fran. "I've been looking forward to getting to know you better." As Fran led the family through the house's cool interior, Karen exclaimed over the antique furniture and thick carpets while Jessa recalled her family's many happy visits there. The close connection her parents had had with the Carlsons brought tears to her eyes. She bent to unsnap Cassie's leash and brushed the tears away as she followed everyone through the house. She wondered if these friends had gotten over her parents' deaths.

"I thought we could sit out here on the deck and talk. I've made iced tea, and there're cookies just out of the oven," said Fran.

"Hurrah," said Michael.

"I like that enthusiasm," said Fran. She opened French doors that led onto the shady deck. As they moved onto the deck, it was like walking into a treehouse. The limbs of a magnolia arched over the table, and the heavy fragrance of the enormous blossoms dominated the afternoon breeze. A pair of cardinals flew across the deck to the bird feeder.

"This is a super place!" exclaimed Michael.

"We like it," said Jack. April headed toward the feeder to have a closer look at the unfamiliar red birds. "Watch out for those deck boards in the corner—they're rotten, and I need to replace them."

Fran brought out a platter of still-warm sugar cookies and a tray with tinkling glasses.

"I hope you all take tea with sugar," she said. "I put the sugar in when the tea's still warm, as we always do, but then I remembered that some people don't sweeten their tea."

"We appreciate being treated like family, Fran," said Karen.

"You folks have a lovely place here," said Ben. "We didn't get a chance to really appreciate it when you hosted Jessa's going-away party last winter."

"We're delighted you're back," said Fran with a smile. "I've got the bedrooms ready, and we have plenty of space. We'd love it if you'd spend the whole summer with us. Jessa's family's house is ready for occupancy, though. Jack was over there yesterday and opened windows to air it out and make sure the water and electricity's on."

Jessa caught her breath. Her house? Without her parents? No! She couldn't go back to that house—that wasn't possible!

"It's great to see you both again, but we wouldn't want to impose on you for so long. We actually had been thinking we'd go back to the motel. They wouldn't take payment for the week we stayed there last fall, and I told them we'd be back," said Ben.

"It'd be good for the house to have occupants again, and legally, there's no problem. We should be able to schedule a hearing about Jessa's custody and her inheritance in a few weeks. The situation for the house and music shop is clear-cut. The farm's more of a hassle because there's no will, but I expect a hearing date later in the year," said Jack.

"These cookies are delicious," said April.

"Yes!" Jessa and Michael chimed in.

"How'd you get along in the Portland school, Jessa?" asked Jack.

"I did okay, Mr. Carlson, but lots of things are different," admitted Jessa.

"In what way, Jessa?" asked Fran.

"There's more homework, and I was behind in math. They put me in geometry, and I hadn't finished algebra here, and I didn't like geometry until a friend in my class helped me get it," said Jessa. "Janie's Negro, and we both play flute in orchestra."

"Schools are integrated in Portland, I gather," said Jack.

"How come they aren't that way here?" asked Michael.

"It'll be a long time before the South gets around to desegregating the schools."

"But isn't it the law? My civics teacher said…"

"Michael, don't be argumentative," said Ben.

"Maybe he's got a career in the law ahead of him," said Jack. "The fact is, the South isn't ready for desegregation, and there's going to be a lot of resistance. There's talk in Landsdowne of organizing private schools for the white students. Radford hasn't got the financial base for that, so I suspect they'll drag their feet and wait to see what happens."

Jessa stood up abruptly, pushing the light patio chair back with a screech. "It's wrong! Segregated schools are wrong! Mr. Carlson, when I lived here, I didn't know that. I just went along with the way things were, but now, I can tell you it's wrong..."

"Jessa, sweet, people here are contented. Nobody wants anyone stirring up trouble over the schools. They have their own school and they're happy with things as they are," said Fran.

"But it's unfair! Part of what's wrong is that it isn't equal—not at all. Nothing about Overbrook is as good as Edison and Hanover and Radford High. Daddy came back from school board tours of all the schools and told us how bad Overbrook was. He said it made him sick at heart to see it!"

"Jessa, sit down and drink your tea," said Jack. "There's no use getting all bothered over the school system. It is what it is. Things are heating up at the federal level, and around here it's a potentially explosive situation. You'd be a lot better off staying out of it."

Jessa slid back into her chair, chastened. She shot a look at Michael and saw that he agreed with her, so she took a deep breath and began to formulate her argument differently: "Mr. Carlson, I think it's really important because of the inequalities, but that's only one way that it's wrong. The other thing I've discovered, a really important thing, is that it keeps people apart—people who might benefit from knowing each other."

There was silence. Jessa scanned the faces of the adults. This wasn't working either. Why did they all want to squelch her?

When Fran met Jessa's eyes, she was disturbed to see her

younger self reflected there. She had been a rebel before she gave up and tried to conform to her parents' expectations. Fran glanced at Jack, and decided that for her safety, Jessa should be discouraged from pursuing this topic. She repeated the argument that her teachers had given her: "Yes, it's true that one purpose of segregated schools is to keep the races apart. Think about it, Jessa, if it prevents Negroes and whites from falling in love, like Romeo and Juliet did, although they belonged to families that were feuding, then it is the right policy," she said.

April looked at her in alarm. "We just read *Romeo and Juliet*, and it didn't seem like the lesson was to accommodate feuds that drove people to kill each other. Wasn't it the feuding that caused the tragedy, not the love?"

"Fran, I'm afraid we have some very outspoken children," Karen broke in. "Jessa has her heart set on getting the school board to extend the music program to serve the colored school. It's something her father was working on before his death, and she wants to fulfill his dream. I hope that isn't pushing the community too much."

"I recall Ted's fight with the school board," said Jack.

"What I learned living in Portland is that when schools aren't segregated, you'll have more chances to get to know people you might really like." Jessa continued, "My friend Janie and I have a lot in common, but if she lived here and went to Overbrook, I would never have met her! I think that's cheating me and cheating her, too!"

"Jessa, you're stubborn, so I won't try to convince you that you're better off associating with people of your own race. It's not so much that we disagree with you, but you need to remember that this is Radford, not Portland. There are a lot of differences. Innocent people can get caught up in controversies like this, and you could end up doing more harm than good. At your age, you can't possibly have the wisdom to appreciate this," said Jack, "so I hope you'll take our advice and let the matter rest."

Jessa looked around the table, but Karen and Ben glanced down rather than meet her defiant eyes. Michael and April were both on her side, she knew, but they had already gotten the message. She could almost hear her mother saying: *Mind your manners. You are a guest...* Her shoulders drooped.

"I'm sorry," Jessa relented. "I guess I get carried away."

"Well, if everyone has finished, I'll show you the rooms where you'll sleep. Jessa, I still have the dog bed I prepared for Cassie when I thought you would be staying with us last winter. You may want to take a turn around the yard before you freshen up for dinner—my roses and dahlias are in full bloom."

"Thank you, ma'am. I know Cassie will appreciate the bed. The tea and cookies were delicious."

Jessa called the dog that had been put in a down-stay by the door. Cassie collected a bite of cookie someone had dropped, then followed Jessa and April out to tour the roses. Carefully manicured beds of roses were planted in a rainbow, from yellow, orange, and peachy shades to pinks, reds, and deep wine-colored blooms. April smelled each one, but Jessa was too troubled to appreciate the smells that April found intoxicating. She'd toured these roses before, and it brought back memories of her family. She ached over their absence and longed for them to back her up. She knew the school integration topic was closed, so she practiced her best behavior and made small talk all through dinner and later on the porch, where they sat and conversed on safe topics until bedtime.

When she and April crawled into the pretty bed in Fran's sewing room, April said, "Jessa, I'm sorry it went so badly about the schools. They seem pretty stuck in their ways."

"What worries me is that the school board may feel the way

the Carlsons do. Don't you hate it when grown-ups tell you that you're too young to understand things?"

"Personally, I think they're the ones who don't understand things. That business about *Romeo and Juliet* was ridiculous. If that's the best defense of segregation they can come up with…"

"I guess it was a mistake to talk about people getting to know each other. They don't like that. I've got to convince them that music is important for everyone and having music in school will make everyone happier. I'll tell the school board that. Don't you think that will work?"

"Maybe," replied April, doubtfully.

· CHAPTER 5 ·

Ben followed Jessa's directions to Marshall's Garage and pulled in at a ramshackle tin building close by the railroad tracks. They headed for the open garage door. Jacob, a handsome, strongly built Negro man, did a double-take. He turned to Marvin, a sandy-haired, bookish young man, pointed at Jessa, and said, "Look! It's the disappeared Miss Jessamine who wanted Eddie to have a fiddle from the music shop."

Jessa smiled and introduced the family.

Marvin said, "Jessa, you won't believe how Jacob's son, Eddie, plays that little fiddle! He came in the other day with his grandfather, and they played a hoe-down! It even got Ray Marshall to clapping and tapping his foot."

"Eddie's mighty smart when it comes to music. I want y'all to hear him play!" said Jacob, who towered over Marvin. "That little fiddle Mr. Carlson delivered to us is the perfect size."

"Oh, I'm so glad," said Jessa.

Ben stepped forward to shake hands, but Marvin and Jacob shooed him away, holding up greasy hands, which they began to wipe on gasoline-soaked rags. Jacob pointed toward a car. "This here's the car we're fixing up for you. Jessa, you probably recognize it—it belongs to your neighbor, Mrs. Forsythe."

"She wasn't able to drive it anymore—too crippled up. She heard about how we got my grandfather's car going and said she'd like you folks to have her car while you're in town," said Marvin.

"That's a nice sedan. We certainly appreciate her offer and your work getting it running," said Ben.

"Marvin, you work at the sheriff's office?" asked Ben. "I gather you were the person who fielded a call from the owners of the motel last time we were in Radford."

"Yessir. I recall talking with them," said Marvin. "Pretty suspicious about you folks. Thought you were Jessa's kidnappers! I had to calm them down."

Jacob said grimly, "Everyone was looking under every bush for kidnappers around here." He let the hood fall and slid into the driver's seat to start it up. The blue and white Oldsmobile's powerful engine hummed. Marvin opened the garage doors widely and Jacob backed the car out. "You can drive both cars to Landsdowne this afternoon, return the rental, and drive home in this one."

"Oh, I knew this would be a problem!" wailed Karen. "I'm afraid I don't drive. Fran offered to help us get the car, but she volunteers at the clinic and isn't free until tomorrow."

Jacob turned to Marvin. "Think you can make the drive and get back in time to fix dinner for your grandparents before you go on duty?"

Marvin glanced at the clock mounted high on the wall of the shop. "No problem."

"Sounds good," said Jacob. "Some of y'all climb in this car and ride with Marvin. He knows Landsdowne—his family lives there. When you get back, I want you to hear Eddie play— maybe Saturday?"

"Oh, yes! It makes me happy that he likes to play!" said Jessa. "I'm so glad the Carlsons got the violin to you. I told them it was what my parents would have wanted me to do, after all the trouble I caused you."

"Bless you, honey! Marv, I'll repack the wheel bearings on that trailer until Ray gets back. You can go straight to your grandparents' place when you get back to town."

Karen and Ben got into the rental, and Jessa, April, and Michael all began to slide into the back seat of the Oldsmobile.

"Gee, you make a fella feel like a chauffeur. Why 'on't you ride up front, Jessa? I want to hear how you survived on your own so many weeks," said Marvin.

As Marvin pulled onto the highway, Jessa asked, "Were you working with Jacob when he was put in jail?"

"No, I was new at the job of night clerk then. That's how Jacob and I met."

"I had no idea something crazy like Jacob getting locked up would happen because I ran away. It must have been awful!"

"Was pretty bad, especially one night when the sheriff and the state patrol guys took the dogs out to track you. Everyone came back angry and exhausted, and although they never hit Jacob, those troopers yelled accusations at him and threatened his family. He just begged them to leave him alone."

"Oh…" moaned Jessa.

April said, "There couldn't have been a shred of evidence against him. Jessa ran away, and he had no part in it."

"That's right," said Jessa. "Marvin, what did he say about me?"

"Mostly he said he didn't know anything about you. I remember he said he had a daughter of his own, and nobody who had a daughter would want to harm someone else's daughter. But don't you worry, Jessa. Everything's fine now. Jacob's a great guy. He doesn't hold a grudge against you—and that little fiddle—I hear about it all the time."

"So how'd you come to work with Jacob?" asked Michael. "I think being a mechanic would be great."

"He's teaching me. I didn't know the first thing about cars, but Jacob's got a completely different kind of education from mine. There's a lot of intuition to it, at least, I can't figure out how he knows what he knows. He knows lots of things that are more useful than what I studied in school, although he's interested in my education, too."

"You and Jacob are friends, right? How'd that happen?" asked Jessa.

"Wouldn't ever have happened if he hadn't gotten locked up. I got to talking with him that first night. Sheriff said he was a mechanic, so I asked him about fixing up my grandfather's Buick, what it would take, and then we talked about our families. Later that night, I got to thinking about it, and I said to myself: *Why not?* It was just as if there was a door that I hadn't known was there, and I opened it and stepped through."

"Your view of race changed?" asked Michael.

"You bet it's changed. Growing up around here, you accept things the way they've always been. The more I thought about it, the more I concluded it wasn't logical. Jacob and I talked most of the night, some nights, and we talked about the barriers. I was lonely, new in town, and needed a friend, and I wanted Jacob to be my friend."

"I have a Negro friend," said Jessa. "She was kind to me when I needed a friend, too."

"It's not easy, around here, but it's possible. I know Ray Marshall loves Jacob like a son. Says he taught Jacob what he knew, and after that, Jacob just took off! Ray defers to Jacob when it comes to diagnosing a problem, and he praises him to the customers who are skeptical about entrusting their precious vehicle to a Negro. I've seen how proud he is of him—doesn't matter what color his skin is!"

"That's it!" said Jessa. You just have to have a chance to get to know each other. That's what happened with me and Janie!"

"So you're on to that? Ted Hufford, the town's reporter, he comes by the sheriff's office after he gets off work and we've been talking. He says segregation is toxic and has got to go."

"There's no segregation in Portland, at least, not like here," said Michael. "There's a part of town that has more Negroes and immigrant families, and their school has received some attention because people said it was ghettoizing, but all the schools have some Negroes and Asians along with the whites."

"Marvin, I came home to Radford to meet with the school board, to represent my father's viewpoint. I'm going to say the colored school should get a music program, just like the instrumental music offered in the white schools, but Michael keeps saying it doesn't make sense to have a separate colored school. Now I don't know what to do. The Carlsons seem dead-set against school desegregation—or not rushing it at least—it came up last night. I've been discouraged ever since."

"People here don't want anything to change. They insist everybody's happy the way things are. And, in fact, Jacob says the Negroes aren't united about it, either. Some talk change, and others say it's dangerous to rock the boat. The Negro teachers stand to lose their jobs because they think Overbrook will be closed if there's desegregation."

Marvin glanced in the rear-view mirror to make sure the rental car was following them. "Michael, what's your parents' opinion?"

"Oh, they personally approve of integration and treating everybody fairly, but they also say things like *When in Rome, do as the Romans.*"

"Mama said that as outsiders, we have to be careful what we say. Anyone resents outsiders telling them what to do," said April.

"But that doesn't apply to me," retorted Jessa. "It's my hometown, and I'm just wanting what my father wanted. He figured that once the school board got used to having music in the white school, they'd want to keep it, and then their argument about "separate but equal" could be used to get music into the colored school."

"That might work," said Marvin. "People might listen to you. They loved your family. That's all I've heard from Florence at the sheriff's office." He stuck his arm out and signaled, then turned into a parking lot. "Well, here we are."

Ben pulled in behind Marvin, and when the negotiations over the rental car's condition and gas use were complete, they all got into the Oldsmobile and started back to Radford. The adults talked about Marvin's transition from English major to apprentice car mechanic, and the kids whispered together in the back seat, making plans. April was eager to visit the farm where Jacob's Aunt Helen lived, and Michael reminded Jessa that he wanted to camp out on Jessa's grandfather's farm. Hanging over Jessa was the plan to move from the Carlsons' into her family's house. She didn't know how she could sleep in that house with her parents gone.

From the front seat, Marvin said, "Jessa, I never found out how you fed yourself all those weeks."

"We ate garden vegetables and nuts and fruit from the orchard. The garden had lots of food, and before the weather turned bad, I could make fires, but after there was a freeze, everything was harder. It got rainy and cold, and I had trouble getting fires to start. We had to depend on winter squash, carrots, dried beans, and potatoes toward the end, plus the fruit I had stored away. The English walnut crop was good, and Cassie loves nuts, so we ate a lot of them. Cassie caught mice, especially at the barn, and we got the hens' eggs. If it hadn't been for needing to find someone to care for Grandad's hens, we wouldn't have met Jacob's Aunt Helen. That's how I found out that Jacob was put in jail on suspicion of kidnapping me—and all that he went through because of me."

"Jacob told me how much it meant when the Carlsons gave him the violin for his son. Says his father-in-law and Eddie have a great time playing together. I bet you'll be surprised when you hear Eddie play that little fiddle. That grandfather must be a good teacher, but I gather Eddie has a knack for music. Real talented, same as his father, 'cept Jacob's talent is with mechanical things."

Ben said, "Jessa, maybe Eddie and his grandfather would like to perform for the community. That might build support for music instruction in all the schools."

"That's a great idea! What do you think, Marvin? My friends wrote me that there's music in the park every Thursday unless it rains. You've heard him play, so do you think he could do it?"

"The kid's got stage presence. I was pretty impressed—not just by the playing, but by how much he wanted to share it. Not the embarrassed sort at all. He and his grandfather put on quite a show. Still, I don't know about playing for the community." Marvin paused, considering. "Jessa, ever since you ran away, the town got paranoid, and Florence at the sheriff's office says that relations between whites and coloreds have been strained. Now that there's talk of school desegregation, the rabble-rousing faction of the town is practicing intimidation tactics against the Negroes. The sheriff's been trying to defuse the situation without opening up a can of worms."

Jessa bit her lip. She knew her running away had caused the town to worry and that they had turned against the innocent Negro population—Jacob in particular. Although he had been cordial toward her, others might still blame her, and the talk about desegregation might make the Radford school board more resistant to her plan now than when her father was alive...

· CHAPTER 6 ·

The grocery store clerk grabbed the bagger's shoulder, pointed and whispered, and then the man behind the meat counter called, "Jessa Olsen! Welcome home!"

People redirected their carts to meet them in the aisle. Everyone greeted them with delight, asked about plans for the summer, and suggested get-togethers. As they checked bread, fruit, potatoes, meat, soap, toilet tissue, and laundry detergent off their list, the pressure mounted on Jessa. From here they would go to her home. Two bags of groceries were loaded next to their luggage in the trunk of Mrs. Forsythe's car as Jessa retrieved Cassie from the shade of a crape myrtle bush. The sun shimmered over the asphalt, and yet Jessa shivered. She sank into the backseat and hugged Cassie to her, burying her face in the dog's tight curls.

When Ben signaled to turn onto her street, Jessa recalled the thousands of times she had made that turn with her family. Nothing could ever be right again without her family there to greet them. Last winter, it had taken all her strength to force herself into the house to get things they needed. Then it seemed that everything depended on her being strong. Now, she was tired of being strong. *How she wanted to be greeted and hugged by her parents.* As the car pulled up to the vacant Olsen house, it had a forlorn, neglected look. No way could she go into that house!

Ben turned into the driveway, and Jessa saw Mrs. Forsythe sitting on her porch. She gripped the car door handle, opened it before Ben brought the car to a stop, and jumped out, announcing, "I'm going to thank Mrs. Forsythe for lending her car to us."

She pulled Cassie out of the car after her, leaving the others to enter her house and unload the luggage and groceries. Settling onto the neighbor's comfortable porch swing, she showed off Cassie's professional clip and described Portland in glowing terms, assuring the older neighbor woman that it wasn't cold at all in Oregon. She answered all Mrs. Forsythe's questions and thanked her for lending them her car. The elderly neighbor seemed more fragile than ever, and Jessa understood why she had given up driving.

Michael emerged from her house and looked across to where Jessa was sitting. "Jessa, where's a lawn mower?"

"Should be out in the garage, way in the back."

From the neighbor's porch, Jessa could hear Michael begin the job of pushing the lawn mower through the grass. The rhythmic spinning of the blades slowed to a grind as he got into the thicker grass. When he emerged along the side of the house, she saw the wave of cut grass blades flying up to coat his feet and pants. *I'm glad he won't have to track that grass across the Carlsons' carpet*, she thought. Suddenly, allegiance to her own home, the modest house that had happily met the needs of her family, rose into her throat. *I like our front porch, our living room, our kitchen*, she thought.

Jessa and Mrs. Forsythe watched as Fran Carlson drove up and got out, waving gaily to them. She headed into the house, balancing a casserole dish and a paper bag. Finally, Jessa could delay no longer, so she said good-bye to the neighbor and wandered over into her own yard, touring flower beds she had helped plant and revisiting the tall trees and bushes where she and her friends had played hide-and-seek. She glanced down the path between the garage and the lilac bushes where she had overheard the news of the accident and shuddered. Then she remembered she'd told Mr. Carlson that she would retrieve the hidden house key. She went to the sun dial and pried up one of the stones encircling its base. There the front door key lay, just where she had hidden it when her world had been complete, her parents and grandparents still alive, and Cassie just a puppy.

Cassie pushed her nose under Jessa's elbow, and she turned to hug the dog. "Good girl, Cassie. Do you ever wonder what happened to Mommie and Daddy? Doesn't it feel like they should be here?" Jessa looked toward the back door. "Right now, Mommie might call me inside to set the table, or to bring a bouquet for the centerpiece." Jessa slumped against the dog, sobbing, and Cassie licked her tearful cheek. Then Jessa felt April beside her, stooping to hug her.

"Sweet Jessa! It must be so hard. I know I couldn't go into my grandparents' bedroom after Grandad died. It just seemed impossible that they were really gone forever when I felt them there so strongly."

"Thank you for understanding, April. I've tried to keep a stiff upper lip and all that, but coming back here is—it's just awful."

"Do you want to talk to Daddy about it? Would you rather go back to the efficiency at the motel where we stayed last winter? I think they'd be glad to do that, to make it easier on you."

"No, April. I love this house, and I want to share it as my parents would have done if they were here." Jessa rummaged in her pocket for a tissue. "I've got to face up to reality. I don't want to mess up my chances to accomplish what my father would want me to do. I'll come in soon."

Jessa circled into the backyard and then set out running, stopping Michael just before he pushed the mower over the bed of lilies of the valley. He knelt to clear the twists of thick grass wrapped around the blades of the mower. "Jessa, I've been studying it. That's a great swing."

Jessa looked at the swing hanging from a large horizontal limb far up in the maple tree. The memory was as clear as yesterday, when her father had climbed that tree and shinnied out on the limb to tie the ropes onto the branch. Then, there'd been the surprise—he'd called *Watch out below!* as he grabbed both ropes and rolled off the limb. Jessa's mother had screamed, thinking he was falling, but he let himself down, gripping the two ropes hand over hand. *Hadn't had any call to do that sort of thing since I left boot camp*, he'd said.

Michael watched curiously as Jessa scraped fragments of grass off her shoes. She didn't reply to his remark about the swing. Cassie trailed beside her as she slowly climbed the front steps and forced herself to enter the house.

The front hall seemed dark compared with the brilliant sunshine outside, but Jessa's eyes adjusted as she ran her hand along the molding that separated the paneled half of the wall from the part covered with the ivy-patterned wallpaper she had helped hang. She bit her lip as she studied the familiar pictures on the wall. This was going to be all right... She swallowed and straightened her shoulders. She could hear Karen's and Ben's voices in her parents' bedroom, so she went there. They had a stack of linens spread out on the bed, and on the floor was a pile of sheets. Jessa thought, *Mommie and Daddy slept on those sheets!*

"Jessa, the embroidery and lace on these sheets and pillow-cases are amazing. We've never seen so much lacework, and someone was not following a pattern at all. The embroidery is a riot of vines and flowers and birds—artwork in stitches! I want April to see these—and look at this one with bumblebees! Who did these?" asked Karen.

"That was Grandmother's love. She made afghans, too, like

the one I took back to Portland. Mother didn't have the patience for it that Grandma had, especially the embroidery, but she knew how to do it. Mommie liked to knit, though. Sometimes she took knitting to the music shop to work on when she didn't have to do orders or entries on the books for the business."

"Well, these are works of art! They should be behind glass, displayed on the wall—and everything smells of lavender!"

"We just always had pillowcases like that. My friends liked them when they spent the night here. Did you find everything you need?" Jessa glanced again at the pile of sheets on the floor but quickly looked away. "Is there anything I can do to help?"

"Ben and I are a pretty good team for getting the beds ready. We're going to be eating soon. Why don't you set the table?"

"Yes ma'am." Jessa backed out of the room and headed downstairs. When she swung around the newel post at the bottom of the stairs and headed for the kitchen, her mother was standing at the counter. Jessa gasped, "Oh!" With the double-take came the hot tears. It *should* have been her mother—what a cheat!

Fran turned. "Sweet Jessa, poor dear, you look more like Cora all the time! How I do miss Cora!"

Jessa halted in the doorway, unable to move. "I'm sorry, I mistook you for Mommie!'

"Then, honey, we both need a hug, don't we?" asked Fran. Jessa bolted across the room, burying her head against Fran's shoulder.

When she could find her voice, Jessa said, "Mrs. Carlson, it's been so hard, just coming into the house—it doesn't feel right without Mommie and Daddy here."

Fran drew back and stared at her. "Jessa, maybe it will help to know that Jack and I feel the same way. He came home after being here to check on the water and power, and the minute he walked in the door, I could tell something was wrong. He said this house, with Paul and Cora gone, made him sick, and it was all he could do to keep himself from running out."

Jessa emitted a moan as she hugged Fran again. They sank into the chairs by the kitchen table, and Fran held Jessa's face in her hands. "You *do* look like Cora!"

Jessa hunched up her shoulders, unable to speak, and broke loose from the embrace to shake her head. Finally, she blurted out, "I'll never be as good as Mommie."

"Jessa, sweet, you are your own person, and I have come to value that person in a new way ever since you came back this summer. You stand up for the rights of the colored kids, and I admire that. Having you back here with the Acrees helps to fill the hole that losing your parents left in my life."

Jessa nestled into Fran's embrace, then cleared her voice to say, "They *should* be here, shouldn't they? Then we could all be happy together."

"Honey, there's no justice in this world. Nothing can explain away the injustice of your parents' and your grandfather's deaths! I don't suppose you can imagine how lonely Jack and I have been. We miss Cora and Paul every day! I know I promised to tell the Acrees about your parents, but when I imagine that conversation, I just break down crying."

Jessa bowed her head. She thought again of her parents' will and the provision for their best friends to care for her in case of their deaths. Her decision to go with the Acrees had seemed natural at the time, but now she felt Fran's tenderness as she stroked her hair lovingly. What if she had known about her parents' provision and had sought the Carlsons' help instead of running away? That would have prevented a lot of the trouble she had caused. Wouldn't that have been better?

Fran rose from her chair, as if sensing that she was overstepping her place. Jessa joined her at the counter. "Let's be friends, can we? I know I can't be the friend my mother was to you, but

I am growing up, and friends can keep in touch, even from as far away as Oregon."

"You sweet dear! Of course we can be friends. I'd like that. I'd love to have a pen pal in Oregon." Fran wiped her eyes and resumed the food preparation, working with Jessa as she had worked with Cora so many times during their long friendship. Jessa stood tall, thinking with pride that she did resemble her mother. It was time to grow up to carry on the work her parents were involved with in Radford.

· CHAPTER 7 ·

Dinner at the Carlsons' was always a delight. Fran loved to cook for company, and she had invited them tonight for fried chicken, sliced tomatoes, boiled corn, pickled beets, and her delicious potato salad, and for dessert, her angel food cake with local raspberries and whipped cream. After they said grace, Jessa announced that she had planned a surprise, but everyone soon forgot about that in their enthusiasm over the food.

Jacob's old truck pulled in front of the house, and he cut the engine. The family sat squeezed together in the narrow cab, gazing across the broad, green lawn. Eddie cradled his violin case between his legs, and his sister wiggled on his mother's lap. What to do now? It all seemed too imposing.

Jacob's wife, Margaret, said, "We don't even know what door we should knock on…"

Eddie was full of enthusiasm. "Let's go in!" he urged, reaching across his mother and Sarah for the door handle.

The truck door swung open, and Eddie slipped out. Margaret helped their daughter Sarah to the ground and climbed out, smoothing her skirt. Together, they moved up the walkway toward the front porch.

April was helping Fran clear away the dinner plates when Cassie barked. Then they heard a hesitant knock at the front door. Jessa and Cassie ran to open it, and there stood Jacob with Margaret, Eddie, and Sarah dressed in their best clothes but looking uncomfortable.

"We didn't know which door to come to," Jacob explained.

"Oh, this is the right door!" Jessa smiled at Jacob, and then Margaret's regal beauty took her breath away. Margaret's straightened hair was pulled up in a broad bun on top of her head, and her dress was navy blue with white piping at the collar and cuffs.

"Oh, hello to everyone," said Jessa, "and you must be Eddie!" She spotted the instrument at his side. "Good! You brought your violin, but where's your grandfather?"

"He thought the four of us would be quite enough," said Jacob. "Eddie can play you some pieces to thank you and the Carlsons for the violin, and then we'll be going."

By this time, Jack and Fran were peering curiously out at the family clustered on the front porch. "Oh, please come on in," Jessa said, and everyone moved back to make room. "This is Mr. and Mrs. Wilson, Eddie, and his sister"—Jessa paused— "hey, what's your name, princess?"

"This is our Sarah, and please call me Margaret," said Margaret, as three-year-old Sarah shyly clung to her skirt.

"Okay," said Jessa. "So, Jacob and Margaret Wilson, Eddie and Sarah, I'd like you to meet Jack and Fran Carlson. Jacob, you have already met Ben and Karen Acree, and Michael and April, and this is Cassie." Upon seeing the dog, Sarah clapped her hands and Jessa smiled.

As they moved into the living room, the partially cleared dining table was visible. Margaret did a double-take and said, "Oh, I apologize. We didn't mean to interrupt your dinner!" She turned, taking Jacob's arm. "We'll come back some other time."

"No, it's perfect! We were just getting ready for the dessert. You came just when I told you to come," said Jessa.

"But we can't possibly…"

"No, it was my idea! I told them there would be a surprise!"

Distressed, Margaret and Jacob searched the faces of the other adults. "You didn't know we were coming?" asked Jacob. "She didn't tell you?"

"Oh, the timing is perfect! We can all have dessert together and then Eddie can play—that's just how I planned it."

Karen said, "Jessa, it would have been more polite to let your hostess in on your plan."

Jessa's face flushed as she sensed the discomfort in the room. She appealed to Fran, "Oh, isn't it okay? You have a big cake, and we can all eat out here in the living room if the table is too small—lots more people were here at my welcome-home party!"

Margaret pulled on Jacob's arm. "We've come in on these people unexpectedly. Eddie can play for Jessa somewhere else. We should go."

Jessa's eyes darted from Margaret to Fran. "Please, don't leave!" She settled on Jack, pleading with him silently.

Jack's arm encircled Fran's waist as he said, "Why, this is a perfect time. Fran, you and Karen slice that cake, and I'm sure you'll have plenty of help with bringing out the dessert. Ben, while there's still daylight, why don't you and Jacob have a look at the home improvement project I started this morning? The deck had some serious rot, so I began tearing it out, but the more I pull out, the worse the situation looks."

"Eddie, let's look, too," said Michael.

After the men and boys left the room, Jessa said, "Mrs. Carlson, I'm sorry I didn't let you in on the plan." She turned to Margaret. "Sorry for the misunderstanding, Mrs. Wilson. I get carried away with what I think are good surprises."

Fran said, "Listen, everyone. It *is* a good surprise. We'll all have dessert and then the music, just as Jessa planned. I'm looking forward to it. Karen and I will serve the dessert as soon as we clear the table."

"Is there anything I can help you with?" asked Margaret, heading for the dining room with Sarah dragging on her skirt.

"Sure, Margaret. Please gather the water glasses and take them to the kitchen sink," said Karen. "Jessa, why don't you give Sarah a chance to get to know Cassie?"

Jessa lured Sarah into a corner where she could sit and pet Cassie. The three women quickly had the table cleared, and April was charged with brushing the crumbs into a little silver pan. By the time Karen put the cake on the table, everyone was more relaxed. Fran got out a stack of dessert plates from her set of fine china.

"Such pretty dishes!" said Margaret.

"Thank you, Margaret," said Fran.

Karen said, "Margaret, we're planning a trip to Jacob's aunt Helen's place soon. Jessa wanted to see her grandfather's hens again, and my kids have been fascinated by the prospect of going there ever since we visited last winter. Michael won a prize for the story he called 'Visiting a Farm in a Snowstorm.'"

"I'd like to read his story. Eddie sure loves Aunt Helen's farm."

"Ben and I were so impressed by how ably Helen is managing by herself. Her independence and how well she's dealt with the loss of her husband was such a contrast with how my father fell apart after my mother died. A real change came over him, so I am particularly sensitive to how some partners seem able to recover after such a loss and others seemingly give up."

"Aunt Helen's a saint—she really is. She's helped me through some hard patches." Margaret recalled the debilitating attacks of morning sickness she had suffered during her second pregnancy. "I don't know what we'd do without her. She and Uncle Adam had a big part in raising Jacob after his father was killed, so she's like a mother to him."

Fran said, "Now, ladies, let's set up an assembly line." She led the way to the dining table and lifted the lid off the cake saver.

"I'll slice the cake, Karen can scoop the raspberries, and Margaret can put a dollop of whipping cream on each serving." She turned to get the bowl of whipped cream out of the refrigerator.

"Please, just a small slice for Sarah. Mrs. Carlson, would it be okay with you if the children sit at the dining table and the adults gather in the living room?"

"Sounds good to me. Please call me Fran, Margaret."

• • • • •

Jack was showing Ben and Jacob the deck, which was partly torn away. Jacob walked out on a part that was still intact, where the deck wrapped around the side of the house, and peered over the edge. The basement door was just below the railing. "You know, if this was my deck, I'd extend it out a couple of feet on this end. That would give you a little overhang above that basement entrance."

Jack looked down at the basement door, and then at Jacob. "You think an overhang like that would hold up?"

"Sure thing—it's the principle of a cantilever. See here how these joists span from the ledger to the beam? They can extend beyond the beam and be tied in with the rim joist. This is the weather side, so you're going to have to replace the railing over here anyway. You can add some bridging to keep the joists from spreading."

"Sounds good to me," said Ben. "A lot of porch roofs are supported that way. They may have posts and columns added, but they aren't important structurally, just there for appearances. I'd like to give you a hand. Will you be working in the afternoon—after church?" asked Ben.

"I could help, too. Sundays are my day off, and I like working construction," said Jacob.

"Can we help? We could move boards and measure and hammer nails." Michael looked at Eddie, who nodded vigorously.

"Dessert is served!"

They reentered the house and Jessa showed everyone where to sit, wiping Sarah's fingers and lifting her up on the dictionary she'd put on her chair. Everyone had iced water in pretty glasses, although a juice glass had been located for Sarah.

The homemade angel food cake with raspberries and cream was truly delicious, and the adults relaxed as common interests emerged and the conversation flowed easily. When the time came to take dishes to the sink, April organized it and Jessa helped little Sarah down, wiped her face and hands, and pointed her toward the living room to climb on her daddy's lap. When everything was cleared, Jessa, April, Eddie, and Michael joined the adults in the living room and sat in a semicircle on the carpet while eleven-year-old Eddie tuned his violin.

When he was ready, he held the violin out. "This is the most wonderful gift in the world!" He tucked the violin under his arm and solemnly announced the first piece: "This is the chorus from Handel's 'Judas Maccabaeus.'"

Eddie played the melody and went on to embellish it with his own variations. After they clapped, he announced, "Next, I'm going to play 'Turkey in the Straw' because it was the first song Grampa taught me that has double stops—that's playing on two strings at a time."

After that, he played a soulful rendition of "Shenandoah."

"Those are the ones I liked best from the early days. Also, Grampa and I play lots of hymns." He played "Swing Low, Sweet Chariot," "Just a Closer Walk to Thee," and a slow and then a rousing version of "When the Saints Go Marching In."

"It's most fun doing the 'Saints' with Grampa. Now, here's the one I've been working on for weeks, trying to make it sound the way Grampa plays it." Eddie studied the violin for a moment as if gathering his powers, looked around at the faces trained on him, tucked the violin under his chin, closed his eyes, and launched into a lilting version of "The Tennessee Waltz."

It brought the house down. When he tucked the fiddle under his arm and bowed to his audience, everyone clapped and clapped. Sarah kept clapping after everyone had stopped, but Fran wiped her eyes and interrupted, "Oh, it made me cry! That's our song, isn't it, Jack? We used to dance to it!"

Margaret said, "Fran, 'Tennessee Waltz' has always been one of my favorites from Papa's repertoire."

Eddie began packing up his violin.

Jessa said, "Eddie, your playing is wonderful! It would have made my parents so happy! My friends wrote me that there's a summer music series going on each week in the park."

"Oh, yes," Margaret broke in. "Choir members from all the churches are going to perform. We've been practicing for months, now."

"Do you think Eddie and his grandfather could get on the list? Would you like to do it, Eddie? Could you and your grandfather play in the summer music series?"

Eddie looked from Margaret to Jacob. "Could I do it?"

"Eddie, you'll show them!" said Jessa. "Perform just like this, you and your grandfather, and it will inspire other kids to study music. I'm going to the school board meeting to ask them to include music in the Overbrook curriculum."

Margaret said, "I'd like to see music instruction at Overbrook. I know the students would love it. I was lucky to grow up surrounded by music, and to get the grounding in music theory as well. I've had ever so much fun singing in the combined choir! We're all looking forward to our performance. But for Eddie and Dad to perform... Jake, what do you think?"

Jacob's concern about driving his family into the white part of town and the initial sensation of being unwelcome had disappeared in the congenial environment. Maybe all that he and Marvin had been discussing would really be possible, and maybe his son's talent could promote it. He nodded. "If Eddie wants to, I think we owe it to Jessa for giving him the violin."

"Oh, no! You don't owe me anything! Eddie and his grandfather did this on their own, and I want people to see what is possible. Music is wonderful for everyone!"

"Then we'll see how Dad feels about it. Now, Fran, we can leave the men to talk. I want to help you with this big job of dishwashing," said Margaret.

"Oh, I couldn't let you do that." Fran was on the point of saying that she would just leave the dishes for her maid when she recalled that it was Saturday night, so her maid wouldn't be coming in until Monday.

Karen said, "April and I are good dishwashers, too."

"I can stay and help," offered Margaret. "Sarah's happy to be on her daddy's lap. I'd really like to do it."

"Then it will be fun. We can whiz through it together," said Karen. "Fran, you did all the preparations, and the cake was delicious. We just need you to put the dishes away, and Margaret and I will do the rest."

Fran pulled out aprons for all three of them, and the women scraped the dinner plates for Jessa to feed the scraps to Cassie. As they were running water into the sink, Jessa rushed in from letting Cassie out to ask if an empty jar could have holes punched in the lid for collecting lightning bugs. Fran turned her attention to that while Karen and Margaret organized the dishwashing job.

Fran handed the jar to Jessa, who darted out the door. She turned to watch the two women happily working elbow-to-elbow at the sink. At first there was an element of disbelief at the sight of the white and colored women talking and laughing together in her kitchen, and the topic, she gathered, was their children. She felt left out. Soon, a stack of clean dessert plates stood waiting for Fran to put away.

Margaret was saying, "I do hope he'll be able to go on with his music. He really loves it! I don't know what Sarah will want to do, but you should watch her dance when Papa and Eddie play together—she's a whirling dervish!"

"Well, she ought to have a chance to pursue whatever she wants to," Fran found herself saying.

"That's right kind of you," said Margaret, turning to her. Fran looked as if she would burst out crying. Margaret said, "Don't cry—tell me what's the matter, honey." She brushed her hands on the apron and reached out to Fran, who was blubbering.

"Sometimes it just overwhelms me. We've always wanted to have children. I'd give anything to have a lovely family like the two of you have!"

"You poor dear! It is sad when it's that way! Aunt Helen and Uncle Adam never could have children, and they just seemed to adopt the whole family to fill the gap."

Karen felt a pang of conscience, remembering that they had taken Jessa away when Jack and Fran had been ready to provide a home for her.

At that moment, Eddie and Michael burst in the kitchen door with Cassie, eager to show the jar crawling with lightning bugs.

"We collected them for Sarah!" exclaimed Michael. "She can have them in her room for a lamp to watch until she falls asleep, just like Jessa used to do!"

The boys were getting along, jumping from topic to topic as they got to know each other. Eddie and Michael's conversation turned from baseball to what was fun to do in the summers. Michael asked, "Have you ever been camping?"

"No—never had a chance. Where would you go camping around here? Anyway, I don't have the stuff you have to have."

Michael looked at Jessa, a question in his face. She'd heard him say camping, but in her mind, Eddie and his grandfather had been playing music in the park. Then it hit her: Michael was appealing to her for permission to take Eddie to camp in the secret hollow tree.

Now, keeping the tree secret seemed unnecessary, so she nodded to Michael and addressed Eddie. "I know a perfect place for camping. It's on my grandfather's farm. You and Michael could stay there overnight if it's okay with your parents."

Margaret said, "Eddie, that sounds like a nice invitation. Why don't you check it out with your father?"

Michael and Eddie rushed into the living room, carrying the jar of fireflies. Sarah climbed down from her father's lap and took the jar, giggling as she watched the blinking insects crawling on the glass under her hands.

"Daddy, may I go camping with Michael?" asked Eddie. "Jessa says there's a good place on her grandfather's farm."

Karen got Jessa's attention and called her aside. She reminded her of what Marvin had said about the heightened tensions between the races and whispered her concerns about the performance and the camping.

Jessa shook her head vigorously. "It'll be okay. Nobody will bother them in the woods." She left Karen in the pantry and dashed into the living room, where Eddie was pleading with his father.

"It will be easy for us to set them up for a night in the woods," Jessa assured Jacob.

"I guess you know that woods pretty well, now don't you?" said Jacob.

"Sure do," said Jessa, with a smile.

"Please, Daddy, please!" begged Eddie.

"Eddie, this sounds like fun to me," said Jacob. "Learn a little self-sufficiency in the process. Are they finishing up in the kitchen? Your grandfather will be wondering what happened to us."

"Oh, let's send him a piece of the cake! It might convince

him that he should play his violin with Eddie in the park," said Jessa. She rushed back to the kitchen and almost collided with Karen and Margaret.

"Jessa, don't be running in the Carlsons' house!" Karen remonstrated.

"I'm sorry," said Jessa. "I wanted to ask Mrs. Carlson to please slice a piece of the cake to send to Eddie's grandfather."

"Why of course I'll do that," said Fran, turning back into the kitchen. She emerged with a big slice of cake wrapped in wax paper and handed it to Margaret.

"Thank you so much for coming. It was a surprise, as Jessa had planned, and we all enjoyed it—and the music was superb!" said Jack. "I appreciate the tip about the deck, Jacob. Glad I hadn't gotten around to sawing off any of the boards. How's two o'clock tomorrow to get started?"

"What's this?" asked Fran.

"I'm going to get some help from Ben and Jacob on that deck job."

"And me and Eddie," announced Michael.

"Wonderful," said Fran. "And, Margaret, I hope to be seeing you and Sarah again soon."

As they filed out the door, saying their thank-you's, Jack held Fran close. When they were out of earshot, he turned to her. "See, dear, that wasn't so hard, was it?"

Fran shook her head, looking into his eyes. "Thank you, Jack." Then she turned to the others to explain. "This is the first time I've ever socialized with colored people. I mean in this lovely way, to invite them into my living room and sit down to share dessert and talk."

Jessa flew across the room to hug her. "You see! It's just having a chance that makes all the difference!"

"This is a wonderful family, and I hope we can continue to get to know them," said Jack.

Fran nodded to him. "Jack, I'm so glad you could smooth things over when I was at a loss. It was just so unheard of! As if we were breaking laws."

"I'm glad it came off so well," said Karen. "Jessa, this time, your surprise worked out. I was afraid it was going to backfire."

"I would definitely characterize the surprise as a success. I'm glad for the chance to get to know these people, too. Jacob would be quite an addition to any team," said Ben.

"Oh, I'm so happy! Isn't Margaret beautiful? And their little girl, Sarah, such a doll! Thank you so much for going along with it, Mrs. Carlson."

"Thank you for inviting them. It never would have happened, otherwise."

There was a knock at the door, and everyone froze. Through the side window, Jack could see the Carlsons' next-door neighbor, whose yard featured a statue of a little Negro boy holding out a ring that would have served as a hitching post if anyone still arrived on horseback. He cringed, anticipating her reaction, and turned as if to shield Fran, but before anyone could open the door, the woman rushed into the living room. She scanned the people standing around and the unremarkable condition of the room, her wild eyes contrasting with her perfectly coiffed blond hair. She fixed her attention on Fran.

"I've been *so* worried about you, dear! We saw that old truck drive up and park, and the colored people stayed here *such* a long time. Harold said to relax, but I wasn't sure what could be going on at this hour, and then we saw the children out in the yard, colored and white, and I wondered what was going on with you and Jack in the house. Did you have something break down that that mechanic was fixing?"

"Gladys, we just had dessert together and some music provided by our guests, and now it's time for everyone to be getting back home to get ready for bed," replied Jack.

The neighbor drew herself up and turned to Jack. "Well, well! So you're telling me that this Negro family came into our neighborhood for a *social* event? Was *invited*? Well, I never!"

Fran said, "You wouldn't understand, Gladys, but Jessa has connections with this family, and I didn't think I could—"

"No, I don't understand. You've got that right, Fran. There's a right way and a wrong way to run a neighborhood, and inviting trashy people in old beat-up trucks here is not right. We care about appearances around here—at least some of us do…"

"Gladys, you're being unfair. These are lovely people, and we enjoyed their company."

"Well, that's good, because you may have to depend on their company a lot more in the future. I bet *these people*," she glared at the Acrees, "are to blame for this outrage!" She turned on her heel and headed across the lawn to her own property.

There was stunned silence as they watched her go. Jack reached out to Fran and hugged her.

"That woman is the boss of the busy-bodies in this town," he explained to the others. "I suspect she'll make it rough for Fran."

"Oh, pooh on her," said Fran, shaking her curls and looking up into Jack's face. "Dear, you invited Jacob to come help with the deck, and we'll go *right ahead* with that. I don't care what Gladys thinks about me!"

Jessa hugged Jack and Fran. "Thank you so much. I've lost a friend, too. Some people around here don't understand, but I bet you gained more than you lost."

· CHAPTER 8 ·

It was just beginning to get dark, and lightning bugs were lilting across the lawns as Jessa and Ben walked the several blocks from her house to City Hall. People greeted them from their porches or waved as they watered their lawns and flower beds. Jessa stopped twice and pulled Ben over to smell full-blown roses that leaned over the sidewalk. When they walked by the corner house with a big patch of mint growing by the sidewalk, she pinched off a blooming stem and stuck it behind her ear. The fragrance reminded her of the spring's crystal-clear water on her grandfather's property, and it calmed her. Surely, the school board would be won over by her arguments! She squeezed Ben's hand as they climbed the steps to the second-floor hearing room.

As they entered the wood-paneled room, board members began to clap. Marvin was right, the town had loved Jessa's family and were glad to welcome her back. The polished table that stretched the length of the room had plenty of seats, but Jessa was invited to sit near the front. A warm, fragrant breeze blew in the transoms of the tall windows and riffled the sheets on the agenda pad clipped to an easel by the chairman's seat. Ben recognized the reporter he'd met on his previous visit to Radford, and joined him in the row of chairs at the back of the room.

When the four board members were seated, the meeting was called to order, and Mr. Jamison, the chairman, introduced Ben Acree and their special guest, Jessamine Olsen. Then he called for the minutes. Across the table from Jessa was Mrs. Brians, her fourth-grade teacher, now retired. She and Jessa had never gotten along. Mrs. Brians had made fun of her for reading in class, and Jessa had stubbornly refused to listen after she had been forced to close her book. The whole year had been an uneasy truce.

The reading of the minutes droned on, and Jessa imagined her father sitting at this table with these members of the school board. He had often been at odds with them, and Jessa could understand that. The board members wielded power as if the local schools were a kingdom and they were the lords and ladies. Her mind wandered to her statement. After the minutes had been accepted, a page was flipped on the agenda pad at the front of the room. The next item was the budget, and Jessa listened carefully but couldn't decide if the information was favorable to her proposal. At the next agenda item, the chairman called attention to the applications for a Latin and Spanish teacher. Several resumes were lined up at the front of the table, but the deadline had not passed, so no action could be taken.

"I encourage you all to examine these applications before the special meeting next week," said the chairman.

The page was flipped on the large pad and "Proposal by Miss Jessamine Olsen" came up. Jessa felt her face grow hot. She stood, looked around the table, and with a wavering voice, began. "You all know—knew," she corrected, "my father and how important it was for him that Radford schools have instrumental music in the curriculum."

There were encouraging nods and smiles from the board members. Mr. Wexler, the bank director, responded, "Jessamine, Paul worked hard to convince us, and for years, I opposed him because I didn't see the need, but our Abby's so proud to be studying clarinet. She's convinced me."

Jessa nodded gravely. "Abby is good. I'm sorry I missed the

performance. I bet she did a good job on her solo. I know that Mr. Alton wanted to feature her."

"Jessamine, you'll be glad to hear we renewed Mr. Alton's contract. I suspect that was the concern that brought you to our meeting tonight, as his three-year contract was coming to an end, but we all agreed that we were glad to have him on board. His classes have been a positive addition to the curriculum. I just wish Paul could be here to know our decision," said the chairman.

"Thank you, Mr. Jamison. I know Daddy would have been pleased. He felt music was important in people's lives."

"We had very positive feedback from the community at large," said Mrs. Brians. "Especially after the orchestra performance."

Jessa nodded at her, grateful for the comment.

"Very well. Thank you for coming tonight, Jessamine," said the chairman, ready to move on. "I think we can move on to the last item on the agenda…"

"But Mr. Jamison, please, I have something to say," said Jessa.

"Yes, Jessamine?"

"My father wanted all the students in Radford to have a chance to study an instrument."

"And we have adopted his plan for the schools, Jessamine."

"But what about Overbrook?" Jessa demanded.

There was silence. They stared at her, studied the wood grain of the table and furtively eyed each other. Finally, the chairman responded, "That's just not possible, Jessamine. The logistics are simply insurmountable."

"Insurmountable?"

"Overbrook's too small to justify adding a teacher, and Mr. Alton already teaches a full schedule. I know he offered to do it, but it just isn't feasible. Overbrook has no vacancies that might be filled by some paragon who could teach music as well as, say, English, Math, and Geography. Anyway, there wouldn't be any demand. People have to be practical, and music isn't exactly going to prepare students for jobs."

"But music would make going to school worth it. It's important to get the basics, I know, but sometimes it's the music that makes you want to go to school. It makes everything seem worthwhile."

"Jessamine, who do you expect is going to pay for it?" asked Mrs. Brians. "The property taxes collected from the colored part of town don't cover the schooling their kids get as it is. I don't see how we can be expected to cover frills for them also."

Mr. Wexler said, "I'm sorry, Jessamine. There's no way we can stretch the budget to add music to Overbrook's curriculum. We're still struggling to cover the salary boost we gave the Overbrook teachers."

At the back of the room, Ted Hufford rose. "Mr. Chairman, may I be recognized?"

Everyone turned to look at the reporter.

"Certainly. *The Radford Post*'s reporter, Mr. Hufford, is recognized by the Chair."

"As you know, as part of my job, I attend the board meetings and report on the deliberations and actions taken. I seem to recall the discussion about the salaries at Overbrook, which were hiked to bring them into line with those at the white schools, after many years of differential pay. The action was adopted to meet the stipulations of *Plessy v. Brown*. At best, it was a halfway measure that didn't address the real needs of the students and teachers at Overbrook. Furthermore, it cannot have escaped the attention of the Board that last year's Supreme Court ruling supersedes *Plessy v. Brown*. It will no longer be enough to maintain a 'separate but equal' status for the colored and white schools."

The board members stirred or leaned back in their chairs, but nobody responded.

They were startled when Jessa spoke up. "It isn't 'separate but equal' if the white kids have music instruction and the colored kids don't. If you have to have salaries that are the same, then don't you have to have instruction that is the same?"

The reporter remarked, "Miss Olsen's logic is impeccable."

"Ted," responded the Chair, "we won't be forced into anything. We're charged to act in accordance with the wishes of the Radford community. This is a troubled time for schools in the South, and we're going to try to keep the lid on, if you get my meaning."

"Mr. Jamison, changes are already taking place in our state, the eastern part of it, and the Supreme Court ruling is something we can't ignore forever. I admit that around Knoxville things haven't always been peaceful. Outsiders promoted discord. Wouldn't it be preferable if our school board seized the chance to make changes rather than being bulldozed by outside forces?"

"Ted, you need to get one thing straight: the white people who run Radford don't want their children exposed to the inferior nature of the Negro," said Mrs. Brians.

Jessa stared at her through slitted eyes. How did she *dare* say that?

Mr. Morton added, "Those children aren't able to benefit from better instruction. Their school is adequate to prepare them for their place in society, and *nobody's* going to tell this school board what it can and cannot fund!"

Mr. Wexler studied Jessa's incredulous face and tried to return the discussion to the finances. "Ted, you know the realities of the tax structure as well as anyone sitting around this table. You also know that this community is peaceable and respectful of all its members. Nobody wants to rock the boat. I'm sure Miss Olsen can be persuaded that the current status is best for everyone."

"With all due respect to the Board, I recall that the county superintendent pushed you to revise the salaries so that there was, at least on paper, no appearance of discrimination. What Jessamine Olsen is proposing is in line with the directives from the superintendent of instruction."

Mrs. Brians glared across the table at Jessa as she slapped her hand down. "Ted, that salary business still irks me! It was forced on us! We predicated our salary scale on the level of preparation of the teachers. Some of the teachers at Radford High, like Mr. Alton, the music instructor, why, they have master's degrees! Some of the teachers at Overbrook don't have a normal school level of preparation. We had good reason for the sliding scale of reimbursement!"

Ted started to respond, but the chairman brought the gavel down loudly on the resonant tabletop. "The meeting will come to order! I hope it's understood that we are not going to get this town up in arms over music instruction. We need to move on to the last item on the agenda."

Ted sat down. As the Board droned on about repairs to the playground equipment at Edison, Jessa drove her fingernails into the varnish at the edge of the table and blinked rapidly to keep tears from welling over. Was this the end? All her father's dreams? Just like that, they'd turned her down and it was over. Despite the warnings, she'd never imagined they would turn her down. Even with the reporter speaking in support of her... She thought of Janie and the wonderful things she'd told her about Tennessee. Now, she wasn't so sure.

Jessa saw Ben conferring with Ted Hufford. He caught her glance, and she thought he winked. All of a sudden, she remembered his suggestion about letting the community hear Eddie play. When the Chair moved to adjourn the meeting, Jessa stood. "Mr. Jamison, may I present a proposal at the next board meeting?"

He sighed. "Jessamine, it's an open forum. I hope you're not going to make unreasonable demands on us. We have a budget to follow and can't operate with a deficit."

Jessa stood tall, thinking of her mother. "That's what I want to help with."

· CHAPTER 9 ·

That night Jessa slept poorly, waking from disturbing dreams, going back and forth over the arguments made by her and by the school board. Gradually, she convinced herself that their opposition hinged on lack of money. That was something she could tackle. The next day she contacted friends to enlist their support and walked with April and Michael to the library. The librarian waved a greeting as Jessa led April and Michael to the large central table.

Jeff arrived first. He was slim and walked with a slight limp, the legacy of polio. He greeted Jessa with a grin and walked around the table to shake hands with Michael. Soon, Cherry and Alice joined them, each wearing sleeveless sundresses with wide, flowered skirts.

"Pretty dresses," said Jessa.

"We sewed them," said Alice.

Cherry's curly red hair was pulled into a big ponytail, and Alice's formerly long blond hair had been transformed by a pageboy permanent.

"Wow, Alice, you look sophisticated," said Jessa. "Turn around, let's see your hair. I like it!"

"You're the one that's transformed, Jessa," Alice responded. "You were so skinny last time we saw you."

"Both Cassie and I gained some weight in Portland. Everybody, you remember meeting Michael and April at the Carlsons' party? We're here to plan an important mission, and I need to pick your brains."

"What's the important mission?" asked Jeff.

"I'll explain in a minute. First of all, has anyone seen Mr. Alton since school got out? I learned that the school board renewed his contract, so that was good."

"Sure, we've seen him. He comes to watch softball games, and I wrote you about Mr. Alton's summer Music in the Park," said Alice. "It's on Thursdays, if it doesn't rain, and people bring picnic baskets and lay out blankets to sit on while they eat."

"That's going to be part of the plan. What music has there been already?"

"Last week, Mr. Grant played his guitar for people to sing along. That was good," said Cherry. "Mr. Alton's been working with this acapella group from the high school, but they haven't performed because members of the group keep going on vacation. The combined choir is next week, and there's a barbershop quartet from Landsdowne scheduled later in the summer."

"Listen, I've got the perfect addition to the music schedule. This little boy who's been studying violin with his grandfather, Jacob Wilson's son, can play wonderfully. His grandfather has agreed to play with him. I want to tell Mr. Alton about him."

"I bet he'll like it. I saw him with his wife at the grocery parking lot. She looks like she's pregnant," said Cherry.

"That awful Mrs. Brians on the school board said people liked the orchestra performance," said Jessa.

"Yeah, that went well—as we told you at the welcome-back party. What we didn't tell you was how close it came to not happening," said Alice. "We originally canceled it after you disappeared, Jessa. You were supposed to have that solo, remember? So it didn't seem right to go ahead. Mr. Alton was real disappointed when we told him how we felt, but everyone was so distracted, we just couldn't focus on it. Then we were talking with

Mrs. Florence at the sheriff's office, and she thought canceling would be a mistake—that it sounded like you really wanted the performance to be well attended, so it would be a tribute to you to do our best."

"Oh, she was so right! I need to give her a hug!" said Jessa. "Listen, guys, here's the plan: Overbrook still doesn't have music in its curriculum. Daddy was planning to turn their claim about the colored schools being 'separate but equal' against them. The hang-up, according to them, is that there's no money to pay a salary. The plan will be to collect money so that the school board will have enough to add a teacher. Do you think we can pass the plate in the park events and gather money that way?"

"I'd be glad to help," said Jeff.

"It should work," said Alice. "Bazaars and bake sales make lots of money."

"Overbrook needs lots of help," said Jeff. "I heard they had to go back to using the outhouses last winter when the plumbing broke down. Everything smelled bad until they finally got it fixed."

Michael said, "Will someone please explain why there's still a separate school for Negroes?"

"It's always been that way. They probably wouldn't want to come to our schools," Cherry said.

"Why not? It sounds like their school is pretty bad off," said April.

"That's what Daddy told me. Jessa, you've forgotten how things work here. When you wrote Barbara about your Negro friend, she told us about it, and she sounded scared," said Cherry. "Her mother found the letter, and when she read it, she hit the roof. She said the Acrees must have filled your head with Northern activist ideas and that you were a disgrace to your family!"

April turned to Jessa. "You didn't tell us. *We* are Northern activists?"

Michael said, "It's not a question of Northern activism. Schools everywhere are gonna get integrated—it's the law. Why do they think they can be different?"

"They won't change until they're forced to," said Alice.

"Why fight it?" asked Michael.

"I've heard them talking. They say colored children are dirty and have diseases—that they're stupid and it will drag down the quality of education," said Cherry.

"Everyone thinks Negroes should be kept in their place. What they're worried about are uppity Negroes. Who knows what they'll demand next?" said Jeff. "I deliver newspapers to the Negro part of town, and it's pretty run down, there, just like their school. Whites around here don't want them to begin to start making comparisons…"

"But doesn't anyone connect the dots?" asked April. "If they could go to good schools with new books and good facilities, the kids would get a good education, grow up to get good jobs, and live better."

Alice said, "That's just what they don't believe. Or," she looked around, "maybe it's what they're afraid of? I know this, though. They'll tell you Negroes have their own music and wouldn't benefit from music education."

"What the school board wants is to pay for just enough education so they can get low-paying jobs and be thankful for them," added Jeff.

"No! I can't stand this!" said Jessa, rising. "Listen, guys, when I went to Portland, I tried out for the junior orchestra. I was seated next to Janie, my Negro friend I wrote you about. She plays flute wonderfully well, and when she saw I was having trouble in geometry, she helped me. Her education was *better* than mine, and she wanted to be a friend and share what she knew!"

The librarian came over and reproached them: "Remember,

this is a library. Jessa, we love having you back, but you have to be respectful of others. If you can't keep your voices down, you'll have to leave."

Jessa sank into her chair. "Yes, ma'am."

"Hey," whispered Alice, "let's walk over to the sheriff's office and talk with Mrs. Florence. She's been pretty wise in the past."

They slipped out of the library and set out down Main Street. Oaks, maples, and sweet gum trees shaded the wide street, even in the commercial district, and they trooped side-by-side down the shady, deserted street.

"Why wouldn't it be better to push for the schools to merge, Jessa? That would be simpler and solve the problem of music classes for everyone," said Michael.

"But I don't know how to do that, Michael," admitted Jessa.

Jeff mused, "Technically, it wouldn't be so hard. There aren't many kids at Overbrook—around fifty from first to eighth grade. I know they have classes doubled-up, like first- and second graders together. It's kinda like the old one-room schoolhouses."

"I never thought to wonder, but where do colored kids go after eighth grade?" asked Jessa.

"They get bussed to the colored high school in Landsdowne," said Jeff. "That's a long time to spend on a crummy school bus every day."

Jessa said, "This is just too big. All I want is to get music at Overbrook. Listen, if I pass a collection plate after the choir sings—Jacob Wilson's wife, Margaret, told me about it Saturday night, and also after Eddie Wilson and his grandfather play, don't you think people will give for a good cause? If we give them the money, then they can add music instruction."

"Phooey, Jessa. I thought you had more fight in you," said Michael. "All this stupid system with separate schools, duplicating everything is going to come crashing down sooner or later, and sooner would be better."

"I'm with Michael," said Jeff. "It'll come to a head soon, and Radford might be able to set a good example."

"Watch what you wish for," said Cherry. "Daddy said this could get nasty. Remember the guys who drove that car in the Mother's Day parade with the 'white pride' flag? They were looking for trouble…"

· · · · ·

When the six burst into the sheriff's headquarters, Florence, the heavy-set clerk, was on her feet immediately. "Oh, how nice! I heard you were in town, Jessa, and wondered when you'd stop by."

"I wanted to thank you for keeping the orchestra performance from being canceled last fall. Alice said you convinced them," said Jessa.

"I remember that. My husband, Bruce, and I attended. They left an empty seat where you would have sat, Jessa, and I looked so hard at that seat, I almost broke down crying."

Sheriff Goodrich entered through the back door, tossing off his cap so that his white hair stood up, unkempt. He'd been cussing under his breath, but when he saw the kids, his face broke into a wide smile as he held out his arms for Jessa. She ran to hug him.

"Young lady, you're looking good! You know, sometimes when things aren't going well, we remind ourselves that at least Jessamine is alive and well."

"Sorry I made it so hard for you," said Jessa.

"You did what you had to, I guess. Didn't make my office look very effective, though."

"What's got you so riled up, Don?" asked Florence.

"Those self-appointed bastions of white culture are parading in front of the newspaper office, reacting to Ted's article in the newspaper."

Jeff snorted. The sheriff looked at him. "You know these guys? I wish you'd fill me in on what they want out of this. I don't know how to talk with them. I can't figure out where this level of anger comes from."

"Yeah, I know them," said Jeff. "Could be Charlie's father who drives the anger. He used to work at my dad's store, but his treatment of the colored customers was intolerable."

"Jessa, you sure can stir up the worst elements in this town," said the sheriff. "Ted's description of the meeting included your demands to the school board."

"But what did he write?" asked Jessa. "I thought the reporter was on my side."

"He said you challenged the school board to add music to Overbrook on the basis of *separate but equal*," said the sheriff. "Getting that school board to do anything they haven't set their minds to will be quite an accomplishment, Jessa. I had to threaten them about Overbrook's roof, but the colored community took the bull by the horns and patched it before I could get the school board lined up to do anything."

"Desegregation would solve the music problem in the Negro school," said Michael.

"Oh, that school desegregation business—I'm getting directives on maintaining peace from the governor," said the sheriff, "but if we can't calm these hot heads, Radford's in for trouble."

"But how are you going to calm them?" asked Michael.

"We've just got to get back to some kind of balance. People are happy with things the way they are, and nobody wants trouble."

"So, just avoid desegregation as long as possible? They can't stop it—it's coming. The Supreme Court ruled unanimously…" Michael broke off as the sheriff groaned and sank onto one of the benches and ran his fingers through his hair.

"I just hope to serve out my term and hand that mess over to a younger man."

"Don!" exclaimed Florence. "This *is* coming, and soon! I'd trust you to deal fairly with everyone. Don't you think the community needs to be planning?"

"Planning for 'Christian schools' like they're talking about up in Landsdowne? That's the kind of planning I'd rather they stay away from."

"What're Christian schools?" asked Alice.

Florence replied, "Christian schools would be for the white kids. Ted, the *Post*'s reporter, told me about it. He thinks it'll ruin the public school system."

"What about separation of church and state?" asked Michael. "Public schools aren't supposed to be associated with religion. It's in the Constitution."

"The Christian schools would be private. That's how they plan to keep the Negroes out."

"Here in Radford?" asked Cherry.

"Ted doesn't think so," said Florence. "He comes here after work at the newspaper to talk with Marvin. Last night I stayed on to listen. Since Marvin's been working with Jacob, he's ardent about promoting race relations. Ted told me how the Oak Ridge schools are already integrated."

"I'm glad to hear there's some spirit around here!" Michael said, glancing at Jessa to see how she would take his challenge.

"Spirit or not, Florence is right. Planning is important, but I don't know how to deal with this anger," said the sheriff. "Young lady, you seem to be part of the problem—you and your relatives. I want to enlist your help. This is your town, too, and long after I'm gone, you'll have to live with the consequences of how we deal with this."

· CHAPTER 10 ·

The news of Jessa's return and her meeting with the school board
had spread like wildfire around Radford. Jacob's aunt Helen had
heard plenty and was worried about the rumblings over Overbrook and the heated response to the article in the Radford paper. The paranoia generated after Jessa's disappearance last fall
was still echoing, and the Negro population had been trying to
keep a low profile.

As Helen swept the porch, she looked out for the visitors
from Portland. Her sun hat partly hid her gray hair, pulled back
into a bun, and her thick glasses reflected the afternoon light.
As she worked, she muttered about the upcoming visit. She'd
liked this Northern family when they visited her farm last winter, but she worried that they didn't understand the local culture. She shook the leaves off her broom and turned to greet the
family that piled out of the Oldsmobile.

Helen led them first to her garden. Tall, tasseling corn supported the twists and blossoms of pole beans, staked tomato
plants were hanging heavy with green and ripening tomatoes,
and there was towering okra with pretty yellow blooms, sprawl-
ing squash, and pepper plants with red and yellow peppers.

Jessa said proudly, "Aunt Helen's garden shows what Tennessee can grow. Hers is even better than Grandad's garden. That's
one of his chickens, though. Look at her babies!"

"Oh, so darling!" April exclaimed.

Helen was especially proud of her sheep, which had recently been shorn. She led them to see her two rams and then the ewes with their lambs. The lambs were white or brown with black faces and were still clean and new-looking. They were used to getting attention and crowded forward to have their foreheads scratched. The last-born was being bottle-fed, and Helen gave that job to Michael, who struggled to hold on as the lamb jerked and butted at the bottle.

The barn was fragrant with the first cutting of hay. They helped gather the eggs, and when a hen jumped down from a nest, they tried to recall whether it was from Jessa's grandfather's farm. Helen said it was, and that she was a good layer.

When they had visited Helen during the snowstorm, her cow had been in the barn, but today she was out in the pasture enjoying the abundant grass. That cow, Nancy, had made such an impression on April that she had focused on milk products for her Home Economics class project. Her research had whetted her appetite for hands-on experience with milking and butter-making.

"Mrs. Wilson, do you think you could show me how to milk a cow?" asked April. "I'd love to see how you make butter and buttermilk."

"Why, honey, it takes getting the knack of it, milking does, but you can learn. Let me see your hands." Helen studied April's hands' potential. "Yes, you have nice, long fingers. Must have gotten them from your father. When I started trying to milk, my hands were so small, the poor cow thought I was just playing with her! Milking time is later, though. Nancy isn't expecting it now, and I made apple pie for you folks. Let's go in and wash up so you can see what you think of my pie."

Michael and Ben had been touring the orchard when Helen called them for pie, so they ran down the hillside to join the others.

"Mrs. Wilson, do you drive the tractor we saw in the barn?" panted Michael.

"Yes! Adam made sure I could carry on with the operation of the farm. We always worked together, but now I drive the tractor to pull the hay mow and the baler to make the bales. Jacob keeps everything on the farm running good. He came by to help out with bucking the hay—always helps me, and Eddie wants to learn how to drive the tractor, so I promised to teach him."

"Boy, that would be great!"

"I do so want someone in the family to be interested in taking over the farm! Adam made me promise to never sell. He worked so hard to hold on to this land. He felt that it made all the difference in terms of self-respect, for a colored person to own his own land." Helen gazed out over the fields and barn, and Michael detected tears in her eyes. She turned back toward the house. "Why don't y'all wash up at the spigot here or in the bathroom and see if you don't have some appetite for pie and milk. I saved Nancy's milk after you called to say you were coming."

When they had washed, they took their places at the table where the freshly baked pie sat on display.

"That's quite a sight, Helen. A little bird must have told you how much I love apple pie!" said Ben.

Helen sliced and served the pie, and this time, she didn't have to be asked to sit down to eat with the family. The pie was made with tart apples that were perfectly balanced with cinnamon, sugar, and a buttery crust.

"My, but that's good! I want to take lessons from you!" said April. "I can teach you how to make lemon meringue pie like Granddaddy taught us, but this is the best apple pie I've ever tasted!"

"And the creamy milk is super with it!" said Michael.

"Delicious!" Ben said, and everyone agreed.

"I do think it turned out pretty well," admitted Helen.

As they sat enjoying their milk and pie, Jessa sought Aunt Helen's advice about the Overbrook issue. "Mrs. Wilson, we were at the sheriff's office discussing my plans with Mrs. Florence because the school board said it was impossible to get music into the colored school. Then the sheriff came in and said the newspaper report was causing problems."

Glad that she had been the one to raise the issue, Helen had an answer ready. "Honey, your plan is stirring up a hornet's nest. Take my advice and drop the whole idea. Who's going to pay for it, anyway?"

"They say the problem is they don't have the money, so it's my idea that we could use the musical events this summer to raise money—like the way we sold magazines to buy the new water fountain."

Helen shook her head. "It takes a mighty lot of money to pay a teacher's salary, Jessa. How come you been talking with the school board?"

"My daddy was on the school board. Back when I was hiding out, I thought if I proved that I could take care of myself then they wouldn't treat me like a child. I wanted to go back to Radford and live at home with Cassie, go to school, and finish what daddy dreamed of doing."

"Just what was your daddy's dream, honey?"

"He wanted all Radford's kids to have a chance to play an instrument. He was an orphan and never had a chance to study music, but he believed it was important for people's lives. That's why he and Mommie started the music shop. Don't you agree? I heard Eddie loves playing the violin. That's what Mr. Jacob said."

"Yes, Lord! Eddie just worships that little fiddle! Did Jacob tell you how well he plays it? Eddie and his grandfather are quite a pair, now. I wish Adam could have lived to see it. He'd have been so proud! But, Jessa, you better keep away from that school board. They don't want to help us. We tried and tried to get them to fix the plumbing at Overbrook, and finally the men just did it themselves, and the roof leak, too. Maybe we can organize something at the church for teaching music. In addition to Eddie's grandfather, several people in the community could teach the colored children who want to study music."

"But it needs to be fair. Now that they have music in the white schools, they ought to offer it at Overbrook. I think the school board could be coming around, Mrs. Wilson. Mr. Wexler, who must be rich 'cause he has a bank—I know his daughter. Abby plays clarinet, and I bet she can convince him to support us. I'm going to get in touch with her."

Helen just shook her head. "I don't want you pushing that school board, Jessa. They can be vengeful. You sure do get some big ideas in your head." With a sigh she turned to April. "Young lady, evening's coming on. Let's get to that milking job you want to try out."

· CHAPTER 11 ·

When Helen's truck pulled in front of the sheriff's headquarters, Florence eagerly opened the door. Helen, wearing a freshly starched patterned dress and carrying a heavy bag, entered.

"Helen, good to see you. I've been hoping you'd stop in."

"The garden's pushing food out all over the place. I brought you corn, tomatoes, peppers, and crookneck squash."

"Wonderful, Helen. We'll have plenty of eaters tonight— the grandchildren are coming, and they love your tomatoes and corn. I hope you have time to sit a spell."

"Don't mind if I do." Helen set the heavy bag of vegetables on the floor and eased herself into a chair. "I've been hoeing in the garden, and I got all worked up chopping those weeds when all I could think about was this school situation."

"The Supreme Court ruling?" Florence was surprised to hear that Helen was following that. "Ted and Marvin keep talking about it. That Thurgood Marshall sure did lay down the law."

"Well, he did and he didn't, exactly. Now, don't get me wrong, he's a great man, but the business end of it is blunted by this 'all deliberate speed'—what that means around here is as slow as Christmas if Santa just don't never visit your neighborhood."

Florence pursed her lips. "Ted and Marvin talk about that, too. Speculate about what the school board will do. Don points out that they weren't exactly eager to help out when Overbrook needed repairs."

"Well, it's my opinion we'd be safer to just lay low. Florence, you know and I know that this town isn't ready for school desegregation. They'll fight. The lid will come off this town if they try to force colored children into the white school." Helen leaned toward Florence and looked into her eyes. "I'm worried sick."

Florence grimaced. "The threat is all one-way. White parents won't allow white children to go to Overbrook, that's for sure!"

"The Negro children trying to attend a white school will be attacked in ways they'll never forget. Sacrificial lambs are what they'll be!"

"It does sound worrisome!" said Florence. "Ted's been telling us what happened in East Tennessee. He's proud of the Oak Ridge schools, but that system's government-run. In another small town, an explosion destroyed the school. You know we don't need that kind of thing around here. He blames that on people who came into the communities from outside and stirred up bad feelings among the locals."

"We don't need outsiders butting in where they don't belong, trying to do good and causing a lot of harm in the process—that's really what brought me here, Florence. I'm afraid this Jessamine Olsen's going to cause trouble. I know she means well, but she's gone North and come back with some big ideas that that Northern family can't advise her about because they don't know any better. They probably think Radford people are broadminded just the same way they are. Those of us who live here know this can't end well."

Florence focused on gathering her skirt fabric into even pleats between her fingers and didn't reply. She was remembering when she was little and Helen had cared for her when her mother was busy with her baby sister's colic. She'd gone fishing and picked plums and generally run around with her colored neighbors. Always, their home had been welcoming for her.

"Helen, when I was growing up, I idolized your family. I

thought you and your brother were super—remember all the fun we had? I loved the way your parents would sing together. Why would it have been wrong if we had been able to go to the same school? Hearing Marvin and Ted talk about desegregation set me to remembering that when you and Larry went off to school every day, I thought I would just join you when I got old enough. I was so disappointed when I was put in the white school!"

"I remember how you complained to my pa about it, and he tried to explain it to you, and you just cried and cried."

"He couldn't explain it. There wasn't any good explanation!"

"Well, that was then, and this is now. To get back to Jessa's meddling, she calls it her father's plan, and I sympathize with her desire to finish some business she knew he cared about, but I wish she'd tone it down and leave us in peace. It's not like we're lacking for music, even if it isn't taught in school. I tried to suggest that she leave it to the colored community."

"Helen, Jessa has a colored girlfriend in Portland, and she realizes that such a friendship would have never been possible here in Radford, the way the races are kept apart. Think about it—the issue of separation. Your family and my family lived side-by-side on that bluff, and we depended on each other— our mothers canned tomatoes together, and when your pa got sick, my mama brought soup and biscuits so your mother could spend her time nursing him. We didn't care who was a darkie and who was a whitey—we were both just people struggling to get along."

Helen glanced up. When their eyes locked, she reached over to squeeze Florence's hand. "You got it right, Flo. That's just how it was! If it hadn't been that way, I wouldn't be here trying to talk through my concerns with you. But don't you see that this desegregation business will let loose a hell of a lot of trouble on us? There's a history in this town you prob- ably never concerned yourself with because that's the way the whites like it—scare the niggers to death in the night but go to church the next morning with their heads held high. I'm afraid for my people!"

"I'm sorry, Helen. I think Don's right that the troubles started with Jessa's disappearance. All that's true, but I keep thinking this separation business has already gone on too long. And to approach it with the schools…" Florence paused to contemplate. "I think that's the right way to go. Forget the parents and start with the kids! Why, I can't imagine my grandkids would object to a mixed-race classroom. They just care about what they did in recess and whether someone's birthday will result in cupcakes for the class. It isn't something they'd even notice, having brown kids in the same class, if their parents didn't make the trouble…"

"I'm not so sure, Flo. I've heard some mean-talking white children echoing their parents. But how you gonna keep the parents out of it?" asked Helen.

There was a long pause. Florence was recalling ugly remarks dropped in her sewing circle, particularly at the organizational meeting for the annual bazaar. "I just don't know, Helen. Jessa's goal is modest, but Ted must have known that the way he reported it would hit a nerve, and he went ahead and wrote it up. I think he's trying to push the issue. Remember the hecklers who spoiled the Mother's Day parade? People are on edge. Jessa plans to collect donations when the combined choir sings next Thursday, but I don't know how that will go over."

"I've been worrying about that, too. Even without her meddling, the choir performance was going to get us some attention we didn't need," said Helen.

"And getting back to the school board, I'd bet they have no intention of doing anything for Overbrook. They'll turn Jessa down and expect her to forget about it, but she couldn't have held out for weeks on her own if she wasn't pretty determined."

"Flo, if you have any influence over her, please steer her energies in a different direction. I talked with Reverend James, and he's in touch with relatives in St. Louis. He thinks we can ride this one out if there's no attention called to the colored community and we keep our heads down."

Florence gave her friend a hug. "Helen, I'll do what I can. I don't know what the future holds, but in my heart, I feel it's time for the people to come together."

After Helen left, Florence thought for a long time about what her friend had said. She recalled her childhood and her misery at being cut off from her friends by the school arrangement. Then she recalled what Jessa had said about her Portland friend. *I know in my heart that it is right*, she again concluded, but she also knew that her grandchildren would be safe, and she wasn't so sure about the children in Helen's family...

· CHAPTER 12 ·

Karen finished up the lunch dishes and dried her hands. The kids were off to the swimming pool, so she finally had a chance to explore her father's early life. She'd grown up hearing stories about childhood pranks and the farm animals but knew nothing about him as a young man.

At the party hosted by the Carlsons last November, Karen had been accosted by her father's closest friend. He'd demanded to know why her father disappeared, and she'd spilled out her father's story in front of everyone: the story she'd learned just before his death. The realization that her gentle father had fled Tennessee after accidently killing a robber had shocked her to the core, and at the time of the party she hadn't come to terms with the information herself. The guests had been kind, and Karen had frequently thought of the loving words of her father's friend. Now, she wanted to talk with him. Florence would know where he lived.

Karen peeled her dress off, dropped the damp item across a chair and chose a fresh one, wondering how people ever learned to live with this humidity. The slight breeze felt good as she set off down the shady street. *People here sure do love their lawns, and the climate really is better for flowers than for people*, she mused.

It was sultry inside the sheriff's headquarters. Florence had been knitting to occupy herself, and three sets of booties were lined up along the desk. She'd been thinking about Helen's visit when Karen stuck her head in the door, so Florence seized the opportunity to advise the Acrees about the local temperament.

"Mrs. Acree, I'm so glad you've stopped by. We need to talk. I'm worried about Jessa's push about music at Overbrook. I hope you can reason with her. The colored community is afraid she'll get the white people riled up. You see, around here, colored people's jobs depend on the willingness of the whites to employ them, and that's just the tip of the iceberg—things can get a lot meaner than lost jobs. Colored people get along by not attracting attention to themselves, and they're afraid Jessa's effort will force a clash."

"Florence, please call me Karen. Jessa's a very stubborn young woman. She means well, but I can see how her pushing might cause trouble. I'm afraid that on top of her father's unfinished goals, there's the fact that Michael is fired up by the dynamic civics teacher he had. He backs her up and urges her along, and April adds her ten cents' worth. Their newest plan is to collect money for the school board."

"My guess is that if her father were here, he'd counsel her to back off. Did the kids tell you a bunch of young men were protesting outside the newspaper office over her meeting with the school board?"

"No, I don't recall they said anything about that. We need to get on the newspaper delivery schedule for this summer. All I heard was full steam ahead with their plans. They went straight over to the Carlsons' to borrow platters to pass around to collect donations when the combined choir performs."

"There's talk going around about people not knowing their place, and the colored people are worried it might turn violent."

"Florence, I can't promise anything, but I'll talk with Jessa and try to get Michael to tone down his remarks. I agree that this is a local issue that we shouldn't get involved in as outsiders…"

"Karen, I'll put it to you bluntly: this town has a few people who talk change, but they are in the minority. The power structure of Radford will fight it tooth and nail. They're invested in maintaining control. Add to that the rabble-rousing fringe looking for any excuse for a fight. The situation's getting explosive."

"Will passing collection plates cause a problem?"

"I don't know about this collection-plate idea. Maybe if she waits until after the performance, it can go off smoothly. I know I'm not the only one looking forward to hearing the choir. The women are proud of what they've accomplished."

"I'm sure it'll be wonderful.

To change the subject, Florence, I came to see you because I knew you'd know how to get in touch with John Morgan. You'll recall that he and my father grew up together, and I want to plumb his memories about my father as a young man."

"Karen, John will be delighted to talk with you."

"Does he live in walking distance?"

"Right down the street in the back of the carpenter's shop, the place he locked up when he went into hiding. Since moving back to town, John has become a regular community member. Don and I were discussing how John was hounded out of town. Apparently he doesn't have any close family, and when the town people branded him a communist, he withdrew to a cabin in the woods and lived like a hermit. That was long enough ago that he was largely forgotten by most people. Those who attacked him are dead and gone, and he's been accepted as if nobody wants to remember those days. He's a regular at the barber shop, plays checkers and chess in the afternoons."

"I want to learn about when he and Dad were growing up together—what they talked and dreamed about. It's been so hard, trying to piece together the missing parts of my father's life, and I know John could help me. Remember how at the Carlsons' party John told us my dad's girlfriend married Jessa's grandfather after dad disappeared?"

"I've thought of that snowy evening so often, dear, the way your father's story came out at John's prompting, and how hard it must have been for you."

"Hard, but good in the end. I needed to confront my father's past, and I came out of it feeling that those good people believed in him—and me. It was important to finally come to grips with what happened and not have skeletons in the closet. Now, I'm lucky John is still around."

"That's true. John's as sharp as a tack, too. He's the champion checker player and spins good yarns all the time he's playing."

"So where can I find him?"

"The carpenter's shop is on Line Street, which runs parallel to Main Street, three blocks down from here." Florence pointed. "The shop doesn't have a sign, but it's just beyond the Chinese grocery. Knock loud or he won't hear you in the back."

"Do you think he'll talk to me?"

"John's a participant in the life of the town now. Something about Jessa's disappearance and her discovery in that snowstorm brought him around. Some evenings he talks with Ted and Marvin about desegregation issues, and Marvin fills me in."

"Good to hear. In the meantime, I'll try to keep Jessa and our kids from treading on people's toes, but I'm glad that there's grassroots support for change, too." She glanced at the wall clock. "I'd better walk on over there, now, before I lose my nerve! Thanks for filling me in, Florence."

• • • • •

Karen knocked loudly and listened. Far in the back, a door opened, a radio announcer's voice was heard, then footsteps approached and stopped. Karen could feel him standing on the other side of the door. Finally, John turned the knob. Recognizing her, his shoulders relaxed, his bearded face softened, and his blue eyes twinkled. "Little Karen, what a surprise. Please come in."

Karen entered a dim, cavernous room lined with dusty work-tables and benches. The floorboards creaked underfoot as she followed him to the back room where the announcer was giving the weather. John swung the door open to reveal afternoon sunlight streaming through two high windows to illuminate his living space. Everything was neat and cozy, and his tabby cat approached Karen with her tail held proudly.

Karen began. "Mr. Morgan, as my father's best friend, I thought you could help me reconstruct his life. I realized that I have a distorted view of how things must have been like here in Tennessee because I focused on his mother and how she drove him away. I know his home life can't have been as depressing as I imagine. I'd love to learn more about my father as a young man and his life here in Radford. Is this a good time to talk?"

"Little Karen, everyone calls me John. Wait a minute, let me turn off this radio."

He indicated a chair by the table and joined her. "Your father has been on my mind lately. If he were here, he would be participating in our discussions, and I imagine his Quaker ideals would fit right in with our concerns. This country is on the cusp of big changes, and if he were alive, Tom would be pushing for them!"

"You're right. Dad worked a lot with young people in the meeting. What they often wanted was a way to make a difference, and he inspired them."

"I'll put us on some coffee," he said. "Hope you like it strong. I got to liking it that way living in France."

He put a pot of water on a gas stove and began grinding coffee beans in a wooden coffee grinder. For a time there was only the sound of the steady grinding.

"Your father cared deeply for people, Karen. In the evenings, we'd go on long walks, and we often talked about how unfair life was. Together, we dreamed of a new order in which merit would be rewarded and everyone could make a good life by contributing to society in accordance with his God-given gifts. No doors would be closed because of race or the accident of not being born a Vanderbilt or a Carnegie. Trade schools and colleges would be open to everyone, free for all. And we didn't leave out the women, either. We were such idealists!"

Tears were running down Karen's face, and she made no move to hide them. "How I loved my father! He *was* an idealist. In Portland, he worked for fairer housing, and his major focus was with the youth. He cared for them and helped them believe in themselves."

"A hole opened up in my life when Tom left. I told you about the doubts and fears triggered by the circumstances of his disappearance, but I still believed in him, and I kept up the practice of talking with him—in my mind. I could predict his responses to the questions I was grappling with. We were that close." John shook his head at the memories. "When Tom left, times were really hard. Other young men disappeared during that period. There was no work, and farming didn't pay the taxes. Then came the war: the First World War. Young men responded to the call-up almost with relief."

"I suppose Dad might have enlisted if he hadn't come under the influence of the Quakers. I doubt it, though, with the horror of that killing hanging over him. Instead of enlisting, he served time in jail as a conscientious objector."

"Good for him! Wish I'd been with him—war is real hell. Sure, some who came back intact claimed it as the peak experience of their lives—the ultimate fraternity. Some, the ones that stay quiet, never gloried in their experiences. Then there were the ones who'd been full of hope for a new country and were sorely disappointed—a reflection of the problems this country is still plagued with."

"What do you mean?"

"It was like this: I served in an all-white regiment, of course, but we were supported by Negro units who hauled equipment, and dug trenches, and after a skirmish, they were the ones set to digging the graves. Sometimes, in the heat of combat, the race lines broke down and we all pitched in and served shoulder-to-shoulder. Those colored boys were dedicated, and they served bravely, and most of us from the South felt at home in their company."

John pulled out the drawer of the coffee grinder and tilted the grounds into a tall glass.

"Those who were interested got acquainted with the colored men's dreams. I don't know if you know your history, Karen, but according to Wilson, America got into that war so the world would be free for democracy." John's penetrating gaze cut Karen so fiercely that she shrank back. "The colored soldiers, those poor devils, what they wanted was a chance to prove they were loyal Americans, too! They risked their lives in Europe because they believed there would be democracy here at home! Then came the triumphal end of the war. The Negroes came home, those who survived—no medals for them, of course—but they were expecting that their contributions would be recognized. What a travesty! Nothing had changed. If anything, it was worse! I traveled to Detroit and Chicago and saw it first-hand there, so it wasn't just in the South."

"The conclusion was unmistakable: the expectation of the Negro for democracy was down the drain. They weren't even asking for the whole ball of string, just a shred of fair treatment. Bit by bit, I watched them face the truth—*get kicked in the face with the truth*. This country had used them as a doormat! 'Jobs for Veterans' the signs said, but not the colored veterans. They were turned away from cafeterias, movie theaters, rooming houses—nobody wanted to hire them for even menial labor jobs if they could hire a white man instead. The inhumanity of it tore me up."

"That's why I went back to France, which had sustained terrible damage but was building on the changes, too. It wasn't home, but with my friends dead in the war or disappeared, it was a good choice. I studied woodworking over there, learned the trade pretty good. Eventually, memories of Tennessee and the good furniture wood here lured me back, so I brought my tools with me and got established as a furniture maker here in Radford."

When he paused, the cat jumped into his lap, so he stroked her ears. Karen saw tears drop on the cat's fur, but he continued. "At first, it seemed like I was going to be able to live here in peace. Some people were suspicious of me from the start, but there was a lot of construction going on, and I fulfilled a need, so I built up a good business. Unfortunately, I never could shed the taint of a foreigner. Mostly, I tried to keep my head down and toe the line, but pretty soon, comments that I made got to grating on people's nerves, especially the people who exert the small-town power. Next thing I knew, there was another war. I would have fought the Nazis, but by the time America entered the war, I was too old—even the Merchant Marines rejected me. The news reports of atrocities and lives lost brought back vivid memories."

He poured the boiling water onto the coffee grounds, added a lid, and sat down across from her. "And after World War Two, the same dang thing happened. Negroes who sacrificed in the trenches for their country and women who'd operated machinery, put rivets in airplane wings, and driven trucks—they were all put back in their places. The women were supposed to be satisfied with cooking, washing clothes, vacuuming, and, of course, having babies, but there was no place at all for the Negro man. Segregation was enforced even more harshly than before the war."

"And when were you labeled a communist?"

"The town caught the Red Scare after the Second World War, and I was their best target. Figured I must be a communist sympathizer, and there was some truth in that. Your dad and I had talked a good socialist line before he disappeared, so I guess I had eased into it naturally. I'd been to some meetings—not around here, mind you, but when I traveled in the North. I never have been a very tactful person, so there was no way I could get along in the town by that time. The communist label put a bullseye on my back."

"Karen, you came here to hear about your father, and all I've talked about is myself. Let me tell you a tale about him. The school we attended was torn down years ago, but it was in a pretty little clearing out where there's a drive-in movie theater now. Out behind the school there were two outhouses, one for the boys and the other for the girls. At the end of the school year, the human refuse had to be dug out and carted off somewhere and buried. One morning, Tom and I happened upon this old Negro man working on that job. What caught our attention was the smell because digging into that mess released a powerful scent, as you can imagine. We walked to the slope down behind the outhouses to see what was going on, and out of the hole this old man looked up. His head was grizzled, and the whites of his eyes were yellowed, but he sang out a cheery hello, proud as could be. We knew him from around town; his name was Joseph. I'm sure he must have been illiterate, but he was known for being able to quote Bible scripture along with the best of them. It seemed that his very language was the language of the Bible. I thought that he would be embarrassed to be found digging out an outhouse, but it was nothing like that. He was glad to have the work. Seems this was a job he did for a lot of people. Tom asked him how much he got for the job, and he said, *I get half a dollar for each of 'em, Tommy—that's good pay!*

"We could see the job was a big one. It must have taken him

all day to dig out those outhouses, haul off the mess, and bury it. When we discussed it, we agreed that it was a job someone had to do. How else can an outhouse remain functional? But it kept bugging Tom. He'd see some example of ostentation, evidence someone had cash to spend on a new wagon or a hat with fine feathered plumes, and he'd think of Joseph. Finally, he came round to where I was fishing and he said, *I'm going to visit Joseph—take him a bucket of our early apples—wanna come?* Of course I went along, took the couple of fish I had on the stringer, and we located Joseph in what you could only describe as a hovel. It was dug into the hillside, and it had one finished side with a door, one window, and a dirt floor. Joseph greeted us with delight and made over those poor apples and the two little fish like they were caviar. It didn't occur to us to give him money, because he was proud of being able to support himself, and anyway, we didn't have any. After that, Tom visited Joseph frequently and he'd take along a gift of a loaf of bread or eggs when the family could spare it. He didn't come away empty-handed, either. Joseph told him wonderful stories. Tom shared them with me."

John turned a piercing glance at Karen. "I always expected Tom to become a writer, with Joseph as his inspiration." With his gnarled hand, John slowly pushed down the plunger he had fashioned to make a coffee press. He walked over and took down two cups from above the sink, poured in the strong, dark brew, and set the sugar bowl in front of Karen. "I recommend you try this coffee with sugar. It's considerably stronger than the local brew. Sorry, but I don't have milk or cream."

"It smells wonderful. You're treating me to a trip to France, minus the hassle of travel," said Karen.

"I have the beans shipped to me from New Orleans and roast them myself. It's my one indulgence."

"John, you're right. If Dad were here, he would be pushing

for equality." Karen sipped the thick, sweetened coffee. "My, isn't that a treat—so much flavor! Did you and Dad often go fishing together?"

"Fishing was part of our way of life, Karen. Both my mother and Tom and Bill's mother would fry up fish for breakfast if we got home too late for the dinner preparations. Fish was a mainstay of our diet! We caught rabbits in traps, too, and skinned them. My mother, bless her soul, would take the skins and tan them and make caps for winter. I still recall a pretty little rabbit-skin muff she made for my cousin."

"Times must have been hard."

"Better here than in the cities, I bet. Sure, nobody had money. Doctors and shopkeepers gave you credit or took something you had to trade, so store-bought things were generally unaffordable, but we always had a big garden and something to eat. When someone was sick, the neighbors turned out to help, doing chores and bringing in food."

"How many people lived here then?"

John stopped to do the calculation. "Maybe a third as many as live here now."

"Sure sounds like a tight-knit group, everyone taking care of everyone else. Maybe that's what we need more of nowadays."

"Oh, every small town has the same list of characters, including the holier-than-thous, the ne'er-do-wells, and the drunkard. Real power is exerted behind the scenes, and everyone knows everyone else's business. Can be pretty hard on someone who is different."

At the memories, sadness swept over his face. His cat rubbed against his leg and rumbled softly, and he responded by rubbing her ears. Karen knew that her father had been a non-conformist, and she now had a clearer view of how much these two friends had supported each other, how much the friendship must have meant to John. She recalled how sad her father had been over the fact that he had never been able to bring himself to contact friends and family in Radford.

"John, the town drove you into hiding, I understand."

He sighed, took a sip of the hot coffee and faced her across the table. "The people of this town are suspicious of anything different from what they grew up with. The country had fought wars that turned the social structure upside down, and then they just wanted to forget it and force everyone back in their place. No lessons learned, no betterment of man's place in society!"

"So now you've come back, and Florence says you play a good game of chess and checkers."

"The town apparently has a short memory. Nothing was being served by my hiding away in the woods, and I wanted to see if I could rejoin the human race. Part of the trick to coming back was outliving some of the people who had it in for me. Actually, learning of your father's deathbed confession made me want to see if I couldn't make some good choices before it was too late."

"The issues are different now. Tell me about the talk that supports desegregation. Florence tells me that you, Ted, and Marvin are working on issues of race relations."

"I wish I could glorify our discussions by saying we're formulating plans. We just share what we hear on the national level, which, by the way, rarely gets in the local news unless Ted slips it into an article. He has to downplay the topic, or he'll lose his newspaper job. We share our dissatisfaction with the way things are in the South—not that the North doesn't have problems, too."

"That's true. Portland's record is pretty sordid when it comes to race relations. Jessa and our kids are focused on school desegregation, which gives them a better impression of Portland than is warranted. I think we need to make sure they're aware of the seriousness of the housing discrimination there. How do you see the South responding to the Supreme Court rulings about the schools?"

"That ruling has people shaking in their boots! Maybe I'm a pessimist, but I predict there'll be riots and people will be killed before it's over. Too many white people are dead-set against change, and they'll fight. As I see it, a generation of whites is going to have to die off, and in the meantime, it's crucial that the colored race take the bull by the horns. They'll lead the fight."

"And can change come through the schools? That's what Jessa and our son, Michael, argue for! Jessa became friends with a colored girl in Portland, and it's made her into an advocate for desegregation."

"Interesting that Tom's family members would have gotten involved in this. I always knew Tom and Bill had it in them to be agents of change. They just didn't catch the rising tide for their ships. We'll have to turn it over to the next generation, but I hope I live to see real change come from all of this, and I'm still ready to be part of the fight."

Karen rose and leaned over the table to reach out to her father's friend. It was almost as if she could hug her own father, and he returned the hug fervently. "Karen, your father is pulling for us to set the world on a better course. I hope we won't disappoint him!"

· CHAPTER 13 ·

When Jessa, April, and Michael returned from the swimming pool, they got a talking-to by Karen about local opposition to change in the schools, and the threat to the colored community.

"But Eddie wants to play in the park! We promised!" objected Jessa, speaking for the trio.

"I want you to talk with Florence about that," said Karen. "Quit saying that just because the white school has music, the colored school should have it also. I know things around here aren't right—we all agree about that—but Florence is in tune with the local community. You should listen to her when she says what you're doing threatens the Negroes."

"Threatens them? School integration is a threat?" asked Michael.

"What's worked for them is to avoid attention. The choir performance is going to be a test, and the whites may object to the mixing of the races, so if Mrs. Florence isn't behind adding Eddie and his grandfather to the list, I want you to know that she has her reasons. Don't you argue with her. A small town has a lot going on under the surface, and we can't waltz in here and think we can revise things we don't like."

With that admonition depressing them, they walked downtown, discussing what they were going to do. When they got to the sheriff's office, they entered and responded to Florence's greeting.

"Mrs. Florence, we need to talk with you," said Jessa as she approached Florence's desk. "We have some more music to add to the summer music series!"

"How nice, Jessa," said Florence. "Bill Alton did say there's an empty slot coming up in July. Are you going to play your flute?"

"No, ma'am. Eddie Wilson wants to play with his grandfather. He plays violin, and he's good, and I think it will show everybody how important music is," said Jessa.

April and Michael nodded, and April agreed, "He's really good, Mrs. Florence."

"He'd be the first child on the roster; that's one hurdle." Florence bit her lip, wondering what the best route might be to discourage the plans that Helen had warned her about. "We should check with Bill. The combined women's choir performs Thursday. I'm really looking forward to it, but there's rumblings against it, and then we've got that barbershop quartet, and after that…" Her voice trailed off as she glanced out the window and saw four young men coming down the street. "My, but don't they look angry!" she exclaimed.

The men surged into the waiting room of the station, forcing Jessa, Michael, and April toward the back. They were dressed in old jeans, tennis shoes, and sweaty button-down plaid shirts, but that's where the similarities ended. Charlie, the ringleader, was thin and angular, with greasy black hair that fell across his face. Matt was stocky, with short brown hair, a bad case of acne, and the beginnings of a beard. Maney's muscular build was apparent through his outgrown clothes, and his sandy hair was botched in an amateur attempt at a buzz cut. Dexter's hope of fitting in with the others was undermined by his clean-cut boyish face and wavy blond curls.

"What's the matter, boys?" Florence asked in her most soothing voice. "I'm sure we can help you. The sheriff's out on rounds, but I expect him back soon."

"We're here to represent the white citizens of Radford. We

demand to know why Radford is cozying up to niggers! Things are getting out of hand in this town, and we're going to set it right," said Charlie.

"Why, Charlie, that's no way to talk," said Florence, surprised by the aggression. "You better clean up your language as long as you're in this office! Now, what's this all about?"

"Music in the Park—in the white end of town—this Thursday! This so-called 'combined choir' is scheduled to perform and"—Matt pulled out a flier and read from it—"*Featured performers include choir members from St. Mark's Methodist, New Hope Baptist, Radford Presbyterian, Bethany Christian, and the AME.* That's the African Episcopal Methodist"—he glanced at Florence—"the Negroes! And it says here: *The whole community.* Get that?" He waved the flier in Florence's face. "*The whole community is invited to bring a picnic dinner and enjoy the park performance this Thursday at six p.m.!*"

Matt slapped the sheet down on the counter. Maney continued: "Since you, Florence Hadford, are known to have been behind the previous 'combined singing' here at the sheriff's headquarters, we figure you must be behind this! Just *who* do you think is going to be picnicking in *our* park?"

Florence drew herself up proudly. "Maney, the park performances are popular. They've been going on for weeks. The women who participated in the first 'combined singing,' both white and colored, enjoyed it so much *they* proposed to get together again. Those women have been practicing for weeks at the high school auditorium."

"Who authorized them to go into our auditorium?" demanded Charlie.

"I guess it was probably the teacher's idea, but the custodian was likely involved, as his wife sings in the choir."

"Ain't going to be no such performance. No white and colored women singing together!" insisted Charlie.

"And what possible harm can come from that? They're enjoying it!" said Florence.

"Mrs. Florence, don't play dumb with me. This town keeps the races apart. We have laws. I expect Sheriff Goodrich to put a stop to this outrage."

The door opened, jostling the crowd in the small reception room, and Ted Hufford, the town's reporter, squeezed in. "I've been trying to catch up with this gang. Looks like news in the making, so I thought I'd find out what's going on," he announced.

"Ted, they're raising an objection to the women's choir performance this Thursday," said Florence.

"What's to object to?" Ted asked, taking out his notebook.

"You know as good as we do, Mr. Hufford, this women's choir will have colored women mixing with our white choir members. *That's* to object to," insisted Maney. "If niggers want to sing, let 'em do it in their own church."

Matt grabbed the flier off the counter and shook it in the reporter's face. "Can you feature it? Pickaninnies playing in Reubens Park? Swinging on the swings? Niggers eating their picnic dinners alongside whites?"

"Sure, I can feature it," Ted said calmly. "And by the way, you'd better clean up your language. *Negro* is the correct term, and drop that pickaninny business. Didn't your mothers teach you that? It won't be long before the schools and public buildings will be desegregated, too. It's already the law of the land, Matt, and it's coming to Radford, whether you like it or not."

"Over my dead body!"

"Oh, really, Matt? Aren't you making a mountain out of a molehill? I say let it come in, easy and slow, to give people a chance to get used to the idea. I think the combined choir is a good place to start."

"We came to get satisfaction from the sheriff," said Charlie. "I know where you stand. You support music at Overbrook. I read your Northern ideas in the *Post*." He noticed Jessa, Michael, and April. "Ha! It's the Yankee agitators! Let's get out of here. We're wasting our time on this bunch!"

The door slammed behind them. Michael, April, and Jessa came out of the corner. "Wow," said Michael. "Amazing. My civics teacher described this, but I'm getting to see it firsthand."

Florence slapped the desk with both hands. "Now, what do we do, Ted? The choir was having so much fun the last time I dropped in on them—just laughing up a storm!"

"It's a problem, Florence," agreed Ted. Ted looked at the 'Yankee agitators.' "We may all need to take stock of the situation. I hope you *agitators* were listening. I include myself in the agitator category, by the way. Those young men can disrupt the performance, and they seem dead-set on trying. I don't know what they have in mind, but Charlie's stepfather's a leader of the white supremacists in this town. Some would call them poor white trash, but that's neither here nor there. I imagine he gets a lot of this racist talk over the dinner table."

Michael said, "What's the role of law and order in allowing the choir to sing? Why can't they do it if it isn't against the law?"

"It should be a non-issue, but these high school graduates have too much time on their hands, in my opinion," continued the reporter. "Just casting around for ways to stir up trouble. Anyway, lots of people around town are looking forward to the singing. Maybe you'd better consult Jim Alton."

Jessa tried to steer the conversation back to Eddie. "Mrs. Florence, mother said our suggestion may be a problem, too. But Eddie Wilson really wants to play."

"Jacob's son?" asked Ted.

"Yessir," said April. "He plays wonderfully well."

"But, Jessa, think about it. Isn't that asking a lot, setting a little boy up to perform, especially now that you've seen this opposition to the choir performance? I know he's taken off playing that fiddle. Jacob told me. But what about the risk?"

"Eddie's good, and he has stage presence—announces each piece and tells something about it, too. He really wants to play. Have you seen how he takes a deep bow at the end of a performance?" said Jessa.

"Yes," said Michael. "He said he and his grandfather are working on special pieces for the park concert, so they're really counting on it."

"Having a colored boy perform is likely to ruffle their feathers, but no worse than the combined choir," said Ted. "Where'd you hear him play, Jessamine?"

"His family came over to the Carlsons' after dinner on Saturday. They had dessert with us—some of Mrs. Carlson's famous angel food cake. Then he played."

"Will miracles never cease! Right there at the Carlson home?"

"Yessum, I planned it as a surprise, but after they left, a neighbor came over and wanted to know what the matter was. She didn't like hearing that it was just a social occasion, including Negroes."

"Well, Jessamine, you sure are one to stir things up! You don't know what you're up against."

"What I want to know is, does this big taboo against sitting down together or singing together come from slavery days?" asked Michael.

Florence heaved a big sigh, but Ted said, "You better bet it does. Them's the 'good old days' as far as the whites are concerned."

"But the Carlsons were okay with breaking those rules," said April.

"Actually, Mrs. Carlson had a hard time," Jessa admitted. "For her, it was a shock. I realized that too late to change things, but she recovered pretty well. I should have known better, after that discussion of school segregation."

"The people in this town have taboos that cover just about everything!" said Michael.

"Not everyone feels that way, Michael," said Ted. "Marvin and Old Man John, the carpenter, he's ardently opposed to segregation and job discrimination. He's traveled all over the world, and he's convinced it doesn't have to be this way."

"We could have told you that. You don't have to leave this country to notice that things in Tennessee are just plain dumb," said Michael.

"Lots of places in the deep South are worse. Tennessee has a level-headed governor, and he's doing what he can to help the state transition smoothly," said Ted.

"Lord help us, yes! Mississippi, Arkansas, Alabama—they're bound to be worse. White people there are outnumbered, and they're afraid!" said Florence.

"But what about Eddie and his grandfather? Eddie really wants to play," said Jessa. "We came here to find out what spots were open. I thought that when they play, it will show people how good music is for everyone. And the schools need to be fair. I'm going back to the school board with the money we can collect after the performances."

"Whoa, Jessamine, what's this?" asked Ted.

"I plan to earn a lot of money, first when the combined choir sings and then when Eddie and his grandfather play. We're gonna pass the plate like they do in church. Getting people involved will be good, won't it? We'll give the money to the school board to convince them to put music in the Overbrook curriculum."

"That school board is a tough nut to crack, Jessa. My guess is you'll have one halfhearted supporter in Mr. Wexler. The others will dig in their heels. I've seen it a dozen times."

"I'll call Mr. Alton," suggested Florence. "Music in the Park was his idea. Maybe he can come over."

"You do that, Florence. I've got to pick up the trail of this band of marauders." Ted gave the children a sympathetic glance. "Bye, folks."

Florence turned to her phone and dialed. "Hello, Jane. This is Florence, down at the Sheriff's office." She paused to listen. "No, everything's fine. I just needed to confer with Bill if he's available. It's about the Music in the Park program. I have Jessamine Olsen and the Acree kids here with me."

She put down the receiver and reported, "He'll walk over shortly. When his wife relayed that you were here, she said he seemed eager. You haven't seen him since you got back, have you Jessamine?"

"No, ma'am. Mr. Jamison said his contract was renewed. Everyone likes him, and he knows lots about music—and plays so many instruments. Daddy said Radford was lucky to attract him, and we better not let him go."

"I get the impression he loves his job. When he was in here the other day, he said he's had free rein to develop the music program, just the way he'd dreamed of when he was in music school."

"Good," said April. "That's how teaching's supposed to be. Our parents love teaching, and Granddaddy felt the same way."

"So, Mrs. Florence, what do you personally think about challenging this colored school versus white school situation head on?" asked Michael. "It sounded to me as if there aren't very many colored kids, anyway—not enough to fill each grade level—and they have to send the high school students somewhere else because there's nothing for them here."

"Michael's got a point," said Florence. "Theoretically, all the Overbrook children could go to the white schools, but what would happen to the Overbrook teachers? My guess is they'll oppose this because they'd lose their jobs."

Bill Alton arrived and greeted Jessa with open arms. "Honey, you look so much better than you did at that welcome-home party last winter! Have you kept up with your flute?"

"I play in the orchestra, and the first-stand flute player is my friend Janie—she's Negro."

"I'm glad Oregon has got the integration thing figured out," he replied.

"We're working on it here in Radford," announced Michael.

"Are we, now?"

Jessa said, "This is Michael Acree and April Acree."

He nodded to April and held out his hand to Michael. "Bill Alton here. I recall you from the welcome-home party for Jessamine. Glad you're back in town." He turned to Jessa. "Jessa, your dad wanted me to teach at Overbrook, but I cover chorus at all three white schools, and then there's all the students who want to play an instrument in the band or orchestra. It's only going to get harder this year as advanced students move up and need new challenges, and there're the beginners who take so much one-on-one time."

"Why don't you try an 'each-one-teach-one' arrangement, like in one-room schoolhouses?" asked April. "Our grandfather told us about that."

"So you come from a family of teachers, too? I think it must be in some people's blood, like farming or a knack for selling iceboxes to Eskimos. That's a good idea about scheduling the classes to let advanced students help those coming along. You learn the most when you have to teach something!"

"Eddie's grandfather must be a good teacher, 'cause he taught Eddie to play the violin just since last winter. We want them to play in the Music in the Park series. I'm going to take up a donation after the combined choir and Eddie's fiddling and donate the money for music at Overbrook," said Jessa.

"Bill, that's why we needed to talk," said Florence. "The combined choir performance is coming up Thursday night, but there've been objections, and I'm afraid we'll be asking for trouble if Eddie Wilson and his grandfather are scheduled to perform."

"Objections?"

"Guys barged in here objecting to Negroes and whites singing together, and to Negroes in the park," Michael summarized.

"How serious is this, Florence?" asked Bill.

"Bill, who knows?" said Florence. "Ted Hufford was here, and he tried to get them to lighten up, but they wouldn't back down. These four just graduated from high school and are at loose ends this summer. Marched after the paper's article about Jessa's proposal to the school board. They said they represent the "white citizens," but I doubt that, although there are undoubtedly others of the same mind. So the question is, do we back down to avoid a confrontation or go ahead, and even add this fiddle performance on top?"

The back door opened, and Sheriff Goodrich entered.

"Don, you're just in time to help us with this decision," said Florence.

"My goodness, a greeting committee," said the sheriff. "What's this decision I need to weigh in on?"

"Don, four young men—the gang of trouble-makers you were dealing with at the printing office—they came in here demanding that you stop the combined choir from performing and keep Negroes from picnicking in the park. On top of that, Jessa and her friends are here to schedule a fiddle performance by Eddie Wilson and Jacob's father-in-law."

"Too much!" The sheriff flopped his cap down on a bench. "I'm going to hand in my resignation! The town's coming apart at the seams and," he turned on Jessa, April, and Michael, "we've got trouble-makers in our midst!"

"But, sir, the problem is these silly taboos!" said Michael.

Florence said, "Don, just focus on the issues: there's the question of who can come on the park grounds, whether Bill should cancel the choir performance to avoid a confrontation, and will another evening featuring Negro talent break the camel's back."

"First, there's no actual law against having colored people on the grounds of Reubens Park," started Don. "There's just tradition and the fact that it's in the white part of town. I kinda don't picture many Negroes turning up, but I guess families of the performers will be there. Bill, it's your baby, this Music in the Park business. People have been loving it, but that was when it was exclusively white, I guess. How strongly do you feel about having the women perform?"

"The choir's been practicing for months. If we pull them off the schedule when it's already been publicized, a lot of people will be disappointed, and the local toughs will think they can walk all over us. Maybe we should let the choir members decide. Florence, they practice tonight?"

"I'm sure they'll be there, Bill—at seven-thirty."

"I'll talk with the choir and get back to you, Florence. I want to talk with this grandfather, too. Let's just pencil in the fiddle performance for the last Thursday in July and see how everything goes in the meantime."

Michael's fist plunged into the air triumphantly.

Florence shook her head in amazement as they followed Bill Alton out the door.

· CHAPTER 14 ·

When Ben and Michael pulled up at the Carlsons', Jacob and Eddie were conducting an animated discussion with Jack on the front porch. Jack led them around the house to a pile of lumber, and they each grabbed a load and headed up the steps and out on the deck. Fran waved at everyone through the kitchen window. Jacob wore a hammer in a nail belt, and it soon became apparent that he was more experienced than either of the other men. He used his pen knife to test the joists to determine the rotten spots and sketched a plan in a little notebook for the overhang he had suggested.

Michael and Eddie measured and marked the lumber and shuffled the boards to the sawhorses. Jack sawed away, and when a board was ready, Eddie and Michael delivered it to Ben and Jacob to nail into place. Everyone's effort furthered the project, and soon they were working seamlessly in the rhythm of people who understand one another. Jack, in particular, was enjoying himself immensely. His job as an attorney was largely solitary because that allowed him to maintain a professional distance from both his clients and the opposing legal team. Now, he could relax, free to just be with friends.

"How about I spell you on that sawing, Jack," offered Ben. "Too much of that can give you a blister."

"Sure enough?" asked Jack, eyeing his smooth hands.

"Yep, so let's trade jobs, and you can bang away for a while," said Ben, moving into the spot in front of the sawhorses.

"Here's the next board, Dad. Eddie supports the end while you cut. We've learned how to not bind up the saw and how to keep it from falling off and tearing," said Michael.

Jack worked with Jacob to place and clamp the boards until Jacob had hammered in a few nails to stabilize their position.

Looking through the kitchen window, Fran watched the team working on the deck and carried on a conversation with herself. It definitely took some getting used to, the sight of her husband, his sleeves rolled up, working and laughing with a black man, and Michael and Eddie smoothly coordinating their end of the job.

The deck work was half completed when Fran called, "Coffee break! Cookie break!"

They brushed sawdust off their arms and knees and scuffed their feet on the doormat before entering the dining area, where Fran had set out coffee, milk, and a platter of warm cookies.

"I've been smelling these cookies for a while, and when the odor of coffee reached me, I knew we were in for a treat, Fran." Jack hugged his wife, appreciating how smoothly she seated everyone and dismissed their concerns about getting sawdust on the carpet.

Again, by welcoming Jacob and Eddie into their home, they were breaking rules that had bound her behavior her whole life. She found her heart swelling with amazement because it didn't hurt at all. Furthermore, Jack was obviously enjoying himself as a member of the work team, and that was what mattered most to her.

While they ate the oatmeal cookies, Michael brought up the plan for camping. "Dad, Jessa told me it's okay to talk about the hollow tree, now, because she never needs to run away to it again."

Fran slid into the empty chair. "Oh, tell me—I want to hear about this tree!"

"It's in the woods on Jessa's grandfather's farm. We saw it

when snow was all over everything, and we helped Jessa get her things out. Jessa says her mother played in it when she was growing up, and it is only more wonderful now than it was then."

"So Cora grew up playing in this hollow tree, too? It's big enough to crawl inside?" asked Fran.

"Sure, we went in it, and she had things stored there—bags of walnuts and dried corn, and her bed, which she shared with Cassie."

"The tree was a little house?" asked Jacob.

"Yes, when we saw it, it was magical, with the tree glazed with ice from the storm," said Ben.

"That's where we camp, inside a tree?" Eddie fixed on Michael with excitement.

"Yeah, it's great. I've dreamed about it ever since Jessa said I could camp there this summer."

"Well doesn't that sound like an adventure," said Jacob.

Ben nodded. "Eddie, you'll love it!"

"So we had a little wood nymph in our midst, and we never knew it," marveled Fran. "That girl has a lot of gumption. At her age, I would have been scared stiff to spend the night alone in a forest!"

"But she wasn't alone," reasoned Michael. "She had Cassie, and Cassie's real good company."

"I suppose that's true, but night after night? Poor Jessa."

"We'll have Cassie to take care of us, and we need to take the thermos jug for collecting water from the spring, some food, and blankets to sleep under."

"Hooray, I want to do it!" said Eddie.

· CHAPTER 15 ·

The next morning, Fran sat at the breakfast table, slowly rotating her second cup of coffee in the saucer. She glanced up at the windowsill over the sink, where her prized collection of African violets was lined up, covered with double velvety flowers in pink, purple, and white. Gazing at their blossoms, she let her mind wander. Something was stirring in her, and she felt heavy with anticipation, full as if she were about to burst. Certainly, things had already been transformed. Jack had been in better spirits than in many months when he kissed her good-bye before heading out to work. He'd practically lifted her off her feet when he hugged her, and since yesterday, when Ben and Jacob and the two boys had spent the afternoon working on the deck repair, he'd begun to whistle again.

Fran's thoughts returned to Jessa's surprise invitation that had brought the Negro family into their home. She pictured their little girl, Sarah, with her face lighting up as Eddie played, radiant with love for her brother. That, and Jessa's plans for the boys to camp out together, evoked memories that Fran had suppressed for many years.

Merrybelle rapped on the back door, as she did every Monday, and then entered, beads of sweat standing out on her broad forehead. "Ma'am, it's going to be a hot one today! Your roses are already looking droopy. Do you want me to put on the sprinkler?"

"Thank you for the reminder. I'll get out there in a bit and cut some flowers, and I'll water them then."

Fran didn't head for some other part of the house to be out of Merrybelle's way, as she usually did. Instead, she poured herself a warm-up of coffee and sat down at the kitchen table. Watching Merrybelle set her bag with her lunch on the floor and get out her apron, it occurred to her to offer Merrybelle some of the still-warm coffee.

"Please join me for a sip of coffee before you get started, Merrybelle. There isn't a lot to be done today, except for the sawdust that's getting ground into the carpet from this deck job. I don't resent the mess, because Jack was happier than I've seen him for a long time." Fran recalled the help she had gotten with the dishes Saturday night, and how full her heart had been over making her house welcoming for the guests she hadn't expected.

Merrybelle peered through the patio doors to see the deck, with its new wood replacing the rotten sections. "Mr. Jack must have worked all weekend on this job, Mrs. Carlson. Sure does look fine."

"He didn't do it alone. He had good help." Fran went to the range, picked up the coffeepot and held it out. "There's a cup of coffee left and it's still warm. Do join me, Merrybelle."

"Oh, ma'am, I couldn't do that! I ate breakfast a long time ago and better get to work."

"Please, Merrybelle, I'd like a chance to talk. You sit right here and tell me how you like your coffee—and I have cookies to go with it."

Merrybelle pulled the proffered chair back away from the table and sat down. She said, "Your cookies are delicious, Mrs. Carlson. We always appreciate the box of sweets you give us at Christmas."

"That's little enough for all your good service."

"I just take the coffee black if there's something sweet like cookies, ma'am."

At a loss for how to begin, Fran busied herself with setting the cookies out on the table and getting small plates for each of them. Merrybelle kept her eyes on her lap. She was about Fran's age, thirty-eight, and had worked for the Carlsons since they were first married. She was familiar with the little giveaways that Fran left for her in paper bags. These were things that Fran would have felt guilty throwing away and took pleasure in passing along, so Merrybelle always played the grateful recipient. Merrybelle steeled herself to deal with another giveaway.

Fran searched for a way to begin. She was ashamed that she didn't even know the names of Merrybelle's children. She did know her husband's name, however, so she asked, "How is George getting along these days?"

"He got a new job at the warehouse, ma'am. He's doing well. It's easier on his back. They let him drive the forklift, and he's good at that. Doesn't have to do so much lifting, like when he was working for the moving company in Landsdowne."

"So George has back problems? I'm so sorry. My mother has such a bad back, it almost has her confined to a wheelchair. In her case, it's weak bones."

"That certainly can be bad, ma'am."

"Merrybelle, I'm sure you know Margaret Wilson?"

"Of course, ma'am. Margaret's a real leader in the community. She organized the after-school program my kids attend, and we sing together at church and in the combined choir."

"Margaret and Jacob and their children came here Saturday night. We had dessert together, and then Eddie played for us and our guests, the Acrees." When Merrybelle didn't answer, Fran continued. "It was Jacob and Mr. Acree who worked with Jack on the deck Sunday."

"I guess I did hear about that," said Merrybelle.

"Really? How did you hear?"

Merrybelle put her coffee cup down in the saucer and centered it carefully in her lap before she said, "Ma'am, maybe I shouldn't say this, but it's pretty common knowledge now. Your neighbor, Mrs. Gladys, she had a Sunday tea party, and her maid, Rachel, had to serve. Mrs. Gladys was complaining to everyone that the neighborhood had been invaded. She took them out and pointed to Jacob's truck in front of your house. What she had to say to the guests and what they were uh-huhing about made Rachel so angry she's ready to quit working for Mrs. Gladys."

Fran sat staring at Merrybelle. "I never liked that Gladys Blakeley. I guess now she'll undermine my position with the auxillary and the garden clubs. She's such a busy-body, I'm fed up with caring what she thinks! If that's the way she wants it, that's what she'll get!"

Merrybelle rose. "Guess I've done as much damage as I should, for this day of the Lord. Thank you for the coffee and cookies. I'd better tackle this carpet."

"Wait a minute, Merrybelle. I've been thinking a lot about the past, remembering things I've never even told Jack. I've got to tell someone, so please sit back down here and listen to me." Fran pushed the plates and coffee cup back and leaned across the table. "When Jessa invited the Wilsons in and we had dessert together, it broke all the training I'd gotten since I was six years old."

"Yessum. That's for sure. It just ain't done, now is it?"

"But why? And why is it any business of Gladys Blakeley what I do? Seeing the Wilsons' little girl has got me thinking a lot about my childhood. I don't care what Gladys Blakeley says about me. What does she know? But the real question is, what do I know? And why? And that's when the memories all began to flood back. Ever since the Wilsons' visit, I've been overwhelmed, like I'm living in a dream world, absorbed in the past."

Merrybelle glanced up to read Fran's face, concerned.

Fran seemed to shiver at the memories. She pressed her hands against her cheeks and stared straight ahead. "You see, Merrybelle, when I was little, I was an only child, and our maid, Sojourner, lived with us. She had a daughter my age named Justine. Later, Sojourner moved across town, but she brought her daughter to work with her every day, and Justine and I played together. It slipped out in something my mother said many years later, that Sojourner had nursed me right along with Justine because Mother didn't want to breastfeed me. Anyway, Justine and I grew up together—we were so close! We did the strangest things, like spend rainy days playing with snails and slugs that we collected at the downspouts of the gutters by the porch—their tentacles fascinated us, and we loved to gently poke them to see them withdraw and then slowly extend." As she spoke, Fran closed her eyes, recalling the good times. "In sunny weather, Sojourner would make up a bowl of sugar water, and we would put it out in the clover patch to watch the honeybees feeding on it, and we would lie side-by-side in the clover with bees all around, watching the pollen loaded on their legs. Of course, we did all the standard things, too: made mud pies that we decorated with dandelion down, collected special rocks to decorate castles in the sandbox, and wove flower crowns and tied long clover chains. At nap time, Sojourner sang to us, and we would fall asleep in each other's arms. We loved each other. It's the truth. We wanted to spend all our time together, and we made each other *such* promises."

Fran dug for a handkerchief in her pocket, and Merrybelle offered her a paper napkin for her eyes.

"Then I had to start school, and so did Justine, and I guess by that time my parents were concerned that I didn't have any white girlfriends I cared for the way I loved Justine. It seems to me now that they were probably worried that I would rebel against being separated from Justine, so we moved to a different part of town and hired a different maid. They kept me busy with school friends and dancing classes, and with all the changes, I'm sorry to say that I didn't make much fuss about not getting to see Justine anymore."

Fran paused to wipe her eyes and blow her nose, and sat shaking her head as if to deny the past. Finally, she blurted out, "It was years before I learned that Justine had died of measles." She covered her face and sobbed. "I didn't even know how to grieve. It was as if it never happened—all our good times together and the promises we made to each other—vanished! Now, it's all I can think about. She probably didn't have proper medical care, I don't know. Maybe if my family had still employed her mother, we could have made a difference."

Merrybelle shifted in her chair, uncomfortable. "Lots of families lose a child."

"All I know is that that part of my life got buried as if it never happened, and I was carefully groomed to play the role of White Southern Lady. I've played that role for over thirty years, and *I've been so miserable!*"

Merrybelle looked up, startled. Many evenings after the kids were in bed, she and her husband would get out their money and count it, worrying over how to make the rent and utility bill payments and provide for their growing family's needs for shoes and clothes. Here was this woman who could pay for anything she wanted saying she was miserable! She repeated the word: "Miserable? You have such a beautiful house, Mrs. Carlson. Mr. Jack's a good husband to you, ma'am. You're lucky to have such a kind man."

"Oh, it's true, it's true. And maybe if we'd been able to have children, it would have been different, but Merrybelle, I've been so bored in this life you wouldn't believe it! Sure, I read. I like to cook. I like to sew. I volunteer at the clinic and on church committees, and I lead the garden club. I do these things that everyone expects of me, but I feel worthless. There has to be more to life than this!"

Merrybelle leaned over and patted her back. "Honey, you're a good woman. I'm lucky to have worked for you and Mr. Jack all these years. You do a lot of volunteering. Most women I know would give a lot to have just a little of what you have. Don't you go bothering yourself about what Mrs. Blakeley has to say about you, because she's being mean spirited. That's the truth!"

"Oh, Merrybelle!" Fran clasped her hand. "I've been such a fool to play this White Southern Lady role. I don't care about Gladys and what she thinks. Maybe she can be excused because she never knew any better. The blinders are so effective; you only see what you're supposed to see, so you never get out of line, but I of all people should have known better, and yet I went along with it. Justine and I were true friends, just like Cora Olsen and I were true friends, but they're both gone. As for all the rest of the women, why, I don't think there's a woman in this town who won't turn against me now that Gladys has—*and I don't care*! All they can do is shun me—isn't that right?"

"Honey, I don't think it's gonna get really bad. Anyway, this is just between the women. They'll talk and talk and then something else grabs their attention and they'll forget about bad-mouthing you. They'll forget it ever happened."

"But I don't want it to not happen again. Jessa's responsible, and she's right. Her instincts are intact, but I have instincts, too. When she and the Acrees go back to Portland, it won't be the way it was, not for me, and I suspect not for Jack, either. The fact is, Jack would love Jacob's friendship, and Margaret and you and I could all be friends."

"Now you got me worrying, ma'am. There're limits, and we'd be smart to respect them. What you're talking about will get us all in trouble."

Fran continued with her fantasy, as if Merrybelle hadn't spoken. "You love flowers the same as I do, and did you know Margaret majored in English in college—same as me?"

"Yes, ma'am, I know she went to college. She's been helping some of the graduates apply to college and trade schools. Our son Lester wants to drive a truck, and she found schools that train you to get a good job doing that."

"Then I could help her—that's something I can do. Oh, Merrybelle, I've felt so worthless. Before it's too late, I've got to find something I can do to make life worth living."

"Why, honey, you shouldn't talk that way. God gives us chances every day to make a difference."

"You're making a difference right now, just by listening."

Merrybelle glanced at the sawdust ground into the carpet and realized that she would have to move the table and chairs to get at it. "It looks like I really ought to tackle that floor. Oh, yes, and next time you go to the store, please remember you're low on laundry detergent. The Tide boxes have a pretty dish towel in them."

"I have a better idea. I have this piece of fabric I've been keeping. Come see." She led the way to the sewing room. "I bought it to make a dress for my sister-in-law, and when I took the material and pattern to show her, what did she do but take me to her bedroom closet and pull out a Sears Roebuck dress almost the same green! I'd like to make this dress for you. I don't need another dress, but it'd look beautiful on you."

Merrybelle watched as Fran spread the fabric on the bed. She gasped at the soft green pattern and felt her resistance melting.

"Ma'am, that's so pretty! Isn't that green what you call a *pastel*? 'Cause for the combined choir performance, we're supposed to wear pastels, pale colors like pink or light blue or green, and I don't have a thing that's right."

"Why yes, it has a fine pattern of leaves, but the overall

appearance is pale green. It would be perfect! Let me get your measurements. You're a bit slimmer and shorter than Jack's sister, but I can adapt the pattern easily. Now, look here at the picture, which style of sleeve do you prefer?"

"In the heat, the shorter sleeve will be cooler. Are you sure you have the time for this? You can take the cost out of my paycheck."

As Fran got out her tape measure and a pad to write the numbers down, she threw back her shoulders, looked at Merrybelle, and took a deep breath. "Merrybelle, I love to sew, and this project has a purpose! I can get this dress ready by Wednesday for a try-on. It will be done and pressed in time for you to wear for the performance on Thursday!"

· CHAPTER 16 ·

That afternoon, when Merrybelle slipped out the back door, her friend Rachel had already started walking up the street. Merrybelle skipped a few steps to catch up with her.

"Rachel! Hold up!"

"What's going on, Merry? You sure look like the cat that swallowed the canary!"

"Rachel, it's strange, that's what it is!"

"What's strange?"

"Mrs. Carlson sat me down and, I swear, she opened her heart right up, and poor me, trying to not spill the cup of coffee she poured for me!"

"Uh huh. It'll be a cold day in hell before Mrs. Blakeley pours a cup of coffee for *me*!"

"You're not going to believe it, Rachel. First, she won't even let me put my apron on, and she sits me down at the kitchen table and serves cookies! Says she has to talk to someone…"

"Now, *I* got some talking-to. I could hardly get my cleaning done with all her gab! You'd think the neighborhood was disappearing into a sinkhole, and it's all because of colored people." Rachel shook her head in frustration. "Practically 'moving in' she says, and with the Carlsons' invitation, too! If we could afford it, I'd quit working for that woman!"

"Mrs. Carlson's aware of the talk, and I tried to comfort her— told her that time will heal and they'll come up with something else to jabber about at their canasta parties, but she didn't seem to care what Mrs. Blakeley thought about her."

"Don't say! So what she want to talk about?"

"Says she's miserable, there in her perfect house with her perfect yard and her perfect husband! Don't that take the cake? Now it's true Mr. Carlson has spells of depression, and that's hard on any woman, but he seems to have recovered. Matter of fact, she said working with Jacob and that Mr. Acree on the deck repair had him whistling, again."

"There! You hit on it! Mrs. Blakeley pins the blame on those Northern relatives of the Olsens!"

"I guess something about Jessamine and the relatives is what started it, all right. But all of a sudden, she wants to cozy up to me and open up her heart—stuff she's never even told her husband."

"Like what?"

"Well, like this. She's got to remembering this little colored girl she used to play with when she was very young. They were real close friends. Then her family moved, and she started school, and somewhere along that time, this colored girl died of the measles."

"Hu-huh. That kind of friendship white parents got to break up. I'm surprised she had a chance to play with a colored child…"

"Said the girl was the daughter of their maid. Seems this woman nursed Mrs. Carlson along with her own daughter while the woman lived with them."

"Ah! So they were titty sisters! That's not so unusual."

"The point is, now Mrs. Carlson wants to change. She's all sorry for forgetting her friend and for what she calls her role in society. She's got dreams of being friends with all the colored women she knows, especially Margaret because she went to college. You should have heard her running her mouth with these big plans."

"So how's she think she's goin' to do that? Teach us colored women to play canasta and have us out there tending the flower beds by the courthouse like the white ladies do, instead of growing food for the table and earning a living?"

"Don't know about that, but she's going to sew me a dress for the choir performance."

Rachel stopped in her tracks and faced Merrybelle. "Now, girl, you're getting in too deep!"

"It's beautiful green cloth—you should have seen it—and you know she has time on her hands. Why shouldn't she sew it for me if she wants to? The fact is, and this is the truth, it's me who's doing her a favor. I figured that out. She's buying off her regrets over the little girl she forgot. When she sews this dress for me, she's paying back her guilty conscience. But she says she can do it by Wednesday, and it's so pretty!" Merrybelle giggled.

"No! Next thing and she'll be cleaning your house!" exclaimed Rachel.

"Well, she wanted to send me home with a bouquet of roses, but I begged her to put them on the dining table instead—said they'd never get home without wilting!"

Rachel shook her head in disbelief. They crossed the street and headed for their homes across the tracks.

· CHAPTER 17 ·

While Fran was opening her heart to Merrybelle, across town, Jacob was dropping Eddie off at Jessa's house as agreed. The plan for the camping trip had been all they'd talked about at home, and Jessa had thrown all her energy into it.

Michael ran out to greet them. "Eddie, that's a great hat! Did you get that feather from one of Aunt Helen's roosters? Hey, look what I found in the garage—a lantern! Dad showed me how to light it and adjust it so it won't smoke."

"Wow! I brought Aunt Helen's ham-and-biscuit sandwiches for us. They're great, and she sent apples," said Eddie.

Jacob greeted Ben and handed over grocery bags with food and a pillow. "Don't know how scary it'll be, out in the woods, but Margaret thought a familiar pillow might come in handy."

The screen door burst open, and Jessa and Cassie ran out. "Eddie! It'll be wonderful. You'll love camping." Cassie danced around at the delight in the air. "Yes, Cassie, you're going. You're gonna take care of Michael and Eddie, just like you took care of me. Michael, did you pack her dinner kibbles?"

"Sure 'nough. Cassie'll remember the tree, I bet," replied Michael.

"Yeah, I'm jealous," said April. "Cassie gets to go, but I don't. All I've heard about is how great the tree is and what you might hear in the night."

"I've got to get on to work," said Jacob. "What time you want to be picked up, buddy?"

Eddie looked to Michael, who volunteered, "I figure we can explore the forest and the barn and walk down to the creek and go wading."

"So maybe tomorrow afternoon?" suggested Eddie.

"I'll pick the guys up middle of the afternoon, then," said Ben. "Eddie will be here with us when you drop by after work, Jacob."

"Come give me a hug, Eddie."

Eddie slammed into his father, hugged him tightly, quickly pulled away, and raced off after Michael. Jacob grinned at Ben and said, "I think it'll be okay. He's never done anything like this before, and he's higher than a kite!"

Karen waved the expedition off. "I want to get out to tour the farm sometime soon!"

April sat up front with Ben; Jessa and Cassie joined Michael and Eddie in the back seat. Jessa said, "I've no idea what fruit is ripe in the orchard, but you're taking plenty to eat. These old quilts April and I found will make great pallets."

"I want to see the forest, now that everything isn't all covered in snow," said April.

When they drove up the drive, the farmhouse looked sadly deserted, with flowerbeds overgrown and the front door padlocked. To escape the depressing scene, Jessa hurried everyone off across the pasture to the edge of the woods. Cassie raced ahead, delighted to be in the country again. As they walked, Jessa pointed out the property boundaries and the direction to the orchard.

When they entered the woods, getting through the tangle of vines and brambles occupied their attention until they intersected a trail. They discovered ferns, moss, bracket fungi, and delicate mushrooms on the fallen logs. When they walked too close to a mockingbird's nest, one of the birds chased and dive-bombed them into a run.

As Jessa led them to the tree, she recalled the many times she and Cassie had trod the path, hungry and sometimes carrying heavy loads. Her stomach tightened as the hardships flooded back, and she halted to examine a spider's web hung with dew drops to get herself under control as Michael and Eddie pushed ahead. Soaring pride brought tears to her eyes when she heard Michael's delighted shout that he'd found the tree.

Cassie was happy to be in the forest, revisiting their old haunt. Jessa called the dog over to give her instructions. "Cassie, you must keep Michael and Eddie. Take care of them. You *stay* with Michael and Eddie. I am *going*, but Cassie is *staying*. Keep the boys safe all night, and tomorrow, I'll come back. Cassie is my good dog, and she has a job." Turning to Michael, she pointed toward the rear of the tree's interior. "Our pie pans and cups should be there still; you can wash them in the spring."

April said, "Let's quickly check your grandfather's bees, Jessa. I thought if there's more honey, we could make some more honey pears—they were so good!" So Jessa gave Cassie a good-bye hug, and they ran along the forest path until they were back in broad sunshine.

They heard buzzing as they approached the hives and saw the vibrant turmoil of bees alighting on the entrance bars or taking off to forage. "They're doing fine! I hoped they had plenty of honey for the winter, and I'm sure they're making more. If Grandad were here, he would already have taken some spring honey. He liked samples from different parts of the year because they taste different. He called the earliest honey, blackberry blossom honey, although it included all the fruit-tree blooms, too."

"Did he use a bee suit to gather honey? It's called 'robbing honey,' isn't it?" asked April.

"He didn't use any special clothing, but he did smoke his

pipe. When he gave up smoking, he kept his pipe to calm the bees, and he puffed smoke at them all the time he was cutting comb out of the hive. They buzzed all around him, but he only got a few stings, mainly if the bee got trapped in his clothing. I think robbing is what you do, all right, but Grandad never took very much at a time—he always left the bees rich."

"So you watched him do it? Would you dare do it yourself? I found that milking Aunt Helen's cow was a lot harder than it looked when she did it. Working with bees would call for steel nerves. I've heard that if they sense you're afraid, they sting you a lot more…"

Ben caught up with them. He'd given the boys last-minute instructions about where to be when he came the next day, but they'd been too enthralled with the tree to pay him any attention. From the orchard slope, he called, "April, Jessa! Look here, peaches and some promising-looking apples. It's a shame we didn't bring picking bags. We can take back a few and get more tomorrow."

They ran down the hill to see a tree loaded with ripe peaches. "Elbertas! And the Gravenstein apples! Wonderful!" said Jessa. "We can make pies!"

Meanwhile, Eddie and Michael stashed their food, bedding, and lantern in the ancient oak tree. The entrance to the hollow interior was an old lightning strike injury that had split the base between two massive roots that arched over the ground. The interior was like a cave with the only light coming in the opening. The ground inside was littered with the debris from Jessa's life in the tree. Forest inhabitants had invaded and carried off anything edible, leaving scattered fragments of the burlap bags she had used for storing ears of dried corn, apples, pears, and nuts.

"Let's brush this stuff out. Jessa said we'd have to clean it out some," said Michael. Eddie sized up the situation and broke off a branch to sweep the floor. When they had a tidy interior,

Michael said, "Let's go for water." They'd brought the big thermos jug that Jessa had used for water when she lived there.

As they walked across the meadow, Eddie said, "Wow, it's hot! This will be a good time for wading."

"The spring water should be great." Michael remembered where he and April had discovered the spring house last winter, and he retraced their path by the garden. The slope down to the spring was steep and littered with tiny rocks that rolled under their feet. The boys ran and then slid after Cassie, with brambles catching at their clothes. Cassie adored the spring water and drank lustily while the boys stripped off their socks and shoes and waded in on the moss-slippery rocks. The water was very cold, so they splashed through a deep pool to explore the sandy beach on the other side, skipped flat stones for a while until they each got the hang of it, and then re-crossed the stream and sat on a rock to let their cold feet dry in the sun. Cassie came to lie next to them.

"What a nice dog!" said Eddie. "She really likes getting petted. What did Jessa tell you about the time she and Cassie were hiding out here?"

"After her parents and grandfather were killed, she heard the sheriff tell her neighbor that she was an orphan. Jessa couldn't stand that idea, because her father had told her about his awful experiences in foster care."

"My dad's father was killed, and that made him a half-orphan, I guess. He doesn't talk about it, but it's bad," said Eddie.

"I'm sorry," said Michael, turning to face Eddie. "I gathered from what she said that Jessa was also worried about Cassie. She figured they wouldn't let her keep Cassie, and she thought they'd send her to the pound, so she took her and ran away. Jessa and Cassie hid here for weeks and weeks, and finally came out of hiding during the snowstorm, when we had driven out here and were looking around."

"I guess she was scared of the sheriff. Daddy got locked up by the sheriff, and we were scared, but he said it was all a big mistake. My fiddle was a gift because of the mistake."

"I think Jessa was most afraid of being taken away to live with people she didn't know."

"She was lucky she had Cassie with her when she hid out." Eddie patted Cassie's head, and she leaned against him for more attention.

"I'm hungry. How about you? We can scrounge, the way Jessa did, but we have food in the tree if we don't find anything."

They filled the water jug with the cold, clear water and climbed the bank after Cassie. Near the top of the bank, they noticed the blackberries hanging heavy and ripe.

"Hey, these look good!" exclaimed Michael.

They almost lost the green water jug because Michael put it down and then they migrated from one clump of blackberries to the next, eating their fill. In the process of hunting for the jug, Eddie found a box turtle grazing on fallen blackberries. They played with it, studied the yellow and orange markings on its shell, and turned it over to watch it right itself, laughing as Cassie barked at it. Then Michael called her away, picked up the jug, and they left the turtle to eat blackberries undisturbed.

"Those biscuits with ham will taste good with this cool water," said Michael, lugging the jug. "Eddie, did you ever try to make biscuits?"

"Nope. When Mama was sick before Sarah was born, Aunt Helen came every day to fix food and wash. I guess I could have learned then, because she liked me to keep her company in the kitchen. Mama's biscuits are different from Aunt Helen's—smaller. She likes to make cornbread, and I should learn that, too."

"I've never made biscuits, either, but my granddaddy made lemon meringue pie, and he taught us how. I help with cutting out cookies and decorating them, too, and if there're jobs like cracking nuts. Jessa collected bags of nuts when she was living in the tree, and we ate them back in Portland."

"What kind of nuts? Aunt Helen grows peanuts, and last year, I helped her harvest them. It's the funniest thing when they're dug up! You can see how the pea plants pushed their pods into the ground, so the pods come up all wrinkly and brown. Inside are the peanuts that grew underground like potatoes!"

"Didn't know peanuts grew on pea plants, but that's what the name says, isn't it?"

"They pull up in bunches. They're kinda sweet, but I got sick, eating too many raw, but you can boil them or roast them."

Cassie ran down the trail across the meadow in front of them. Suddenly, she jumped back and barked. She looked around for Michael and Eddie, turned back to the path, growled low, and circled stiffly. Eddie grabbed Michael's arm and said, "Listen, hear the rattle?"

"Oh, no—I hate snakes!" said Michael. "Cassie, come here. Don't fool with that!"

Eddie stooped down and called to her, but Cassie wouldn't leave the snake. They advanced, and the dry rattling grew more insistent. The large snake was coiled, its tail vibrating in a blur, ready to strike.

Michael said, "That snake'll kill Cassie if it strikes her. *Please, please* come here, Cassie," he pleaded, but the dog circled the snake, barking frantically, alternately advancing and jumping back.

Eddie called Cassie, but she wouldn't obey. Frustrated, he slapped his thigh, hard, not knowing that that had been the wordless signal that Jessa had used to command Cassie to come. The dog stopped her attack and reluctantly went to Eddie's side, her focus still on the snake, which flicked its red tongue and rocked its head to menace her. The dry rattling continued. Eddie got his hand around Cassie's collar and moved back, pulling her. He continued to hold on to her collar until they were safely out of range. Then Cassie ran with them, and they didn't stop until they were in the shade of the woods, panting and resting on a log.

Eddie hugged Cassie. "Good dog! You were trying to protect us, weren't you?"

"Whew! I hate snakes!" said Michael with a shudder. "Always have. April thinks they're cool and interesting, and she will handle the harmless sort at the pet store, but they all give me the willies."

"I don't like them much, but Aunt Helen, she defends them. Says they have to go down mouse and groundhog holes and kill pests. I found a snake once—it was just a little one—she wouldn't let me kill it."

"They also climb and steal eggs and baby birds out of nests. I guess they're a mixed blessing." Michael's hunger was settling in despite the snake. "Let's get those biscuits!"

They ate sitting in front of the tree, where Jessa had eaten so many times, and Cassie leaned forward to remind them that dogs liked biscuits, too. They lay on their backs and looked high up into the intense green of the leaves.

"Wouldn't it be great to be a monkey and swing through those branches?" mused Michael.

"Squirrels climb and jump around up there pretty good," said Eddie.

"Jessa said Cassie pointed out a squirrel with a nut in its mouth, and that was how she knew that the English walnuts were falling off the tree."

"It's too early for tree nuts. Can we explore the barn?"

"Sure, let's do that next. Better put the biscuits in that cake tin, though. Jessa said mice ate some bread she got from her grandfather's refrigerator."

They were more cautious as they set off across the meadow.

Cassie knew *the barn*, so she led them there, nose to the ground. She stopped at the back, where Jessa had always entered, but knowing nothing about that, Michael circled around to the front of the barn and opened the two big doors to let in light.

The boys toured around the stalls and examined the row of chicken nesting boxes. Doves were cooing from the loft, where lots of interesting items were stored.

"Let's climb up!" exclaimed Eddie.

Eddie led the way, and Michael was right on his heels. At the top of the ladder, they had to punch through cobweb tents covered with dust before hauling themselves over the top of the ladder onto a plank floor scattered with straw and bird droppings. Down below, Cassie had left her digging and stood on the barn floor looking up, whining.

"Good dog, Cassie. We'll be okay. Don't you worry!" assured Eddie.

The loft had been used for storing broken or obsolete equipment, and at one end, the frame of a pony cart, with padded leather seats, had been hoisted up. The boys climbed on it. They pretended they were chased by robbers pursuing their stagecoach. Finally, when their horses were tired, they slid off the seats and explored the other treasures.

They moved cautiously, sensing the struggle to make a life that the relics reflected. There were metal foot lasts used for cobbling shoes, a corn sheller, a worn out two-man saw, and pieces of equipment they couldn't figure a use for. On the walls, saddles, harnesses, and plow attachments hung. There was even a strange saddle that Michael figured out was a side-saddle for a woman to ride wearing a dress. Buckets of fence materials and nuts and bolts were rusting away, but nothing that might possibly have a value had been thrown away.

Eddie whispered, "These things are very old—back from the time before cars or tractors."

The boys were drawn to the pair of identical bicycles hanging side-by-side. Michael explained, "These belonged to my grandfather and Jessa's grandfather. They were twins. They grew up here, but Jessa didn't know her grandfather had a twin brother. When she asked him why there were two bicycles, he wouldn't answer her—just told her she couldn't ride them because they had rotten tires." Michael squeezed the tire of the nearest bicycle, and bits of rubber crumbled in his hand.

"Twin brothers? That's pretty special. Why didn't Jessa know?"

"It's a sad thing that happened to our family. Nobody knew because my grandad ran away after he accidently killed a man. He told us when he was dying, about how he was trying to stop a robber but got angry when the robber shot his dog. He was so mad that he strangled the man."

"Must have been really strong," said Eddie.

"I don't think so. He was pretty young, had just graduated from high school. He didn't know it was going to happen that way. His dog had tried to protect him when the man had him down. But he always grieved over killing that robber. He left that very night because his mother forced him out, saying he would burn in hell."

Eddie brushed his hands thoughtfully against his jeans before he spoke. "What happened to my dad's father is the sad story in our family. My daddy's father was lynched."

Michael jerked around to face him, shock in his wide eyes. Gradually, a deep flush made its way up to his hairline. "Eddie, I'm real sorry. I've read about that kind of thing. It's hard to believe. Awful." The stories his civics teacher had told the class filled his mind. "Was it the KKK?"

Eddie shrugged. "I don't know. Daddy doesn't talk about it. Mama found out from Aunt Helen and Uncle Adam." Eddie sighed. "Mama told me because she thought I needed to know. She hasn't told Sarah. Aunt Helen said it was because his father was a good farmer, and his farm made the neighbors feel infe-rior. He was showing them up, and they wanted his land."

"That's terrible, Eddie. I've seen a lot of bad things in Ten-nessee, but nothing like that. Your dad was a little boy then?"

"He was the oldest. Aunt Helen said his mother had till morning to pack everything into the truck, and her brother drove them to live with her family. The whites took the land and burned the house. Said she didn't have any claim to it."

Michael put his hands over his face. "That's just like in Mis-sissippi—all the bad things I've read about. It's not supposed to be this way!"

From the floor of the barn, Cassie's whining reached a new pitch.

"It worries her for us to be up here," said Michael.

"I think she knows we're unhappy," said Eddie. "Let's climb down."

When they reached the bottom of the ladder, Cassie jumped all around them. Eddie laughed in delight. "Cassie's a fun dog! Michael, your face is pretty dirty. Guess mine is, too. Should we go back to the spring to wash up?"

They pushed the barn doors closed, latched them, and head-ed for the spring. The sunshine was blinding at first, and step-ping into the sunny meadow had an unreality for Michael, who was still reeling from the news of the lynching. Together, they crossed the broad expanse and watched Cassie run ahead and flush a killdeer, which went into the broken wing imitation to lead the dog away from her nest. The boys watched, fascinated, as the bird seemed to falter and almost tumble to the ground in front of the dog. Cassie wore herself out, circling under the bird, which led her far away before finally returning to its nest.

The odor of mint greeted them as they neared the spring, and as they scrambled down the bank, the coolness rising from the water engulfed them. They splashed the cold water over their hands and faces, then scooped up handfuls to drink. Cassie waded in, drank for a long time, and stood in the current, panting. Then she joined the boys as they lay on the rock above the deep pool and drank in the peppermint fragrance.

"Wow! That's refreshing!" Eddie said.

"Let's look in the spring house. Jessa's bike should still be there, and if Dad puts it in the car when he comes to get us, we can take it back to town."

Michael unlatched the door of the stone building that emerged from the hillside and stepped aside so that Eddie could enter the cool, dank space. "Gee, it's neat in here," he said. The spring flowed out under a large ledge of limestone, and there were shelves on one side.

"There's the bike. Its tires are flat, and it seems pretty rusty," he said, running his hands along the handlebars, "but we can push it up the slope and leave it by the porch. You have a bike, right?"

"Sure do. Love to ride around town and out into the country."

"I bet Jessa will let me borrow her bike. We'll oil it and get it running fine, and you and I could go places together."

"I know great places to bike. I'm hungry. Let's eat. I brought real sweet apples from Aunt Helen's farm."

It was beginning to get dark when they reached the tree, and inside, it was even darker. Eddie located the apples and ripe tomatoes, and Michael pulled out boiled eggs and crackers. "Cassie needs her dinner, too. I've got kibbles."

They sat outside the tree to eat, leaning against the tree's trunk and massive roots. They finished up the meal with cookies and spring water from the jug. As shadows began to take over the forest, a robin began his evening song, perched high in the canopy. Birds flew swiftly through the trees, heading for night shelter. In the distance, a whip-poor-will began calling and bob-whites joined in.

"Dad gave me a flashlight. We can use it to lay out our quilts if it's dark in the tree, and then we can light the lantern," said Michael.

"That'll be fun. I'm not sleepy yet. Jessa talked about gnawing sounds we might hear from inside the tree?"

"Yeah, nothing to be afraid of, though. I hoped we might see a raccoon. The raccoons robbed Jessa a couple of times. You know that black mask they have as face markings? Well, they really are robbers, but I'd love to have one for a pet."

"What I want is a puppy. Mama said she would consider it when Sarah is a bit older. She said she wanted to make sure we could take care of the puppy, and Sarah could understand to be gentle. I know Sarah, and she would be gentle now."

"Do you know the book called *Beautiful Joe*?"

"Oh, yes, that's good! My teacher read it to us last year for quiet time. Maybe I'll get it out of the library."

Michael thought of their visit to Radford Library. No colored children were in the corner reading group, and he couldn't recall seeing any Negroes while they were there.

"What library do you figure would have a copy of *Beautiful Joe*?"

"Our school's got a small library, and the teacher was going to add that book to it. But in the summertime, we can't get books out of the school library."

"Jessa used to work at the Radford Library. I bet she could check out *Beautiful Joe* for you."

"I'd like that. Summers are sure long. I help Mama with the garden, babysit Sarah, practice on the piano at the church, and now that Grandpa is here, it's been great because we play our fiddles a lot. We're working on some special pieces for the park concert, but I've read all our books over and over."

"I depend on reading a lot, too, and Jessa's offered to get me books."

"Grandpa was a teacher in Kentucky, and he's been working with me on my spelling. He says if you want to be respected in this world, you should be able to speak and write the king's English. What do you make of that—*the king's English?*"

"Seems funny to me. That would be England-English, not America-English, and I know there are differences. Some words are spelled differently, like p-l-o-w and p-l-o-u-g-h. Lucky for us, the American is simpler!"

"It sure gets dark in a hurry in the forest. Let's lay out our beds, then sit out here with the lantern. Cassie, wait back till we get it ready."

They crawled around inside the tree, spreading the quilts. Eddie added his pillow, and when he saw Michael folding the quilt over at the end to make a pillow-like mound, he offered to share it. "Look, it's big enough for both of us." Cassie was invited to come inside. "Good dog, Cassie, this is your bed." The dog circled a couple of times on her assigned throw rug and settled down.

The flashlight beam was weak and had threatened to go out before they got the bedding down. Michael switched it off. "I'll light the lantern. Let's go out to that rock for that. Dad said we have to be very careful about fires. Here, Eddie, hold the flash-light but wait to turn it on until I have everything ready."

"Now," he said. In the flashlight's flickering beam, he struck the match, cranked up the lantern's chimney, and touched the flame to the wick. The wick caught, producing a lot of black smoke and flooding them with the smell of kerosene. Michael turned the knob one way, which made matters worse, and then back the other way. Finally, the wick was adjusted to provide a nice light.

"Your daddy teach you how to do that?" asked Eddie.

"Yes, he did a demonstration and then blew it out and had me light it myself."

"Let's go for a walk with the lantern!"

They scrambled to their feet, and Michael called Cassie out of the tree. "Come on, Cassie—we're going on an adventure! I want to see if I can find the place where Jessa made her fires. It's down this path a ways—it'll be on our left."

It was hard to distinguish features along the path when large shadows shifted ominously with every movement of the lantern. Michael searched in vain for the fire pit with its ring of stones.

"You want to carry the lantern? Dad said proper etiquette is to hold it down, like this, so someone walking behind you can see the ground." Michael demonstrated. "Don't touch it, or you'll get burned."

"This way?" asked Eddie, taking the handle. "It's hot coming out the top, too."

By the time they had circled back to the tree, it was feeling like bedtime. The whistle of the night train started up, and they stopped to listen. "Jessa said that train whistle was her connection with the town while she was living here. She loves trains— we all do—Jessa and our mom rode a train to Oregon last winter to get Cassie home, and then we all came out here on the train. It's the very best way to travel!"

Michael yawned. Eddie caught the yawn. Michael asked, "Why d'ya figure yawns are catching?"

"I guess it keeps people feeling the same way, getting sleepy together and then they'll be awake together?"

"I saw a special zoo program on TV, and it showed baboons that will yawn if you yawn at them. Dogs can do the same thing—yawn when they see a person yawn."

"So people and dogs living together will sleep together and then be awake together!"

"Except for that owl—listen! It's his time to be awake. Must be what they call a screech owl."

"We hear them all the time where we live—we're close to some woods."

"I bet there are bears, mountain lions, and wolves hunting for something yummy—like a nice juicy dog? You hear that, Cassie?"

He held the lantern up to illuminate the tree's interior. Cassie was curled up, and she barely moved. "She looks settled," said Eddie.

"How 'bout we join her?"

Michael cranked up the chimney and blew across the flame. Immediately, darkness engulfed them. Michael left the hot lantern on the flat table rock, and they crawled into the tree.

Eddie lay on his quilt and smelled his side of the pillow, for the comfort of it. Then he rolled over to look up into darkness. "Would be good to have one of those jars of lightning bugs like the one we gave Sarah to go to sleep by."

"Yeah, I'd like that, too." Michael settled in beside him. In the darkness, they could hear the screech owl and some rustling, but no chewing. High up, the tree's branches moved with the night breezes. "Isn't it great to be *inside* a tree!"

"Super great," agreed Eddie.

· CHAPTER 18 ·

Ben drove Jessa and April to the farm the next afternoon, with the car loaded with buckets and bags for the fruit. Ben whistled a tune as they drove to the farm and Jessa and April planned their camping adventure. Ben gave a horse-whistle as the car pulled in front of the farmhouse, and right away, Michael whistled back—a family practice that had served them well on many occasions. Michael and Eddie ran across the meadow and joined them at the farmhouse porch. They were carrying their bedding and the jug. They pointed to the bike that they had pushed to the porch, and Jessa was delighted to see it.

"I think I can get it in the trunk," Ben said. "The fruit will have to go in the interior, but we've had a change of plans, so these quilts will stay here. Jessa and April decided they'll spend tonight in the tree. Now, let's go pick apples and peaches."

"Jessa, blackberries are ripe and they're super," said Eddie. "We ate all we could and played with a turtle."

"Oh, good! We'll have some to eat, too, and let's pick enough for blackberry pies!" said Jessa.

"Did you know there are rattlers on the farm, Jessa?" asked Michael as they climbed the hill to the orchard. "Cassie showed us it was there before we got to it."

"I've never seen a rattler here, but I saw a copperhead down by the creek when I was with Grandad."

"Aren't there good snakes, harmless snakes, around here, too?" asked April.

"For sure there're good snakes," replied Jessa.

"We'll watch out for snakes. We're picking peaches and apples for us and Eddie's family," said Ben as he distributed the picking vessels.

The fragrant peaches came off the branches readily, and they quickly filled two bags.

"Can we climb the apple tree?" asked Michael.

"I always did," said Jessa. "Grandad didn't mind."

"Michael, you and Eddie climb up and pass apples to us."

Soon all the sacks were full, and everyone had a heavy load to carry down the hill.

"We'll leave you and April the small buckets for blackberries, Jessa," said Ben. "It's getting late, and Eddie needs to get back into town. Jacob's going to pick him up."

They loaded the fruit into the car and parted company in front of the house. Eddie stroked Cassie's head before climbing into the car with Michael. "She's a wonderful dog, Jessa. The camping was great. Thanks for sharing your special tree! I'd like to come back and play my fiddle in the forest sometime, to sing with the birds!"

"I'll bring my flute!" said Jessa.

"I'm looking forward to my night in the tree, too!" said April, waving good-bye.

The girls gathered up the quilts, water jug, and their own food supplies. April had brought her sketch pad, filled with the many landscapes she had drawn with colored pencils on the train trip. "Before it gets any later, I want to find some of those wonderful mushrooms to sketch!"

"We'll follow the trail. I think I remember where they were," said Jessa.

They plunged into the deepening shade of the forest, walking slowly and peering around logs and at the base of the trees. "Here's some—we didn't see these yesterday," said Jessa.

A cluster of parasol-shaped mushrooms with tiny red warts scattered across their fragile white caps were ranged around the litter of a mossy log. "Oh, lovely! I'll sketch these!" exclaimed April.

"I'll take the stuff to the tree—it isn't far—and bring you back a cookie. Come, Cassie."

Jessa continued down the path with Cassie cavorting by her side and dumped her load inside the tree. "You think we're going to go back to living in the tree again, don't you, girl?"

She sat just outside the tree and stroked the dog. Everything felt so different, now. Warm instead of cold, safe instead of hunted, loved instead of lonely. Jessa buried her face in the dog's wooly head. If she cried, now, it would be with a full heart, a happy heart. The previous day, she'd been overwhelmed by memories of the tree, her refuge, when she was cut off from everyone. Now, she could see the beauty and wonder of it through the eyes of others, and a feeling of love for her tree and her grandparents' land swept over her.

Leaning back, she looked up at the trunk spreading its strong branches high into the sky. She addressed it, "I *love* you! I *love* you!" Cassie squeezed past her into the interior, and Jessa followed her and caught the dog in her arms and hugged her. "I love you, too, Cassie!" She opened the tin of cookies and got a couple each for herself and April. "Cassie, here's one for you, too! There's plenty!"

Jessa retraced her steps with the cookies. She sat quietly and watched while April's swift strokes captured the magic of the population of mushrooms growing by the rotting log. When April closed her sketchpad, they called Cassie and set out for the tree together.

April crawled in and commented that the shredded burlap

bags pillaged by raccoons and other animals were missing. "I guess the boys cleaned them out." Then she noticed the pile of stones and crawled over to examine them. "Jessa, tell me about these rocks."

Jessa joined her inside the tree. "Oh, I forgot them. That pile is the ones I transferred, one each night, to mark our days in the forest. The day of the snowstorm, I left without thinking about them. Let's count them." She opened the cookie tin and used the lid to receive the stones as April handed them to her and counted aloud. There were forty-five stones in all. "I think I should keep those stones together, and maybe someday I can make something with them, like a steppingstone with these stones embedded in cement."

"That's a good idea," said April. "These are such smooth, interesting rocks, with different colors and markings."

"I'll slide them into this bag and we can take them back."

That night, Jessa and April lay on the quilts, listening to the songs of crickets and katydids and looking up into the tree's darkness, just as the boys had. Jessa tried to explain how she felt. "When Cassie and I ran away, April, everything about my life was ripped apart! We'd been so happy, always so close, always doing things together. Mommie and Daddy would play records in the evening—new recordings that they ordered for the music shop. I remember so well the time they played 'The Magic Flute' by Mozart. That was when I decided that I just had to play the flute. I wanted to play that music so much!"

"I can't imagine how awful it would be—to have my parents killed," said April. "We had it hard when both my grandparents died. First, sweet Grandmother, we knew she was suffering so much, but she never complained. I think she felt she had to be strong to help Granddaddy. When she died, we felt so sad, but it was something we had to accept. After that, mother tried to keep going for everyone's sake, but Granddaddy was never the same. It seemed that he didn't care about anything. He'd always loved eating with us, joking and telling stories, but after Grandmother's funeral, eating was just something he did to please my mother. His mind was always somewhere else, somewhere inside himself. After he died, there was an enormous hole in the family. You know" —April turned to Jessa— "it made such a difference, when you joined us in Portland—the house was happy again."

"I was happy, too. I'd thought I'd never feel part of a family again. When I was hiding out, I imagined living just with Cassie in our house in Radford. I planned to cook and mow the lawn and go to school. I know now they'd never have allowed me to do that, and it seems like such a lonely life, when I think about it now."

"Poor Jessa!"

"April, I'd always wanted to have a sister. You've been wonderful, sharing your room and your stuff. It may sound funny, but I love wearing hand-me-downs—I love being part of the family that way."

"We are so happy you chose us!"

"But it's not simple. Why is nothing ever simple? My decision was a problem for the Carlsons, more than I realized, when I chose to go to Portland with you. I wonder what Daddy and Mommie would have wanted me to do. The Carlsons loved my parents so much, and I know they would have tried to give me a good home."

"Jessa, I'm thinking about it this way: the Carlsons are truly your godfather and godmother—like in fairy tales—special people with the power to rescue you if you're really in danger!"

"Thank you, April. That's a sweet idea!" Jessa hugged her. "I think I can go to sleep now."

The next morning, sunshine entered the tree filtered through green leaves. Birds were singing all around them, and April said, "Oh, it's magical, you feel you're part of the forest!"

They sat in the dappled sunshine in front of the tree and ate peaches and peanut butter and jelly sandwiches with their spring water. A line of ants was crawling along a log by the tree, and Jessa sprinkled breadcrumbs on their trail to see what the ants would do. The first ones just climbed over the crumbs, but then one picked up a piece and threw it aside. April and Jessa elbowed each other as they watched as the next ant picked up a crumb and carried it along. Soon, there were ants coming back to collect the crumbs.

"What interesting creatures!" said April. "Jessa, I would never be bored, living here!"

They set out to explore the entire farm. Jessa led April to the place at the edge of the forest where the May apples grew in a broad swath. The plants were about a foot tall, and their two leaves spread to form a droopy parasol. In the summer's heat, the spring plants were turning yellow, and the leaves of some plants were missing, revealing the bifurcation where, in some cases, fruits were still attached.

"I remember when Mommie showed these to me," Jessa said. "She shared the places where she played as a child, and introduced me to this grove of special plants."

"Are they edible?" asked April.

"Yes, Mommie and I ate some together. The fruits have seeds and are okay but not great. I think she said that the rest of the plant is not edible. Now let's find the ginseng."

As they walked through the forest, April exclaimed over many things that delighted her and wanted to sketch the stand of fiddlehead ferns. Jessa headed up a slight slope to a tree, put her hand on its trunk, and pointed up. "This is a tulip poplar tree—my father's favorite kind of tree. Look how straight the trunk is. Daddy told me they were used for ship's masts. In the spring, they have big blooms shaped like tulips."

"Oh, I would love to live here year-round," said April.

"Now, we're coming to the ginseng. Watch where you step. Grandad didn't want me stepping on the littler plants. See," she stooped and pointed one out, "the shiny leaves spread—it looks like a hand with big flat central finger leaves. That one over there has seeds. See the red? When granddad was young, he dug ginseng roots to sell. I guess your grandfather must have dug them with him. He told me he had to clean and dry them very carefully, and when he had a shipment of the roots ready, he'd mail them off and eventually get paid. They're pretty valuable in China. He said what makes them valuable is that the root looks like a little man with two legs and sometimes a penis between them. Little naked men—isn't that funny? The more they looked that way, the more they were worth. People believe they have special power."

They walked to the hot west-facing bank of the forest where dewberry vines bore glistening round berries similar to blackberries. They had mostly finished bearing, but Jessa stooped and lifted the slender, thorny branches, which formed a web over the ground, and found a few of the berries to share with April.

"They're delicious! The seeds are small, too. How come nobody grows these for the grocery store?" wondered April. "Can we go see the walnut tree where the wonderful English walnuts came from?"

They cut back through the forest toward the creek and walked through the stand of slender persimmon trees, looking up to see fruit that wouldn't be ripe until frost. The walnut tree was heavy with clusters of nuts covered by green hulls. April scanned the big, spreading tree, taking in the enormity of the crop.

"It's going to be a good year for nuts. A shame we won't be here to collect them," said Jessa, petting Cassie, who had run up to join them.

"I'm sad to not have lots of those nuts to take back to Portland," replied April.

From the forest, they crossed the meadow to the farmyard, and Jessa showed April around the flowerbeds and told her what spring bulbs were planted in each. The roses her grandfather had called "Emily's roses" were blooming, and they both stopped to smell. Jessa explained how she had come to understand that her grandfather also loved the roses, even though he always called them Emily's roses.

After the tour of the yard, they got their buckets and began to pick blackberries. The largest, most perfect berries draped over the creek, and the footing along the bank dropped off precipitously. Their lips were stained with blackberry juice, and their fingers were pricked, but each had collected a bucketful when Cassie cocked her ears and emitted a low growl at the approach of a car. Jessa reached for Cassie's collar to keep her quiet.

"It's too early for Daddy," whispered April.

Cassie struggled against Jessa's hold on her muzzle. The car advanced up the drive to the farmhouse and stopped. As she restrained the growling dog, Jessa's fear returned.

The car doors slammed, and their voices could be heard. "Come on!"

"Isn't this trespassing—on private property? We could get into trouble…"

"Ain't a crime to pick berries, and nobody but us is going to be picking these blackberries this year. It's like nobody at all owns them. I bet old-man Ellis didn't bother to pick them back when he was alive—good blackberries going to waste!"

The young men scrambled down the steep bank.

Jessa and April could still hear voices, but now they couldn't make out the meaning. They tried to move around the bend out of sight, but Jessa lost her footing. As she slid toward the creek, she spilled her bucket of blackberries as she frantically grabbed at sumac saplings. Furious, she leaned into the crumbling bank, pulling the dog to her, shaking with dread.

April was more worried about Jessa than the men. She moved so that she could help control Cassie, who was growling despite the fact that Jessa had grabbed her muzzle to suppress barking.

Jessa was clearly beside herself. Memories of being the quarry flooded her brain.

"Here, grab this tree. I think we can climb up over here and get away," April whispered.

Jessa inched along the steep bank to grasp the tree April indicated and transferred her hold on Cassie's collar over to April, who guided the dog up and over the bank while Jessa hauled herself up through the brambles. By this time, both of them were badly scraped by thorns and smudged with dirt.

Meanwhile, with whoops and yells, the young men ran down to the gravel by the spring and almost didn't stop before landing in the water. Jessa and April heard curses and the clanking of buckets as they shoved one another.

"My mother says she'll bake us a pie if I bring her berries," said one. They began to pick, all the time making a lot of noise exclaiming over the berries and thorns, and one of them nearly fell in the creek. The others were shoving and knocking, ready to push the unlucky one in, but he yelled, "Hold your horses! Push me any more and you'll have to walk all the way back into town!

"Now, Dex, be a good sport!"

"I'm here to pick blackberries, not roughhouse with you guys. I'm liable to get in trouble just for going out here with you, but I happen to like blackberry pie!"

"You guys are lucky to have a mother who'll bake a pie," said Charlie.

· · · · ·

Jessa and April raced across the meadow toward the forest. From the safety of the trees, they took stock of the damage. In addition to the loss of Jessa's berries, their hands were scraped, their clothes dirty, and thorns had torn April's sleeve, but it could be mended.

"We can go back to that boysenberry patch you showed me and get berries there to replace the ones you lost, Jessa," suggested April. "Anyway, I think there's enough in my bucket to make two pies."

Jessa hugged Cassie, who was still intent on the men. From the safety of the forest, the girls gazed across the meadow toward the farmhouse. They were checking their hands and knees for thorns when April grabbed Jessa's arm and pointed. They watched as the men climbed over the bank, crossed the back of the farmyard, and circled the house to climb into the car.

"I recognize them! They're the guys who came into the sheriff's office objecting to the choir performance," said April.

"I think they're also the ones who came here looking for me last fall. Cassie and I had to run out of the garden, and when we hid in the blackberry brambles, one of them said it'd be a good place to pick blackberries."

"Well, that's not bad—going someplace they think is deserted to pick something that grows wild."

"I guess so. Sorry I got so scared. I felt that they could grab me now and get the reward. That other time, I heard them talking about a reward for finding me. It was hard to hold on to Cassie then, just like now, and we got worse briars, didn't we, girl?"

April glanced at Jessa. Her eyes were brimming with tears. "I think you were brave, Jessa. It must have been terrible, to be hunted like an animal!"

· CHAPTER 19 ·

Jessa sat on the phone bench in the front hall and looked up Abby's number. She twisted her loose hair in her free hand to get it off her sweaty neck and kicked her shoes off to wiggle her toes on Cassie's curly back. She described the plan to Abby and asked her to appeal to her father for his help. They talked for quite a long time. When she finally hung up, Jessa bent over and hugged her dog, saying, "I love my friends, Cassie!"

That night, Ben again walked Jessa to City Hall. They climbed the stairs and were turning down the hall when they overheard a woman saying, "...just a spoiled only child who's used to having her way..."

Jessa and Ben paused. Ben watched the grimace on Jessa's face transition to determination. Lips pressed into a thin line, she pulled herself to her full height and entered the room. Ben ducked back to sit beside the reporter as Jessa joined the four school board members at the long table. Mr. Wexler smiled, but the others barely acknowledged her. *So much for being a celebrity*, she mused.

The issue of the new teacher was raised, and one candidate was the clear favorite. A motion to offer the position was made, seconded, and voted on. Then the Chair recognized Jessa.

"Mr. Chairman, I understand the school board has had lots of expenses and doesn't have much money," Jessa started. "I have a plan to get money for the school board to spend however it thinks best."

"Miss Olsen, how are you going to get us some money?" The chairman hardly masked an indulgent smile.

"I'm going to collect money at the next Music in the Park performance. We'll pass a plate, like in church, and I'll tell them that more music in Radford—lots of music in the future—depends on their support for music in the schools."

Mrs. Brians leaned forward. "Jessamine, is there any coincidence that the next Music in the Park performance will be the combined choir?"

"No, ma'am, it's not a coincidence. This music features residents of Radford, so I thought it would be appropriate to ask for support. When an outside group like the barbershop quartet from Landsdowne performs, I didn't think it would be appropriate."

"I've heard objections to opening the park up to Negroes, especially the picnic part of these events. Has anyone else gotten wind of that?" asked Mr. Morton.

"That's why I was inquiring," said Mrs. Brians. "The choir members were questioned about whether they would be willing to go ahead with the performance, given that some in the community objected."

"But Mrs. Florence said they wanted to sing, no matter what!" said Jessa.

"Young lady! Mr. Morton and I were talking."

"I'm sorry," said Jessa.

"I think the combined choir performance will be a fine community event, and Jessa's plan to collect money for the school board is a generous one," said Mr. Wexler. "I'm prepared to match any amount she's able to collect."

Abby! thought Jessa. She must have convinced her father!

"I don't like the connotation of a public collection. It makes it look like we can't cover the needs of the school program without begging," said Mr. Morton.

Jessa's hand shot up.

"Yes, the Board recognizes Miss Olsen," said the chairman.

"I thought the cost of the Overbrook salaries and repairing the playground equipment made it impossible to consider expanding the curriculum. Isn't that what you said at the last meeting?"

"Adding a teacher to the payroll is different," Mr. Morton replied. "A collection at the park might fund a new bleacher for the gymnasium or a cabinet for displaying sports trophies, but not a new teacher, Miss Olsen! That calls for several hundred dollars. You have no idea the magnitude of what you are proposing!"

The gavel came down loudly. "Do I hear a motion to accept Miss Olsen's proposal?"

Mr. Wexler said, "It's my understanding that Miss Olsen would like the funds collected at the park events to be earmarked for the Radford school music program. I therefore move that we graciously accept any money collected at events featuring local musicians and use it to enhance the music program."

Mr. Jamison, the chair, cleared his throat and eyed the reporter at the back of the room. "A motion has been made. Do I hear a second?" There was silence.

He scanned the committee. Everyone turned to Jessa. As the silence dragged on, she was close to tears, but she turned to Mr. Jamison and faced him squarely, defiance in her eyes.

"Jessamine, doggone it, you remind me of your father. In his name, I second the motion." He turned to the others. "All in favor?"

Mrs. Brians and Mr. Wexler assented; Mr. Morton stared silently at the table.

"The motion passes. This meeting is adjourned."

· CHAPTER 20 ·

The Esso gas station was located at the edge of town. The services it offered were limited to pumping gas, checking oil, and cleaning windshields, but it was the closest Charlie had been able to get to training as a mechanic. His friends admired him for landing a job at all; they depended on the extra cash to fund a steady supply of bummed cigarettes. The Esso station had become their hang-out as the lazy summer months dragged on. Dexter was the only one with access to a car, although Charlie was occasionally allowed to drive his stepfather's truck.

"We got to plan out our strategy for this park event. Looks like they're going ahead, despite our warning," said Maney. "That sheriff's a real pussycat."

"You know what I think got Radford messed up? That runaway girl coming back with her Yankee relatives." said Matt. "She's been messing with the school board, like it said in the paper."

"Pussycat's nicer than what my stepdad calls the sheriff. He's got some choice words for how he lets the town run over him," said Charlie. "I'm itching to put him to the test!"

"Listen, I say we arrive at the park after the choir starts singing. They'll not be expecting anything, and whammo, we let them have it."

"What do you mean, 'let them have it'?" asked Matt.

"Do we attack the singers or the colored audience?" asked Maney.

"I favor the colored families on their blankets. We ain't just gonna yell—we'll have to draw some blood to get their attention," said Charlie.

"Don't know about that, guys. You think whites in the audience will back us up? We've got to make it clear we're objecting to the coloreds invading the park. Then they'll support us," said Matt.

"Agreed. Make it obvious the coloreds are the targets. To put them back in their place. I think a good cudgel's what I want."

"*Cudgel*? Maney, you sound like you're back in English class—cudgel or stick or baseball bat won't matter, just so it's plenty heavy. We'll take them by surprise," said Matt.

"Dex, can you get your mother's car that day?" asked Charlie.

"Dunno. She works at the bank until four o'clock. Sometimes she does errands after that," replied Dex. "But by six she should be home."

"We need you to get us to the park. I don't have time to walk to the other side of town. I'm on duty here, and if my boss gets wind I left the station unattended, I'm in trouble. I waited in line and licked boot to get this job pumping gas. I aim to earn enough to move out. Tired of being picked on."

"Business is slow. You probably wouldn't have any customers, anyway," said Dexter. "I'll get here with the car soon as I can."

"So, it's agreed? We'll each bring a good stick, and when Dex gets here, we'll head for the park."

· CHAPTER 21 ·

Merrybelle arrived at the Carlsons' early to finish cleaning and get home to dress and prepare her family's picnic dinner. Before she could get started, Fran insisted she try on the dress again to make sure the fit was perfect. The ironing board was set up in the sewing room, and the pressed dress was draped across it.

"I feel like it's Confirmation Day—I've got such butterflies in my stomach! My daughter and her friends are just dying to seeing this dress—I've told them so much about it!"

When Fran stepped out to give her privacy, Merrybelle slipped her work dress over her head and dropped it on the floor. She took up the green dress and held it out. It had been years since she had had a new summer dress. She slipped the green, gauzy fabric over her head, and when she zipped up the side zipper, the dress settled around her shapely body. Fran knocked and re-entered.

"My, doesn't it look pretty!" Merrybelle said, turning to view it in the mirror on the closet door. "Whee!" She spun around so that the full skirt billowed out from her slim waist, making her feel like a princess.

Fran couldn't help admiring her own work. "You look *so* pretty in it, Merrybelle. I'll take my camera and get a picture of you tonight!"

Merrybelle sang her way through the housework and hugged

the package with the dress in it when she waved good-bye to Fran and hurried off home.

A storm had threatened earlier, but by the afternoon, the sky cleared and the sun beamed hot. Families began to arrive, walking from nearby homes or parking along Main Street and carrying their picnic baskets to the park; the sultry air made the shade of the big trees welcome, and the grown-ups selected smooth spots to spread their blankets while children ran to the playground area. The entire community was represented, with young families joining grandparents, aunts and uncles; members of all the churches proudly supported their singers. Friends called across the crowd to greet one another as they settled their families and spread the picnic dinners on the blankets.

Segregation of the audience was apparent early. While the white families took the shady spots on the smooth lawn in front of the gazebo where bleachers had been set up for the choir, the Negro families spread their blankets in a fringe in front of the playground. Reverend James, the natural leader of the Negro population, appeared to be organizing the families. Michael, on the look-out for Eddie, noticed him gravely pointing and apparently warning the children to stay away from the slide, swings, and merry go 'round.

While the audience assembled and unpacked their picnic dinners, the choir gathered by the bleachers. Boyfriends and husbands recognized their special choir members with cat whistles. Dressed in their array of pastel summer dresses, the singers were both proud and self-conscious over the attention they were getting. They ranged from nubile teenagers to white-haired women of both races, and for all of them, the practice sessions had become one of their favorite summer activities. Teenaged girls out of school with time on their hands had been gratified when their suggestions for including popular songs had been adopted, and for the older women, escaping routine chores to sing with women who shared their love of music had become the highlight of their week. The practice sessions had gradually bound the women into a cohesive group, forged by appreciation of each other's talent.

The pianist arrived, directing four men to push the piano from Bethany Church down the sidewalk and across boards laid on the grass to a position next to the bleachers. She carefully positioned her chair on the turf and sat on it, wiggled to force the chair's feet into a stable position, and looked up to where the choir director would stand.

There was laughing and hugging as choir members greeted and challenged one another. A careful observer would have noted a novel situation for Radford: the clusters of women were assorted by age rather than by race. Friendships they barely acknowledged had grown across the race line as they had come to admire one another's talents and had shared aspects of their lives. Today was a triumph they had worked together for, and everyone was having a good time, although those with solos were more nervous than the others. As they climbed over the bleachers to the positions they had been assigned, the young helped the less nimble, adding a heartfelt greeting to the helping hand.

The Acrees and the Carlsons spread their blankets side-by-side so that they could share food and company. Cassie was one of several dogs in attendance. Jessa put her in a down-stay off the blanket with strict orders to not beg. When Michael spotted Eddie and his grandfather spreading a blanket for Sarah, he called, "Back in a minute!" before tearing across the park to greet his friend.

In the settling-in period, several singers traveled back and forth between their families' picnic spots and the bleachers, instructing more competent older children to keep the younger ones in line until their fathers located them after work.

Merrybelle had older, well-behaved children, and Margaret could depend on her father to help Eddie with little Sarah until Jacob showed up. Aunt Helen joined them with deviled eggs and fresh biscuits just as Michael ran up.

The pastel-clothed singers made a pretty sight in front of the decorated gazebo. Fran fretted until she saw late-arriving Merrybelle, surrounded by friends admiring her new green dress. Soon the waving and calling stopped and the women closed ranks on the bleachers. There were a few last whistles from the audience, and Fran stood and took a picture of the entire group.

Finally, there was a shushing as the choir director from Radford Presbyterian turned to address the audience. "Thank you all for coming this evening. We hope you enjoy our program as much as we have enjoyed preparing it for you!" She turned to face the singers, whispered something the audience couldn't hear, raised her arms, and nodded to the pianist, who struck a chord of intro for the first piece.

They began with arrangements of songs made popular by Frank Sinatra, Frankie Lane, and Patty Page. Soon, the audience was rocking back and forth to the beat and singing along. Everyone was involved with the music, calling compliments back and forth between family groups and cheering the soloists. The picnic dinners were shared as children carried cookies and slices of cake between the blankets.

The program was punctuated by sessions of enthusiastic clapping and little children were allowed to dance alongside the picnic blankets, providing a show all their own. The first half concluded with popular songs from musicals, and the audience joined in. April and Jessa sang the songs everyone knew, and Karen and Ben encouraged the Carlsons to join in.

When the music reached a halfway mark, the choir director turned to face the picnickers. Her face was glistening with sweat, but her pride in the performers was clear. *"Thank you!*

Thank you all for joining us to celebrate this beautiful summer evening with song! We'll take a little break here, and our pianist has agreed to play a medley while we get something to drink. Keep your ears tuned, and when the pianist plays 'Pop Goes The Weasel,' you'll know the second half is coming up. "

The white children ran for the swings, slides, and merry go 'round, where their shouts of delight rang out. Michael tapped April's shoulder to point out that the colored children were looking toward the playground equipment but not making a move in that direction. He gave a thumbs-down, but April prevented him from sharing his observations with Jessa, who was leaning across to the blanket where Fran and Jack were sitting, engaged in animated discussion.

All around them, a festival-like atmosphere prevailed. People visited with neighbors, the choir members checked on their families and were hugged and greeted with congratulations as drinks were shared. Some of the singers grabbed a quick bite along with something to drink, but those who had solos in the second half stuck to water or lemonade. Some people were fanning themselves, but a pleasant breeze had sprung up, making the sultry afternoon more tolerable.

Soon, the pianist pounded out several rounds of "Pop Goes the Weasel," and kids ran from the playground equipment to rejoin their families. More drinks and cookies were distributed, and everyone settled back to focus on the choir director as she mounted her platform in front of the bleachers. She turned to the audience, which burst into spontaneous applause before she could begin to speak.

"Thank you for your enthusiasm for our first half. I know I speak for the choir members when I say we love this chance to share this music with you. We will now return to our usual repertoire, familiar hymns, and highlight more of the talent our town is blessed with. Most of you know the first stanzas of these hymns, and everyone knows the refrains, so feel free to join us. After the first stanza, one of our soloists will sing the other stanzas and we can all sing the refrains together."

As the choir began to sing, the audience joined in. Well-loved hymns unified the community, and the sound of the sing-along rose and spilled out of the park. Merchants and shut-ins unable to attend listened in amazement. The unfamiliar stanzas were claimed by the lovely voices of soloists from each of the town's churches. Soon, it became clear that differences between white and colored renditions had been embraced by the choir director. This had been a closely guarded secret, which they had explored during their practice sessions, when it had been agreed that "colored" renditions should be offered by the colored solo-ists. The colored families far across the lawn were surprised to hear the soaring embrace of the hymns, as only their soloists could render them. Some among the white audience shrugged at each other, some raised their eyebrows in indignation at the liberties taken with the melodies, but many wiped tears from their eyes.

Few in the audience heard the car screech to a stop in the car-lined street. Facing that way, the choir members were the first to detect the disturbance at the fringe of the park, but when their voices faltered, everyone turned to see four young white men dash into the park, waving sticks and yelling.

"Out of our park! Niggers get out!"

"Got no right to be here—get out!"

Children shrieked and mothers clutched them like chicks as all eyes turned on the young men yelling and swinging sticks. Babies wailed and dogs barked.

The men kept shouting: "Join up! We're defending white rights!"

"Help us drive niggers out of our park!"

The sheriff, his deputy, the fire chief, and others in the

audience moved quickly to block the young men's advance toward the performers, but this opened up a path toward the cluster of Negro families who were already rising and grabbing blankets and baskets.

"Go back to Niggertown! Get out of our park!" they yelled, leaping over the blankets of the white picnickers as women and children shrieked, and drinks and picnic baskets were overturned. The sheriff called on white men close to the intruders, soliciting their help, and soon the young men were apprehended. Men confiscated the sticks and pushed three attackers to the ground, but one broke free and took off running toward the street.

The sheriff pushed his way to the action. "Maney, Charlie, Matt—I'll charge you with disturbing the peace! You'll spend the night in jail!"

The car roared away, and the three attackers realized Dexter had abandoned them. From his position on the ground, Charlie pounded the grass with his fist and yelled, "You all know it ain't right! It goes against nature, mixing the races—there're laws against it!"

From the white population, there came a murmur of support. The sheriff turned toward the supporter and snarled, "No laws were being broken before these boys showed up!"

Jessa, the Acrees, and the Carlsons were far from the action. They initially watched the scene frozen with horror while Cassie growled and lunged. Jessa had difficulty holding on to her, and when April reached to hold the leash, she overturned their pitcher of iced tea, causing everyone to jump up. Ben and Michael set off to see if they could offer help.

"Unreal!" Michael muttered. "This is the *genuine* South!" He accompanied his father to the semicircle that surrounded the sheriff and the three intruders. Disgruntled picnickers complained all around them. Jessa was holding one of the platters intended for the collection as the choir melted off the bleachers and scattered to join family and friends. Adults focused on comforting distressed children and collecting their disrupted picnic spread. Everyone was busy packing up, and the usual friendly exchanges were lost in the haste to retreat. Colored people disappeared especially quickly, and by the time Fran turned from watching the young men being led off to search for Merrybelle, the bleachers were empty, and the piano player was again instructing the men to push the piano back to the church.

Jessa decided to try anyway. She took the collection plate to the family on her right, but when she began to explain the purpose of the collection, they said, "Honey, we just want to get out of here!" She turned to watch the sheriff and deputy. How she wanted to hurl the collection plates after the young men! They'd ruined everything—stolen the final triumph, the applause and congratulations the women deserved! This had come so close to being a wonderful event, but Jessa's chance to address the picnickers and pass the collection plates was lost. Maybe the dream of influencing the school board was lost, too.

Karen and Fran both tried to comfort her, and Cherry and Alice ran over, but Jessa didn't want hugs—she wanted to punch something. She took the dog's leash from April and pulled the dog close, bent over, hugged her, and whispered, "Girl, you knew they were bad, didn't you? I want to bite them, too. I could chew them to pieces!"

Ben and Michael returned from talking with the sheriff, and they began to gather the picnic spread. Jessa helped bag up the picnic things and the soaked blanket. It was a long walk home, and they trudged along in silence. April carried Mrs. Carlson's heavy platters. Cassie walked by Jessa's side with her tail at half-mast, dragging her leash on the sidewalk. No one could think of anything helpful to say.

Finally, Michael ventured, "Jessa, it seems pretty bad, but

I don't see it as a total defeat. Did you see those white people stand up and knock those guys down? More people are on your side than you think!"

"Yeah? Well how much money did that put in the collection plates?" said Jessa.

Ben said, "Jessa, that's not the major issue here. What's important is how the community will respond to events that involve both races. Michael's right. There was local opposition, although some people did support the intruders, but the sheriff put them down."

"Mr. Wexler said he would match any money I collect, but zero plus zero is still just zero!"

"This whole situation in this town bothers me more than I expected it to," said Karen. "I thought this segregation was just something everyone had to put up with, a sort of parallel existence, but seeing the audience so unfairly segregated made me angry. White people were comfortable with colored people taking the picnic spots in the sun, but if they had competed for places in the shade, there probably would have been objections."

"That's not the half of it," said Michael. "None of the colored kids dared to play on the swings or slide. This place is sick! I thought the worst stuff was in the past, but it's alive and well."

"I still think music is a good way to get the races together, and wasn't that a stunning rendition of 'Amazing Grace'?" asked Ben. "It's still ringing in my ears."

"It would have been a wonderful event—it really was—all the way up until the end," said April. "I think Jessa would have made lots of money collecting donations after that performance!"

"Do you think those guys listened to the music at all before they crashed the party?" asked Michael. "How can you attack someone singing church music?"

"What do you think made those men do it? I mean, what's in it for them? At the sheriff's office, they were angry the sheriff was allowing their 'white' park to be used. The sheriff said there weren't laws against it," said April.

Jessa said, "I agree with April. This doesn't make sense. I need to know what drives them. I've been telling Janie more about Tennessee in my letters, but this is so awful I don't know how to explain it to her. Before I write, I need to understand what makes them so angry."

· CHAPTER 22 ·

Dexter steered the old Studebaker through side streets, unsure where to go. He'd dropped his stick and been desperate to head for the car after he'd seen his mother sitting on a bench with her friends. He touched his brow tenderly, where a welt was growing under the blond curls. He decided to head for the Esso station. He'd no sooner pulled into the back parking area and gotten out of his car when the owner of the station pulled in next to the pump. His faded blue work shirt was open down the front, and Dexter smelled alcohol on his breath. The old red station wagon was jacked up in the back, and lumber was sticking out the rear window.

"Hey you! Where's Charlie?" asked the owner.

"He—he got sick," Dexter responded. "Sent me over to cover for him at the station."

"You know how to pump gas? How do I know you won't rob me blind?"

"Just trying to help out. Charlie needs this job. He felt responsible, but he had to leave in a hurry. Asked me to help him out."

"Pump the gas. Make it fast. What happened to your head, anyway?"

"Yessir, I'll pump it. Ran into a tree. Wasn't looking where I was going." Dexter struggled to look competent as he set the pump running and dipped the cloth in the bucket of water and began to wipe the windshield.

"Skip that. Just let me get out of here!"

Dexter returned the nozzle to its slot. Without offering to pay for the gas, the man scratched off, leaving Dexter in a cloud of dust.

He went to the chairs lined up in front of the station, sank into the nearest, and cradled his head in his hands. "Mamma warned me to not let those guys get me into trouble. I'm really in for it now." He again touched the surface of the goose-egg and tried to gauge its size.

• • • • •

At the sheriff's headquarters, Marvin gawked at the young men's injuries. "They gonna spend the night together in there?"

"That's what they'll have to do," said the sheriff, forcing Charlie, Matt, and Maney down the hallway to the single jail cell.

"You ain't going to lock us up, now are you, Mr. Sheriff? We're just defending the town against this outrage!" said Matt. "Standing up for whites like somebody's got to do."

"Shut up," hissed Charlie.

A crowd was forming in the reception room. First, the reporter, then Maney's father, shoving and cursing, followed by Charlie's distraught mother accompanied by her neighbor.

The sheriff returned from locking the attackers in the jail cell to face them.

"Could I get a statement from you? What happens next with these young men?" the reporter Ted Hufford demanded.

"Charlie's a good boy, Sheriff. He don't mean no harm. My husband just gets him agitated over the nig..."—she looked around and continued—"...over the taking of liberties in this town."

"You think you can lock my boy up over a little tussle in the park, Sheriff? You got another thing coming if you think that.

Why 'on't you lock up some of those nigger families. They're the ones breaking laws!"

Florence pushed her way in the door. "Excuse me, excuse me. A burning shame, that's what it was!" She marched down the hall and squared off against the young men. "Breaking up the singing when everyone was having such a good time! *Shame on you*! You can rot in jail, as far as I'm concerned. Those poor women worked so hard on that wonderful program!"

"What are you charging them with?" the reporter persisted.

"Threatening the public, unlawful conduct, disturbing the peace!" answered the sheriff.

"Gotcha," said Ted.

"No, not my son!" shouted Charlie's mother. "Charlie's a good boy!"

"Now, ladies and gentlemen, it's past closing time, and we're only open for emergencies, with Marvin here on duty. I advise you all to go home. This here emergency is under control, and I want everyone who doesn't belong here to clear out," said the sheriff.

"But what about my boy?" asked Charlie's mother.

"Ma'am, I figure to keep these young men here overnight and the town council can meet tomorrow morning to decide their fate. Ted, you can come to the meeting with the mayor and anybody else who wants to weigh in on the process around nine o'clock tomorrow. That will be plenty of time to get something for your paper."

He ushered them all to the door. Florence questioned the inhabitants of the jail cell, "Any of you hoodlums hurt bad enough to need medical care?"

"No, ma'am," they each said, followed by groans. They sat side-by-side on the single cot.

She studied them, went to the closet, and got out three blankets. "I recommend you pull the mattress down on the floor and use it as a pillow." She shoved the folded blankets through the bars. "These accommodations are too good for the likes of you!"

When she was gone, they started in on Dexter. "That rat fink!" said Charlie.

"Takes off running and leaves us to face the heat," said Matt.

"He's such a mamma's boy. Doesn't have any background to fall back on."

"Got no right to save his tail running off that way. I'm goin' to get even with him!"

"Told you we should have taken my dad's shotgun!" said Maney.

"What you goin' to do with it, shoot the sheriff? That's real smart!" said Matt.

"Sprinkle 'em with birdshot, those darkies! Do 'em good! They've no right to Reuben's Park! Somebody's got to put them in their place!"

"Did you see how those colored families scrambled out of the park? Wish my stepfather could have seen that! We really cracked the party up, didn't we?" said Charlie. "I doubt they'll try something like this again. Wait till my stepfather hears about it."

· CHAPTER 23 ·

Jessa, April, and Michael sat around the breakfast table. Jessa's elbows were on the table, her hands under her chin. She had no interest in the bowl of cereal, with or without peaches. April left her alone, but Michael tried to get a conversation going. Jessa resisted. Finally, she said, "I lay awake last night, trying to sort this all out. I want to talk to Mrs. Florence about it, but most, I want to talk to those guys."

Karen said, "Remember, we have to get to Landsdowne by one o'clock for the court hearing. We can't be late for that."

"Am I going?" asked April.

"Ben and I thought it would make sense for you two to stay here. You can keep Cassie company."

"Aw, I wanted to see a real courtroom," said Michael.

"So what time do we need to leave? I have to get dressed up, don't I?" asked Jessa.

"If you can get back to change into nice clothes by eleven o'clock, we should be able to have a light lunch before we leave."

"Then let's go now, April." Jessa clipped on Cassie's leash, and she and April walked her to the sheriff's headquarters.

· · · · ·

Florence greeted April and Jessa with, "What a fiasco! I guess we should have known they'd try something, the way they barged in here. I'm just so sorry for the choir members."

Jessa invited Cassie to jump onto one of the wooden benches, and Florence turned her attention to her. "Oh, I saw Cassie at the park, but I've been wanting to see her cool summer clip up close! Doesn't she look feminine, with those silky ears—quite different from the little black bear we saw last winter!"

"She's a lot cooler. She was hot, even in Portland, before we got her clipped," said April.

April looked down the hall and saw the door to the jail cell standing open. "Where're the guys that ruined the choir performance?"

"The sheriff took them over to the courthouse where the town council will decide their fate," said Florence. "Treating them with kid gloves, it seems to me, but Don doesn't want to alienate the community."

"Alienate the community—that's what *they* were doing!" said Jessa.

"They'll come up with some community service. They're a lot better off with that than going to reform school, and they know it. This way they don't have anything on their record. I've heard a lot of complaints about what happened, especially from the choir members. Lots of people were infuriated."

"We were, but I also want to understand…" said Jessa.

Florence said, "They wanted to spoil the performance, that's what. They couldn't stand…" She broke off, looking out the window. "Oh, there's Helen Wilson going into the bank. She usually stops by to say hello when she's in town. Have you kids met Jacob's aunt Helen?"

"Oh, yes—she has a super farm and makes the best apple pie!" said April. "She was there last night. I want to hear what she thinks about this."

Jessa recalled Helen's admonitions about getting involved in the music program. She had admitted that Eddie loved to play the violin. *Maybe she knows more about how to go about this music goal than I do*, she thought.

Florence asked April, "Tell me how it went when Eddie played at the Carlsons' home. I've been trying to picture that."

"It was nice, at least until their neighbor came over and insulted her about inviting Jacob's family to visit. It was a shock to Mrs. Carlson."

"I believe that, April. To be honest, I was surprised when you said the Wilsons had dessert at the Carlsons'. That part of town where the Carlsons live is so strictly segregated; the only Negroes you see at white events are waiters and cooks."

"Firstly, I have to admit I invited them without asking," said Jessa, "and Karen told me it wasn't polite to do it that way. I wanted it to be a nice surprise, but it was a shock for Mrs. Carlson. I hadn't figured out that the Carlsons' attitude about the schools was part of a larger picture. It just surprised me because I'd assumed that the Carlsons felt the same way my parents did. I know I should understand better how it is around here, but some things are hidden. I'm beginning to wonder if my friend Janie helped me because she was lonely, too. Maybe things weren't so perfect for her in Portland, but if she lived here in Radford, we would never have met!"

"Michael says Tennessee is worse than the wild west," said April.

"I sympathize with him," said Florence. "I'm ashamed that this happened in Radford! Oh, here comes Helen, now."

Helen headed for the sheriff's headquarters after dropping an envelope into the mailbox. "Come on, Helen," said Florence. "Look who I have here. We've been discussing the disruption of the choir's performance."

"Now wasn't that a burning shame! Our choir members are

declaring that's the end. They don't want any part of the white folk's park and all the trouble it caused."

"But, Mrs. Wilson, Mrs. Florence, do you understand *why* they attacked? They just seemed like regular guys," said Jessa.

Florence answered, "I think at the core, it's fear, Jessa. Those young men have caused trouble all through school. Now they've graduated, and they're at loose ends. They don't have college plans or a position in family businesses, so they're scared about the future."

Helen rose to accost Florence. "You listen to *me*," she countered. "Here you are, bending over backwards making excuses for those white boys after what they did to this town! What about the people they were waving their sticks at? What about their foul language! You're so sympathetic with those *poor white boys*, so pitiful with all those strikes against them. Well, they ought to try getting along in the world with brown skin! Those white boys can go wherever they want, study whatever they want to study, and eat in restaurants and sleep in hotels along the way. If they think they're so bad off, they ought to try it with a real handicap!"

"It's true, Helen," said Florence. "There's really no comparison. I sometimes wonder why colored people stay around here to be discriminated against. Your relatives who made it out of the area—how are they doing? Rochester, Cincinnati, and the last went to Akron, Ohio, wasn't it?"

Helen patted her shoulder. "I'm on edge, to fly at you like that, Florence," said Helen, "but it touched a raw nerve. I was at the bank today taking out money to send my niece Crystal, to tide her over. They're the ones that went to Akron. Her husband got laid off and hasn't been able to get work. Crystal's torn up over how things are going. The construction workers' unions won't let him join, because he's colored, mind you, and there Crystal is, looking at how she's going to have to stop working in a month or two because she's expecting a baby. She says it's destroying Murphy's pride to not be able to support his family."

"Michael keeps saying Tennessee is sick," said April, "but maybe it isn't just Tennessee."

"Honey, it's hard all over," said Helen. "Nothing's fair in this world. We're supposed to look to the afterlife, but it angers me to see good, hard-working people like Crystal and Murphy treated this way!"

"What's the matter with people? What about the school board? Do they feel threatened if colored children study music?" asked Jessa. "Or are they greedy and want all the school funds for their own children?"

"I can't speak for the school board members, Jessa, but I know a lot of white people were enjoying the combined choir," said Florence.

"Yes," said April, "but our mother said it was troubling the way the Negro families had to put their blankets down in the sunny spot, as far away from the whites as possible…"

"I can fill you in on that," said Helen. "It was a compromise Reverend James was coordinating. You may not be able to appreciate it, April, but just having Negro families present for the performance was an achievement of sorts."

"But that's pitiful—ridiculous!" said April. "I agree with Michael—this place is sick!"

"But will they come back? Will they come back in a few weeks if Eddie and his grandfather play?" asked Jessa.

"I know we'll support Margaret and Jacob. At least before this happened, Margaret said Eddie's really looking forward to playing. He and his grandfather have been working on new pieces."

"The sheriff had better protect everyone! I don't want people driven away again!"

· CHAPTER 24 ·

The town council gathered in the board room, greeting with handshakes. Mr. Wexler, the banker, headed up the group, which included Jack Carlson, Florence's husband the fire chief, and Ted the reporter. They had conferred by phone and had come up with ideas for dealing with the town's problem kids. *The devil finds work for idle hands* was repeatedly quoted, so the men proposed community service jobs as well as plans for individual internships.

When the sheriff and deputy arrived with the three offenders, the stench of sweat accompanied them into the room. The young men definitely looked the worse for their confrontations with their captors and the night spent in jail. They slouched into the chairs and began picking their noses or cracking their knuckles. The sheriff eyed them critically but chose to ignore their behavior.

Mr. Wexler cleared his throat and began: "Young men, it was clear last night that your actions were aimed at the Negro citizens of Radford. They were peacefully attending a public event, not breaking any laws. You were the ones breaking laws. Your actions offended all the people of Radford. Sending you off to reform school won't address the injury. Instead, we want to give you a chance to compensate the Negroes as well as the community at large. I've suggested that the three of you start by replacing the roof of Overbrook."

Charlie's hair swung aside as he jerked his head up to look at Wexler. He pushed back his chair and rose to leave.

"Sit down, son. We're not through with you."

"My stepdad'll scalp me if I have to work on that shit-hole!"

"This isn't about your stepfather, Charlie. It's about you and what you're doing with your life. You need to get on a path to a productive future," said Mr. Wexler.

Charlie sank deep into his chair. Matt and Maney squirmed but kept their eyes down.

Mr. Wexler continued: "The mornings will be devoted to re-roofing Overbrook, and after that, repairing the playground equipment at Edison and general work on the school grounds. In the afternoons, each of you will start an internship with a local business. That's where we thought we'd solicit your input, so the choices line up with your interests."

"What about my job?" asked Charlie. "You're keeping me from my job right now."

"Actually, we're not, because when this issue was raised last night, I contacted your boss, and he said you were fired."

Charlie jerked around to face him. "No! You can't do that. I've *got* to have that job! I've gotta earn money. I'm saving to move out."

Ignoring his response, Wexler asked, "Charlie, what sort of work would you do if you could choose anything you desired?"

Charlie looked at him with interest. "I'd fix up cars for drag racing."

Unfazed, Wexler pursued the lead. "So that calls for the skills of a mechanic, am I right?"

"Right. You gotta build performance to get lots of power."

Wexler made a note. "How about you, Maney. What do you want to do in life?"

Maney had difficulty finding his voice. "Sir, uh, I like making things. Designs. Using my hands. Maybe construction?"

"Then the roofing job will be a good start. Unfortunately, we don't have a construction contractor in Radford." Wexler cast around the table to solicit ideas from the other men.

The deputy said, "What about carpentry? That's making things. John Morgan's been making sounds about opening up his shop…"

"All we can do is ask him. Might be good for everyone."

Wexler wrote a note on a pad, then turned to the third offender. "How about you, Matt?"

Matt was ready for the question because he thought he could win their game. "I want to study law."

From the other side of the table, Jack Carlson eyed him with interest. "Really, Matt?"

Matt realized his mistake. He could be assigned an internship with the town's only lawyer. "Yeah," he said. "Bet you never imagined that."

"Actually, knowing your father, it doesn't surprise me."

Matt looked at him with amazement. "Really?"

"Sure. He usually beat me in debates. We tried to start up a debate club in high school."

"I will make arrangements for the internships," said Wexler. "Does anyone else want to comment on the plan?"

The mayor said, "My wife sings with the combined choir, and she was hopping mad after the disruption of the performance, and there's lots of other townspeople equally mad. We need to get a report of this meeting in the newspaper so that our response is publicized."

"I'm on it," replied the reporter.

The sheriff said, "Thank you all for taking time from your own schedules to help us deal with these young men." He addressed Charlie, Matt, and Maney, "You boys will report to work at Overbrook at eight sharp Monday morning. I'll see to it that the internships get ironed out by then. You are free to go home and get cleaned up now."

After the three had filed out, they could be heard running down the steps. Wexler addressed Jack, "Are you willing to take Matt on, Jack?"

"Sure, I'll give it a try. Nothing like a challenge. What time will these internships start?"

"I figure we work them at Overbrook until noon, allow them time to eat lunch, and they should show up at their internships around one o'clock. Will that fit with your schedule?"

"Fine. I'll see how well Matt can parse legalese…"

Wexler addressed the deputy next. "Could you talk to old-man John about taking on Maney?"

"I'll see him this afternoon," said the deputy.

"Sheriff, can you discuss Charlie's internship with Marvin?" continued Wexler. "That's the hardest nut to crack. Putting him out there at Marshall's Garage will be hard on Jacob, and I don't know how he'll take to that."

"I don't see he'll have any choice, but it's guaranteed that foul-mouthed Charlie will be unpleasant to Jacob," the sheriff replied.

That evening, when Marvin arrived to take over the desk job, the sheriff said, "Marvin, the committee wants me to approach Ray Marshall about taking Charlie Mains on as an intern."

"Don't see any reason why he can't come to the garage," responded Marvin. "There's plenty of grunt work to go around. Ray doesn't do so much hands-on anymore—he manages the records and the office side of the business."

"It's bound to be hard on Jacob."

"My impression is Jacob's over a barrel about the race issue. His own life was changed when Ray took him in and taught him a trade, so he's got a foot in both camps, but the preacher and the rest of his community are warning about keeping a low profile."

"Charlie has been in my sights for years now. He was the oldest, and it hit him the hardest when his father was killed, and he's never gotten along with his stepfather, who is, in my opinion, a first-class bigot."

"Charlie really wants to be a mechanic?"

"I get that impression. Wants to hot-rod cars, probably so that he can destroy them drag racing. Seems like there's a destructive urge behind everything he does."

"Well, I'd put it this way: if he's interested in cars, wants to fix them up, he and Jacob already have a lot in common. I went into the garage knowing zilch, and I'm hooked now. Jacob's a great teacher—leads you to discover the right answers on your own. Might be just what Charlie needs."

"That's the most positive thing you've said."

"It's worth a try. I'll duck out of the garage for a few days, just to let Charlie settle in."

· CHAPTER 25 ·

Jessa and April ran all the way home from the sheriff's head-quarters and Jessa headed for the bathroom to wash up and get dressed for the court hearing. Karen had a quick lunch ready, so they all assembled around the breakfast table to eat. April reported what Florence and Helen had said, but the others were too preoccupied to engage with the information. Cassie caught the tension in the air and broke training to sneak under the table and press her head onto Jessa's lap. Jessa furtively patted her head, and when the meal was over, she took the dog aside and told her she would have to stay home to take care of April and Michael.

Ben, Karen, and Jessa set out in good time for the estate hearing in Landsdowne. Jessa's custody status had been the ma-jor issue hanging over them the last few months. Jack Carlson had arranged to meet them at the courthouse.

They were all dressed in what they felt was respectful attire for a court hearing, which for Jessa meant wearing a starched dress that was much hotter than the shorts she had worn that morning. She rolled down the window despite the fact that the wind would muss her hair. They tried to find something to talk about, but all attempts fizzled. When Jessa described the visit with Florence and what Aunt Helen had said about her rela-tives in Akron, it just reminded them of the disaster of the pre-vious day and added to the general anxiety. When they pulled into the town, Ben circled the Landsdowne square, looking for a place to park, and Jessa caught sight of Mr. Carlson standing under a huge sycamore, a tall, lonesome-looking figure. They joined him in the shade, delaying going into the courthouse as long as possible.

Jessa kicked last year's sycamore balls with her tight patent leather shoes, then gave it up as undignified. She swallowed and took several deep breaths, but it didn't seem to help. Her stomach was becoming queasy, her throat tightening. How could this go wrong? She glanced at Ben and Karen, and they seemed nervous, too. Mr. Carlson pretended to be absorbed in sorting the papers he carried and avoided her gaze. Soon, he checked his watch and nodded for them to follow. They climbed a broad staircase to a pair of doors that opened into the courtroom. Mellow golden light reflected off the wooden paneling and benches, and the warm air released furniture polish.

Following Jack's lead, they sat close to the front. Jessa concentrated on breathing deeply as she methodically counted the panes in the tall windows, their upper sections cranked open at the level of the lazily circling ceiling fans. Scattered along the wooden benches were paper fans with biblical verses on them, which Karen examined with curiosity. The clerk called the court into session, and everyone stood to acknowledge the entrance of an impressive, white-haired judge. When he had seated himself, everyone settled in and there was silence.

"I've reviewed the records," he said, putting on his glasses after gazing at the small assemblage. "The will of Paul and Cora Olsen was submitted to probate by the executor of the estate, John Carlson, Esq. Will he please stand?" Jack stood. The judge nodded familiarly to Jack and proceeded. "The Olsen estate seems to be in order. All debts and obligations have been paid, and an accounting of the assets has been filed. A trust has been registered with the State of Tennessee, and funds have been set aside to cover the costs associated with maintaining the buildings."

The judge again scanned the small group in the courtroom. "We are gathered here to consider the guardianship of Jessamine Olsen, age twelve, and the management of the estate and real property to which she is heir. I have before me documents in which Paul and Cora Olsen expressed the wish that, in the event of their deaths, their daughter Jessamine Ruth would inherit their entire estate and, if she were still a minor, her guardianship would be assumed by family friends, Francene and John Carlson. Both couples appear to have signed the document in nineteen-fifty-one."

Jessa thought, *Where was I when this happened? They never told me!*

The judge paused and peered over his glasses into the courtroom and cleared his throat. "However, I have before me a statement signed by Mr. Carlson and Mrs. Ethyl Richardson of Child Protective Services to the effect that Jessamine Olsen requested, in November of 1955, to remain with her relatives, Benjamin and Karen Acree. As the guardians under the will, John and Francene Carlson agreed at that time to give the Acrees temporary custody, allowing Jessamine to accompany this couple to Oregon."

The black-robed judge paused again to scan the small group gathered in the courtroom. "It is now the responsibility of this court to determine Miss Olsen's permanent guardianship. The court would like to hear the opinion of the custodians specified by her parents. Will John Carlson clarify this issue for the court?"

Jack Carlson rose slowly. His reluctance contrasted with the dynamism he usually summoned for his court appearances, and the judge noted this. He began:

"I clearly recall the evening when my wife and I met with

Paul and Cora Olsen to go over the details of their will. What stood out was how anxious Paul was about Jessa's future. I was perplexed by Paul's level of concern, but I attributed it to the fact that Paul was himself orphaned, and the experiences he had in foster care represented a very traumatic period in his life. Obviously, he feared that Jessa might suffer a similar fate. I couldn't imagine…" At this point, Jack had to take off his glasses and wipe his eyes. "Please excuse me. They were very close friends." Once he pulled himself together, he continued: "That night, Paul and Cora asked us to agree that if anything happened to the two of them, my wife, Fran, and I would adopt Jessa. It seemed to take a weight off their minds to have the issue formalized. We had no children and were very fond of Jessa, so it was easy to comply with their wishes. However, Fran and I have discussed it at length, and it is our mutual conclusion that we want to respect Jessa's decision. We do not wish to stand in the way of her choice." He bowed his head and sat down.

The judge scanned the people in front of him. "Then I believe the court needs to hear from the minor, Jessamine Olsen, on her preference regarding the assignment of her custody."

Jessa wasn't expecting this. Jack realized that he should have warned Jessa that she would be called upon to make her preferences known. He looked back and saw that the color had drained from her face.

While Mr. Carlson had been speaking, Jessa's mind had been set spinning back through the tragedy and her response to it. She'd had no idea of the agreement between her parents and the Carlsons. *Where was I when they met in our living room?* She recalled the meeting at the sheriff's headquarters six months ago, when she had chosen to go to Portland with the Acrees. At that point, she had been with the Acrees for almost a week, learning to trust and love them. They had welcomed her into their family. When she'd learned that her parents had provided for the

Carlsons to adopt her, she had been shocked. If she'd known that, she probably wouldn't have run away, and so much would have turned out differently! The Carlsons had been her parents' best friends for as long as she could remember, but it had never occurred to her that she herself meant anything to them. Since then, she had learned how much they had done to try to find her, including posting a reward and preparing for her to live with them. This was so hard! She rose on trembling legs and gripped the bench in front of her. When she began to speak, her voice was barely audible. The judge leaned forward to hear her.

"When I ran away, I had no idea my parents had provided for me in their will. I know Mommie and Daddy wanted the best for me, and I love them for it. The Carlsons have always been very close friends of our family. I knew and trusted them. They're wonderful people."

The judge cleared his throat.

Jessa swallowed hard and forced herself to continue. "After I had been hiding out a long time, the Acrees came to my grandfather's farm, and I overheard them talking. It was cold and snowing hard, and I had been struggling to take care of myself and my dog, Cassie. From what I heard the Acrees say, I realized that they must be relatives. I called out to them because I couldn't stand to see them leave. They seemed to be my only chance."

Jessa turned to Ben and Karen. "My parents never knew the Acrees, but I wish they had. By the time I left Grandad's farm with the Acrees, I already felt like I belonged with them. I've come to love all of them. I don't want to be adopted or change my name, but I choose to stay with the Acrees."

Jessa sank onto the hard bench. She couldn't stop the pain her decision had caused the Carlsons, and it made her head swim. She put her hands to her temples to steady herself.

The judge studied her curiously, looking for evidence of

coercion. Turning to the Acree couple, he said, "Will Benjamin or Karen Acree please speak for their relationship with Jessa, and specifically address their suitability and willingness to accept responsibility for Jessamine's custody?"

Karen squeezed Benjamin's hand as he rose to address the court. "Your Honor, we have felt greatly blessed by getting to know Jessa. We came to Tennessee to explore a schism in my wife's family, the separation of brothers caused when Karen's father, Tom, left Tennessee as a young man. For the record, Karen is Jessa's second cousin, as Jessa's mother, Cora, and Karen were first cousins. Last November, I contacted City Hall and was directed to the sheriff's office. The sheriff called me back and urged us to come to Tennessee because he was desperate over the family tragedy and Jessa's disappearance. What we discovered, because Jessa chose to reveal herself to us, was a girl who had been hiding out for weeks at her grandparents' farm, managing to care for herself and her dog. Her grit impressed us, and we bonded almost immediately. It seemed natural for her to join our family. Karen and I have two children near Jessa's age, and Jessa fit into the family seamlessly. We're both teachers and, therefore, have a stable financial situation that will allow us to support three children."

The judge looked to Karen. "Do you have anything to add?"

Karen stood and placed one hand on Jessa's shoulder, squeezing it gently. "Only that we love Jessa and want what is best for her. We want her to be happy, and we appreciate that her parents were making a good provision for their daughter when they designated the Carlsons in their will."

"Very well. It is then the judgment of this court that the directives of the will shall be overridden due to the unanticipated claim of a blood relative and Miss Olsen's stated preference. I have a signed and dated statement from the designated guardians, who have amicably relinquished custody to the Acrees.

This court therefore rules that legal custody of Jessamine Olsen, until the age of eighteen, shall be assumed by Benjamin and Karen Acree. Appropriate paperwork will need to be filed with this court."

Mr. Carlson nodded.

The judge continued, "I will now turn to the property settlement. According to the terms of her parents' will, Jessamine Olsen is the sole beneficiary of all property belonging to her parents, Paul and Cora Olsen. Until she reaches majority, on September 8th, 1961, the property will be managed by the individual designated in the will, Mr. John Carlson, who has already posted bond and been assigned a tax number for the estate. It will be the responsibility of John Carlson, esquire, to file paperwork related to management of the properties and pay the property taxes. These reports will become a matter of public record."

The judge looked up from his papers and addressed the subdued group in the courthouse. "Funds can be made available from the estate to the beneficiary, Miss Jessamine Olsen, as needed for education or medical expenses. The real properties, namely, a residence and a music shop, were owned outright by Paul and Cora Olsen at the time of their deaths and may not be sold without express permission of the court. The properties must be maintained in a manner that will preserve and grow the value of the estate until Jessamine is eighteen. At that time, the inheritance will be turned over to her to use as she sees fit, although she is counseled by this court to continue to rely upon Mr. Carlson for advice over the management of her properties. The executor must file a final accounting in 1961 with the probate division of the Sixth Circuit Court."

Jessa sat on the hard bench with tears running down her cheeks. The will's testament to her parents' love, reaching across death to provide for her, had broken open floodgates. The shock of learning about the car crash and her subsequent struggles with hunger, cold, and loneliness in the forest came flooding back. The trouble she had caused Jacob and his family by running away, and the pain she had caused the Carlsons when she chose to stay with the Acrees was crushing. It just wasn't possible to do the right thing and not hurt someone.

Karen hugged her and Ben reached around Karen to squeeze her shoulder. Mr. Carlson was sitting alone in the row in front of her, his head bowed, so Jessa reached across the bench to touch his shoulder. When he turned, she saw that he was crying also. "I'm sorry," she whispered.

He patted her fingers, nodded, and pulled a handkerchief from his breast pocket.

· CHAPTER 26 ·

That night, Jessa wanted to write another letter to share everything with her best friend in Portland. She opened the drawer of her desk to get stationery, and there, staring up at her, was a photograph she'd been planning to paste in her scrapbook. In it, Jessa and her mother were standing by the family car in front of her grandparents' house. The faces were clear in the dappled sunlight, and her mother's arm was around her shoulder. She recalled the feel of the smooth metal of the car as she leaned against it, and how happy she had been as her father wiggled his ears at her when he took the picture. She closed her eyes as a moan escaped her.

April, lying on one of the twin beds, heard it and looked up from her book. "Poor Jessa. I'm so sorry about the disaster in the park."

Jessa put her head down on her folded arms and sobbed. April rolled over, sat up, and reached up to rest her hand on Jessa's shoulder.

"It isn't about the music deal, April. It's that sometimes I miss my family so much. Look at this. I was going to put it in my scrapbook, but I never got around to it."

April studied the photograph. "Your mother's hair looks so much like my mother's. They could have been sisters. I'm so sorry, Jessa."

"Last winter, when your family was exploring Grandad's

farm and your mother was describing your granddad's adventures with my granddad, I was desperate to hear more, to understand—but you were leaving—leaving me behind. I just couldn't stand to see you go, so I called to you. Remember when your mother ran and hugged me, April? To me, that felt like my own mother was hugging me. It felt so right! I know they would have been such close friends, if only the families hadn't gotten separated."

"I remember, Jessa."

Jessa sighed. "Life is mean—horrible, sometimes—but at least we have each other. Now we're getting to be real sisters, and I love it. What if your family hadn't figured out that your grandfather had family in Tennessee?"

"We're so glad it happened the way it did. All of us are—I heard Mama and Daddy talking about it."

"Still, I can't help missing my Mommie and Daddy so much, and at the court hearing, it just tore me up, how they loved me and wanted to provide for every possible catastrophe. Then there's the worry that they might be disappointed by my decision to stay with your family. It's all a big mix of emotions. I'm going to try to write back to Janie and tell her about everything here."

"Did you tell her about the humidity yet?" April fanned herself and moved to a cooler part of the bed to escape the dampness. "It's definitely one thing that's hard to get used to if you're from Portland."

"Humidity is bad," agreed Jessa, "but mostly the way they treat Negroes is bad. I thought Janie might come here someday, but now I can see all sorts of problems with that."

Jessa took out a sheet of stationery and began to write:

Dear Janie,

Thank you for writing and describing the trip your family made to the coast. It sounds like you are having a better summer than I am, although April and I got to spend a night in the tree together.

Now, I'm really discouraged. I wrote you from the train about my plan to go to the school board meeting. When I finally got to do that, it was a bust. They said they couldn't afford it, so I came up with a plan to collect money at the park performances that feature local musicians. We were all ready when the combined choir sang. It had choir members from all the churches, including the colored congregation, and the performance was so good. Everything was great until these high school guys ran in with sticks and...

"April, how do you spell sabotaged?" asked Jessa.

"I think it's s-a-b-o-t-a-g-e-d. Sabot is a wooden shoe, so throwing shoes at something sabotaged it," answered April.

"That looks right," said Jessa.

She continued writing:

...they sabotaged it totally. Messed it up for everyone.

I told you Tennessee is beautiful and the people here are wonderful. The part about the beauty is still true. In Portland, I missed the fireflies, the mockingbirds that sing in the night, the cardinals and blue jays. (I'll put a few of their feathers in the letter.) The honeysuckle and magnolias are blooming, so it smells heavenly, and, of course, the roses in people's yards are lovely. It's the people, some of them, that are messing everything up. Michael calls them bigots, and Karen says to not call them that, but I think he may be right. I am trying to understand why.

Anyway, they attacked or tried to attack the Negro families in the picnic area. The sheriff and others stopped them, but it totally ruined the ending, when I planned to pass the plates for donations. April said we would have made a lot of money, but instead, everyone left in a hurry. The sheriff took them to jail. April and I went to talk with them this morning, but they were already at a meeting to be assigned community service jobs.

Then we had to drive to Landsdowne for the custody hearings, and there was no way that was going to be good, because my parents' will said I was supposed to be adopted by their friends the

Carlsons, and Mr. Carlson actually cried because I chose to stay with the Acrees. I felt terrible.

It's late now, and I need to get ready for bed, but I'm sorry to tell you how bad it is. I used to think it would be fun for you to come here with me, but now I'm not sure.

Your loving friend,

Jessa

She reread the letter, folded it carefully, and chose a soft red feather, a barred blue jay feather, and a gray-and-white-tipped mockingbird feather to insert into the envelope. She got out Janie's most recent letter and copied the return address.

"April, I still didn't know what to say to Janie about why those guys messed up the performance. What do you think?"

"Well, when you have people like Mrs. Carlson saying it's better to keep the races apart, I guess it's part of the same way of thinking. I don't know what they're worried about, talking about it being unnatural. Remember that interracial couple in our Meeting? They have two of the most beautiful little girls I've ever seen, and I've babysat for a lot of children. So even if members of different races fall in love, it's not a disaster like Mrs. Carlson thinks."

"It looked as if Mrs. Carlson was coming around after the Wilsons' visit. You saw that pretty green dress she sewed for her maid? That's one good thing." Jessa smiled at the recollection, then grimaced when she recalled the way the entire performance had fallen apart when the attackers arrived.

"Do you think something bad will happen if Eddie and his grandfather perform at the park?" asked April.

"That, I don't know. It has me worried. Your mother keeps cautioning me to not step on people's toes and respect the way things are here. Do you think the same kind of attack will be planned again—or worse? I so want this thing to work, for my father's sake, but I'm getting scared about what might happen."

· CHAPTER 27 ·

Ted's article appeared in the Saturday edition of the paper with big headlines. The lead photograph showed Charlie, Matt, and Maney lined up with their captors, and the sheriff and deputy behind them. A picture of the choir accompanied the interior continuation of the long article. This represented a first for the *Radford Post*, as photographs of colored people had never before appeared; traditionally, white people, such as the graduating class or girl's engagement announcements, were accompanied by photographs, but only the names of the Negro graduates or brides-to-be were listed.

The young men involved in the attack were identified by name. Ted let the story unfold through the outraged statements he and Joel collected from white people as they packed up; there had been no chance to interview the colored people, as they had disappeared quickly. It was clear from the reactions that the white people had been captivated by the music and felt cheated when it was disrupted.

Hand-delivered letters to the editor began to pour into the printer's office and were published in the Sunday edition. Some praised the singing and pleaded for Music in the Park to continue. Choir members wrote to express their disappointment at the disruption. A few expressed outrage at the sheriff for jailing young white men, but the predominant sentiment was that the men should compensate the town for their actions.

· · · · ·

At church that Sunday, lessons were drawn from the attack in the park. Psalms celebrating God's love of music were followed by admonitions against violence and injunctions to love one another. Reverend James was thankful the choir members and picnickers were safe and that his worst fears hadn't been realized. There was a deep undercurrent of resentment over the attack, so his sermon addressed this. First, he read *Luke 6:27-29*: *But I say unto you which hear, Love your enemies, do good to them which hate you. Bless them that curse you, and pray for them which despitefully use you. And unto him that smiteth thee on the one cheek offer also the other; and him that taketh away thy cloak forbid not to take thy coat also.*

Jacob bowed his head as the anger he had spent a lifetime trying to quell boiled up inside him. *White people can't be trusted! Do your best and play by their rules and they still put you down. Let those white people get along without our music!* Sitting beside him, Margaret dug her fingernails into her palms as she shook her head at the memory of the young men with their sticks heading for her family.

As the long sermon progressed, Reverend James turned his thunderous voice to *Romans 12:17-21*: *Recompense to no man evil for evil. Provide things honest in the sight of all men. If it be possible, as much as lieth in you, live peaceably with all men. Dearly beloved, avenge not yourselves, but rather give place unto wrath: for it is written, Vengeance is mine; I will repay, saith the Lord. Therefore if thine enemy hunger, feed him; if he thirst, give him drink: for in so doing thou shalt heap coals of fire on his head. Be not overcome of evil, but overcome evil with good.*

As Brother James developed the theme, Margaret bowed her head and tears dropped onto her lap. Her friends had begged her to sing with the choir this morning, but Margaret couldn't sing. Her knees had been shaking as she climbed down off the bleachers with the other choir members. It had been too mean. Just when she and the others had been feeling so good, suckered into trusting the whites, it had backfired. As the tears continued to flow, Jacob offered her his big white handkerchief and put his arm around her. Through her tears, Margaret could see that Merrybelle was wearing the green dress Fran had made her, and she felt like screaming *No! We don't want their charity, their do-good gifts!*

Margaret thought about Fran, standing to take a picture of the group as she had promised Merrybelle, but that image was replaced by the men running with sticks held above their heads, threatening her people. She couldn't shake that.

Jacob led Margaret down the aisle and out of the church. Eddie took charge of Sarah, who was concerned about her mother. Margaret felt Jacob's arm around her and wondered what he was thinking... He, who had so much more reason to be angry than she did. Now, she wanted to have the conversation he had tried to initiate last night. Knowing his personal history, she wondered how he could be so forgiving. What was he feeling now?

· CHAPTER 28 ·

Fran was full of plans to build bridges with the colored community. She seized on Merrybelle's comment about Margaret's effort to help the high school graduates apply for college and training programs. She baked cookies as an excuse to drop in at Jacob and Margaret's home. When they were still warm, she set out.

·　·　·　·　·

Margaret looked up from reading the newspaper as a late-model Lincoln pulled in front of the house. "Now who can that be? Dad, you know of anybody coming today?"

"Nothing I've heard about, Margie."

As Margaret watched, Fran Carlson got out of the car and made her way up the walkway to the front door. She was carrying a flat package.

That white woman—the last *thing I need right now*, Margaret thought. Stifling a curse, she stuffed some of Sarah's toys under the sofa cushion and headed for the door, ready to put on a brave, polite act.

"Why how nice, Fran!" said Margaret once she opened the door. "Please come in. I'd like you to meet my father."

"Thank you, Margaret! I love your red geraniums—so vibrant!" said Fran.

"Dad, this is Mrs. Carlson. You remember, Eddie played his fiddle for the Carlsons and the Acrees. Fran, my father, Sam Rayburn."

"I'm so glad to meet you!" said Sam. "Appreciated that slice of cake!"

"You're so welcome. We wished you'd come along. Eddie's a charming child and a natural performer, and everyone concludes you must be quite a teacher. We're hoping the town can rise above the disgraceful treatment of the women's chorus, and I'm looking forward to hearing the two of you play in the park."

"I wouldn't have pursued that, but it means a lot to Eddie. As for the teaching, I set an example and showed him how to hold the fiddle and the bow and he just took off. He already knew how to read music, so *he* was pushing *me*. We have great fun playing together."

"Wonderful when talent meets opportunity, isn't it?" said Fran, smiling.

"It does take talent. The fiddle's a challenging instrument. You can have a tin ear and still play the piano, because if the piano's in tune, the correct notes are right in front of you. To play the fiddle, your ear has to tell you how to shape each note, because there're no frets. Eddie has persistence and a good ear."

"I'm sure you're minimizing the role you played. He told us you were his inspiration for how to play the 'Tennessee Waltz,' and I adored his rendition. It's almost magic how he makes a lovely sound come out of that little box!"

"Sure is," agreed Margaret.

"Here, some cookies I baked this morning."

"My goodness, Fran, I appreciate that!" said Margaret. "Jake loves cookies—he comes in here so hungry! And, of course, the kids and Dad like cookies, too. Please have a seat, and sorry there're toys scattered all around."

"I'm glad if you can use the cookies. I seem to have too

much time on my hands, and it's nice to have someone to give them to."

"I know you do a lot. I loved that dress you sewed for Merrybelle—she's proud as punch of it!"

"I enjoyed doing it, and she looked lovely in that green. I was so sorry over the way the choir performance was disrupted!"

"Makes me furious whenever I think of it! Merrybelle and all of us put so much of our hearts into the rehearsals, and we were getting to be a good group, don't you think? But it's all ruined—nobody has any stomach for getting together, now. It's such a shame!"

"Margaret, Merrybelle tells me that you found a truck-driving program for her son to apply to. If there's any more researching about career options that's needed, I wanted to offer my help. It's so important to orient young people to the opportunities for training after high school."

Margaret paused, considering. The last thing she wanted was any more attention from the whites of this town. Those white boys had shattered her delusions about the benevolence of the white community. However, Fran's offer might solve a problem she could not work around. She bit her lip, but said, "What I really need, Fran, is to get up to Landsdowne. The library there has information on education programs. I've been writing letters, but that's a slow way to find out anything. Fanny's son wants to be a teacher, and he'll need financial assistance to go to a teacher training college. I think there are programs that allow him to study one year and get a temporary certificate so he can begin teaching and then finish up his degree at night and in summer school."

"So you need a lift to Landsdowne? That's easy. I could go in the library with you and learn how this information is researched. This is the time for getting applications in, isn't it?"

"Yes, in the next few weeks a lot of things have to come

together. The Landsdowne school hasn't been able to provide copies of transcripts, and I've been tearing my hair out over that."

"I have tomorrow free. When should I pick you up?"

Margaret looked at her father. "Dad, can you take care of Sarah and Eddie?"

"Sure! The kids are the best company in the world!" said Sam.

"Can we go early afternoon?" asked Margaret. "Say, leave whenever it's convenient after you finish your lunch?"

"I'll be here at one o'clock. I'm looking forward to it!" said Fran, who then glanced from the books on the bookcase to the wooden rocking horse with a rag doll sitting astride it. "What a charming horse and rider!"

"Jacob made the horse, originally for Eddie, and his aunt sewed the doll for Sarah," explained Margaret.

Fran longed for an excuse to stay. She couldn't think of any, so she said, "Guess I better get on home. Jack will be back from the office pretty soon."

As she drove off, Margaret collapsed on the sofa. "Whew, Dad. What do you make of that? She's offering something I really need. I think her heart is in the right place, but part of me wants to tell her to just get out of my house and never come back! I'll feel funny riding up to Landsdowne with her in that big car."

"Margie, you be proud of yourself. You have nothing to be ashamed of. You're talented, and I bet you're just as educated as she is. I'm looking forward to getting your mother's piano down here so that I can hear you play again. This Mrs. Carlson seems sincere. Take her offer of help and just play it by ear—I know you'll do the right thing."

"Oh, Dad. It's so good to have you with us!" Margaret hugged her father.

That night, Rachel dropped by to chat. As she sat with

Margaret at the kitchen table, Margaret began, "Hon, get this: that Mrs. Carlson drove over here with cookies—wait, I'll get you one—they're good. And she's all full of wanting to be helpful… Uh huh, and she drives this big black car… At first, I thought the driver must be lost, to come into our neighborhood…" Sarah pulled at her skirt. "Just a minute, Rachel. What do you need, honey?"

"Sarah doll. Baby doll," said Sarah.

"Oh, I know where it is." Margaret went into the living room and pulled Sarah's doll out from under the sofa cushion. "See? She was hiding from you!"

Margaret returned to the kitchen. "Rachel, the fact is, I really can use her help. If I can get to the Landsdowne library, I can dig up information for Fanny's son Dawson and the girls who want to be secretaries and nurses. But what will people think? She's picking me up tomorrow in that snazzy car. Here Jake was, worried about driving our truck into their ritzy neighborhood, with all their gossipy neighbors, but when that big black car slides in front of our house, people are going to think we're running a bootleg operation!"

"Well, I say there're worse problems. She tell you the ladies are all turning against her?"

"How's that, Rachel?"

"I have to listen to a lot of rubbish, and it's been getting worse lately. Today I couldn't help but hear the almighty Mrs. Gladys Blakeley on the phone. She made call after call, laying out her revenge. She's planning to take over the retirement-home program from Fran. They're going to vote tomorrow."

"Well that's a shame! Fran's offered to take me to Landsdowne tomorrow. I wonder if she knew about that meeting?"

"It's just been called, and she wasn't going to be told until it was over. I told Merrybelle, and she was sorry to hear it. She's been benefiting from this change of heart Fran has undergone, but she says Mrs. Carlson's real dedicated about her volunteer work. According to Merrybelle, Mrs. Carlson's volunteering is one of the things that keeps her sane, when she's bored stiff with her perfect life."

"Those women are getting back at her for associating with colored people?"

"You got it!"

"Well, I guess I feel for Fran. I resented the way she turned Merry's head with that green dress, but she didn't mean any harm by it. In fact, she doesn't seem affected at all—a genuine good heart. She needs someone to be a friend. I'll just do as Dad suggested and play it by ear!"

· CHAPTER 29 ·

Margaret cleared the lunch dishes away and pulled out her satchel with notes on the training programs she needed to locate in Landsdowne. In the bedroom mirror she checked her hair to be sure it hadn't been mussed when she slipped on her purple cotton dress with white lace around the collar. She took a deep breath. *Hope this will turn out well*, she half-prayed as she clipped on her earrings. When she saw the car turn onto their street, she stepped out of the house and waved good-bye to Sarah and her dad. Eddie was in his bedroom, playing his part of a duet, and the notes floated out the window to greet Fran when she pulled up to the gate.

"Eddie took to that instrument like a fish to water, Margaret!" Fran said as she slid over to open the passenger door.

"That's true, Fran." Margaret settled into the perfectly maintained car, wondering if she was shedding dust on the black carpet on the floor. "He's so thrilled about playing, he's pestered his grandfather to learn new pieces," said Margaret. "They both have to get them down by heart before Thursday. Dad's been grumbling because he hasn't played from sheet music for years, and the memorizing is harder on him than it is on Eddie!"

Fran steered them onto the road and made a wide right turn to head toward the highway.

"Is it necessary to memorize everything?" she asked.

"Well, it's best. They've been propping up the music in their fiddle cases. They need music stands, but Jacob hasn't had a chance to build them. Knowing the music by heart is best because it frees them to focus on playing, and there're no pages to turn or the risk of wind blowing the music away."

"Do you play an instrument, Margaret?"

"Both my sister and I studied piano. We had Mother's piano to practice on. She was a first-rate pianist—she played in church, but also at home for us. She and Dad loved popular dance music, and at night she played Chopin and Mozart for us to go to sleep by."

"How lovely! I understand your dad moved down after your mother died."

"Yes. He took the bus with his violin and a couple of suitcases, leaving the household goods stored away. My mother's quilts are something I would love to have, but I need to see how my sister feels about them—I'm sure we can divide things up. Lindsey, that's my sister, she said I should get the piano because Eddie plays. We haven't had time to go to Kentucky with Jake's truck and haul it down here."

"Did you get to be with your mother before she died?"

"No, ma'am. I haven't been home to Kentucky but once since I married Jacob."

"That's hard. My mother lives with her younger sister, so she's been able to continue living at home with assistance as she's become feeble. It's almost an hour from here, and I get over there as often as I can. How did you and Jacob meet?"

"I was studying at Fisk in Nashville, singing with the Fisk Jubilee Singers, and Jacob was the driver of the bus that took us to Landsdowne for a performance at City Hall. He and I got to talking, and I don't know—I just fell head-over-heels in love with him."

"That's so sweet, Margaret. He's handsome, that's for sure."

"It was hard for us, though, because he was shy about not having much education, and I wrote him letters, but he could scarcely write back. He was making good money from temporary driver work in addition to his job with Ray, and he hitch-hiked to Nashville to see me as often as he could. He was awfully determined—I had other beaus, but Jacob just had to have me. He would work all week, and then he sometimes had to walk a good part of the way to visit me, but he always arrived with his fingernails clean and wearing a clean shirt, and he'd pick a honeysuckle bouquet or whatever wild flowers were blooming... I never knew when he was coming, but my dorm-mates would greet me giggling, when the house mother had put his bouquet up in our room!"

"Oh, that's a love story!" said Fran. "Sounds like he was the one who fell head-over-heels in love, Margaret."

"I guess you might say that, ma'am. It didn't go too well with my mother, though. That was the fly in the ointment. She wasn't happy that I was in love with a man who wasn't a college man—said after sending me away to college she thought the least I could do was make a good match!"

"From all I can tell, you made an excellent match, Margaret."

"Oh, yes, ma'am. Jacob's great. My mother never did understand, but Dad supported my decision. When we got serious, Jacob's aunt Helen and uncle Adam drove Jacob to Nashville so that they could meet me. They just won me over! Don't you think the quality of a prospective husband's family is important? Eventually, you're going to depend on family."

"Yes, that's an important consideration. It can't patch up a bad match, but it sure does affect the quality of a marriage. Tell me more about the Jubilee Singers. I think maybe Jack and I heard you—that group performed in Nashville the last year I was there. Jack was in law school at Vanderbilt University, and I was at Peabody College, which is really close, and he took me as his date. My friends called him the beanpole! So the two of us may have been in Nashville when you were there."

"Could have been, ma'am. I graduated in nineteen-forty-three. The Jubilee Singers traveled, and I had a scholarship to sing, which is why I went to Fisk. How I loved being part of that group! You know that expression *the whole is greater than the sum of its parts*? Well, that's how I feel about singing in a choir—you're part of something greater than yourself! It made me so happy when the combined choir was organized here in Radford—I do love singing!"

"Now I understand where Eddie gets his musical talent!"

"Yes, he's talented. My mother loved her piano, and you'll see how my father plays the fiddle. My parents used to perform together."

"Wish I could have heard them!"

"Fran, that was the meanest thing, the way those men disrupted our performance. I could chew nails over that! They ruined everything! The choir members still won't consider getting together again. They're cowed." Margaret put her hands up to her face, then turned toward Fran. "I have to admit I don't trust the white people in this town. Do you think it's dangerous for Eddie and my father to play in the park?"

Fran hesitated. "Frankly, Margaret, I'm worried. Jessa thinks Eddie's example will inspire the town to appreciate what music can give people. It seems a shame to let a handful of young men spoil music for the community. I hope they're too busy to plan another attack. They've been put into internship programs and set to repairing Overbrook. I know because Jack was assigned one of the hoodlums who claimed he wanted to be a lawyer. Still, it is a risk, and Radford has some hard liners when it comes to race."

"You're telling me? Things have been on edge ever since that accident and Jacob got locked up… Oh, I pray it'll be okay.

I took Eddie's part against Brother James and Jacob because Eddie begged to play. The responsibility is all on my head, and I just couldn't stand it if something happens!"

"The sheriff and community members will try to keep everyone safe. Did you know that Jessa had been planning to pass a collection plate to give money to the school board after the choir sang? Of course, that didn't come off, but with her irrepressible optimism, she's focusing on appealing to the audience after Eddie's performance."

"Pass a collection plate? Why?"

"Music at Overbrook. It was uncompleted work her father believed in. Jack and I were close to Cora and Paul, and we knew he worked for years to get music education into the Radford school curriculum and was disappointed that when they finally hired a new teacher it was only for the white schools. Jessa probably heard plenty from Paul about how unhappy he was over that decision, and she's come back to Radford resolved to fulfill her father's dream, but she's butting up against the same problems her father had with the school board. They told her there was no money to add a teacher, so Jessa's response is to appeal to the community to get the necessary funds. I'm afraid she has no idea what amount is involved. Margaret, you're a musician. What do you think about adding music instruction at Overbrook?"

"Hmmmm," said Margaret. "That girl's downright pushy! Overbrook has a lot of problems, but the teachers do try to give the children a good education. There's no doubt in my mind that music instruction would be a real plus. Of course, I'm biased because I'm a great believer in music. Art instruction would be an asset for Radford's students, too. I know from helping our five high school graduates write their application essays that it would have been good if they could have added music involvement to their personal statements. Part-time jobs are good, but involvement in music or art would add another dimension."

"Well, here we are in Landsdowne. The library is one of the places I hang out while Jack is busy with a case. I'll head for the courthouse parking lot—it's close and usually has plenty of vacant spaces," said Fran.

As she pulled into a shady parking spot, Fran caught herself remembering the pleasant time she and Jack usually spent in a coffee shop after he got free from a case, and she pursed her lips when she realized that no such experience was possible with Margaret, because they could not sit down together in public.

"Shall I roll up the window or leave it down?" asked Margaret.

"It should be fine to leave it down because this black car collects heat like you wouldn't believe," said Fran, shutting her door and joining Margaret on the sidewalk.

The sight of two attractive women walking together, one white and one colored, turned some heads. Fran's petite stature and narrow hips were a contrast to Margaret's height and full figure. Luckily, the library was a safe haven, with no signs barring Negroes. They mounted the stairs and entered the cool interior.

"Oh, I'm so glad to be here, Fran! Thank you so much!" Margaret headed to the bank of file cabinets on the far side of the main room and Fran followed.

"Here's my list of terms. Could you please search for nursing programs?" Margaret whispered. "And take notes on work-study programs, because Rhondalee needs part-time work."

"Will do," Fran whispered, getting out her pad and pencil. "Primarily Tennessee or possibly Kentucky, right? How about part-time work as a nurse's aide? The retirement community in Radford really depends on the candy stripers to work with the patients, and they get lots of practical experience."

"Yeah," Margaret replied dryly. "Rhondalee applied for those positions but was turned down."

"I'm sorry, Margaret. I serve on the board, and maybe I can do something about that."

Margaret recalled Rachel's comment about the vote to re-move Fran from the board and shook her head. "Probably not. She's beyond that now. Anyway, any part-time jobs, but if it's related to their studies, all the better. Check on jobs in the dining hall or doing laundry for the dorms. I guess you didn't have to work to get through college, but we don't all have family fortunes to rely on."

Fran bit her lip and accepted the criticism. She fingered through the cards, searching for schools that Negro students could attend.

Margaret turned back to the file she was looking through and exclaimed, "Oh, this is just what I was hoping for! Fran, you're a godsend!"

When Margaret's goals at the library were accomplished, they put their notes in Margaret's satchel, smiling conspiratori-ally at each other. They made their way out of the library and down the broad steps guarded by benign stone lions. As they walked into the courthouse parking lot, a woman was getting into a nearby car. First she noticed Margaret and looked down her nose at her. Then she recognized Fran. "Fran Carlson, what are you doing up here without Jack?"

Fran got out of the car to respond. "Hi, Cheryl. We were doing research at the library."

"You and *your maid*?"

Fran took a deep breath. "No, Cheryl. I'd like you to meet my *friend*, Margaret Wilson." Fran peered in where Margaret was already seated in the car. "Margaret, I'd like you to meet Cheryl. She's a stenographer for the court."

Margaret opened the door and stood by the car, enduring the inspection. "Pleased to meet you."

Cheryl drew herself back. "Hello, Margaret." Turning to Fran, she said, "Next time you're in town, we need to get to-gether, Fran."

Fran and Margaret got back in the car, and Fran backed out of the parking spot and into traffic. After several miles, she broke the silence. "Margaret, I'm sorry Cheryl assumed that you are my maid. The fact is, I'm able-bodied and don't need a maid. I've become uncomfortable about employing Merrybelle, and I don't know what to do about it. I hope you weren't insulted."

"Fran, of course I was insulted," said Margaret. "But working as a maid is honest work. It's the way maids are treated that makes the work demeaning. That woman's assumption was a perfectly reasonable reflection of society. It assumes that a Negro woman can't possibly be involved in anything but menial labor. Of course it hurts! My mother told me and Lindsey she didn't want us to grow up to be anyone's maid because there's no recognition that maids have families of their own and might like to be home for holidays or birthdays or when their children are sick. It's the employers who act like they own their maids that make the work demeaning."

"I imagine it's more than that, Margaret. It's an insidious mindset. The white community thinks giving away old clothes or leftover food is being generous. I remember my mother giving away jars of bacon grease. What she said to me was *They cook with a lot of grease.*"

Margaret nodded. "When I was in school, my friends would be dressed in hand-me-downs from the families their mothers worked for, and they were proud when they were young, but after they got things figured out, they were ashamed. It takes a while to understand your place in society, but the most spirit-crushing part is how we're supposed to bow and scrape and be ever-so-grateful for the charity."

Fran drove in silence, recalling her many acts of charity and how good she'd felt. She gripped the steering wheel aggressively to center herself and thought again of her childhood friend Justine and wondered how, if Justine had lived, things might have been different. She knew she could never have employed Justine to clean her house the way she employed Merrybelle. Furthermore, there was the fact that Fran knew that she didn't need a maid. When she and Merrybelle had worked together, digging and dividing the spring bulbs, she'd enjoyed sharing their mutual love of growing things, and had given many of the bulbs to Merrybelle. At the time, she had felt very close to Merrybelle, and it had seemed like genuine sharing, but now, she wasn't so sure. The pattern of handing out largess and feeling good about it was very ingrained.

Fran swallowed hard before she turned to Margaret. "I'm so sorry, Margaret. Truly sorry. I've been on the side of handing out charity, with no sensitivity to the position it puts the recipient in. It's the pattern I grew up with."

"And what about the pattern I grew up with? I'm supposed to accept my *place in society*, and if I forget it for one minute, people like your friend Cheryl come along and slap me down. Any attempt at self-respect is interpreted as *putting on airs*, a taunting threat to the white community. And, Fran, the sanctimonious whites are blind to the fact that their Christianity says one thing while they do the opposite."

Fran was silent. Tears ran down her face. "Margaret, tell me what I can do to get above this, because I've been a part of this system for so many years now."

Margaret spoke gently. "Fran, honey, there's no way in hell you can know what it feels like to be colored. You grew up with a sense of entitlement—it was just up to you to choose what you most wanted in life. You don't know what it's like when people assume that you are dirty, ignorant, and untrustworthy—when they draw back from you as if you're contagious... So why *should* we be trustworthy and not yield to the desire to steal something just to get even? Why should we pursue an education that will never open doors for us? All our lives, it's ground into us that we are inferior. It can become a self-fulfilling prophecy for our kids if there's nobody affirming good choices and showing the way to success. But I can tell you, there's a lot of anger out there—there's a lot of anger in me, too."

Fran slowed the car and pulled off the road. She switched the engine off and sat with her hands over her face. After a long pause, she said, "Margaret, did you read Faulkner in college?"

"Yes, ma'am."

"He thought that the very soil of the South was poisoned, Margaret. That the crime of enslavement would curse the white race out to the end of the world."

"Well, I do hope things can be patched up before the end of the world, Fran. But I want it soon. We haven't got lives to waste, waiting. It not only impacts me and Jacob and our generation, but I want it fixed up so that our children can dream big and be blessed with the financial security they deserve to have along the way. What we need is for the white race to just leave us alone instead of putting obstacles in our path." Fran's sobs continued. Margaret leaned over and squeezed her arm gently. "Honey, don't you take it personal. I know from Rachel and Merrybelle that you are kindhearted. This is a trap we were both born into. Your trap looks pretty from the outside, and you've had all the privileges, but it's still a prison that is hard, maybe impossible, to escape. Jacob's trap was set when his father was lynched. Did you know about that? He grew up with that tragedy weighing on him. His father was an innocent man whose only crime was that he was working hard to create a good life for his family. He was too smart and too good a farmer, and his white neighbor didn't like being shown up by a colored man. That neighbor wanted the Wilson property, and he managed things so that he got it. We have to live in a town with that kind of injustice."

A shudder passed down Fran's body. Finally, she found her

voice. "That's horrible, Margaret. I know that Jack went into the law because he wanted to help people who needed representation. For my part, I'm resolved to change what I can, even if it doesn't amount to a lot. I'm going to speak out to the clubs and resign from the ones that don't want to hear what I have to say. And that business about the candy stripers having to be white girls—I'm really going to work on that!"

Margaret nodded encouragingly, and Fran pulled back onto the road—with new determination building within her.

· CHAPTER 30 ·

Rachel added drops of green food coloring to the cream cheese and mashed it in until the color was uniform. She spread it on slices of bread, added several sprigs of watercress, put on a top piece of bread, trimmed the crusts, and cut each sandwich from corner to corner to make four wedges. As Rachel stacked the little sandwiches into an attractive pyramid, Mrs. Gladys bustled around with the linens for the card tables, muttering about the trouble she had had over finding a substitute to fill in the third table.

"Are the flowers going to be ready in time?" she asked Rachel.

"Yes, ma'am. I'll get to them next."

"Be sure you wipe the bottoms of the vases. I don't want any water getting on the tablecloths."

"Yes, ma'am. I'll be careful of that."

"And it's time to start the coffee. Some women want a cup of coffee, even in this heat!"

"Yes ma'am."

The doorbell rang. "It's only one-forty! Who could be arriving so early? Well, go to the door, Rachel. What are you waiting for?"

The woman at the door was new to Rachel, who recognized all the card-party regulars. The fill-in player, Dexter's mother, was a dumpy woman whose blue pillbox hat contrasted with the yellow print dress she had decided was suitable attire for a canasta party. She explained to Rachel that she had left home early because she had not been sure how to find the house. Rachel led her into the living room, where three card tables were set up.

Rachel returned to the flower-arranging job and carried a miniature bouquet and a polished ash tray to each of the card tables, smiling at the guest seated on the sofa.

"You were one of the choir members who sang in the park, weren't you?" asked the guest. "My friends and I enjoyed that performance so much."

"Thank you, ma'am," said Rachel.

"Certainly was a shame the way it was disrupted. Nobody was more surprised than me, to see my own son running around with those juvenile delinquents! I've been telling Dexter for years those boys would get him in trouble! Dexter's lucky he got away this last Thursday, or he'd have been with the boys who landed in jail."

Rachel knew Mrs. Gladys was listening and didn't want her conversing with the guests. Still, she was interested in the topic and didn't want to be impolite. "That attack sure was a shame, bad for everyone involved."

"I think I talked some sense into Dexter. Told him he was disrespecting his father—just when he graduated from high school, too."

Mrs. Gladys Blakeley made her entrance, shooing Rachel back to the kitchen to take care of the coffee service. "So glad you had the afternoon free to join us for some cards, Susan."

"Oh, I just love canasta. I play a pretty cut-throat game if that's all right with you?"

"We do play a pretty relaxed game I suppose you might say. It's just an excuse to get together and talk."

"I can do that, too," Susan replied. "Was just telling your maid how my son was involved in that attack on the choir performance in the park."

"Is that so?"

"Yes, I told Dexter his father would roll over in his grave if his son was thrown into jail!"

"Well, Mrs. Strickland, I'm sure you *are* glad—it disgraces the family name…" Mrs. Blakeley's voice trailed off as the doorbell rang, and Rachel answered it to let in two more women. Soon, the spacious living room was milling with twelve women chattering over the lovely flowers and how pretty the yard was, despite the heat.

"Everyone, Janice couldn't make it today, and Susan Strickland was kind enough to fill in for her," announced Gladys. "Susan says she plays a mean game of canasta, so you are warned to watch your cards!"

Coffee was offered, with the reminder that they would have a chance to have some later with their sandwiches. Soon the seating was determined, and the card tables were all full; someone at each table began shuffling the decks of cards, a task that prettily showed off manicured fingernails and expensive rings.

The stand-ins Gladys usually counted on had all had other plans for the afternoon, and someone had recommended Dexter's mother, a widow who had moved to Radford a few years earlier and worked at the bank to support herself and Dexter. She had only a passing acquaintance with the other women, so as they began gossiping, she had little to add. Instead, she paid close attention to the game and noticed that they tossed away discards that they could have played on their own melds and made other errors that she could have pointed out to them.

Conversations floated across the three tables, as an interesting tidbit recounted by one woman was picked up by a woman at another table.

"That Jessamine Olsen tragedy has hurt this community! Nothing good can come of having those Northern relatives of the Olsens in Radford! I'll breathe a sigh of relief when we see the last of them!"

"Oh, don't you know, the Carlsons have had their brains washed by that family!" said one woman.

"Gladys, I've felt sorry for you, having to live so close to all that!" another woman said.

"I've told Fran what I think, on several occasions now," said Gladys, "and the last time I called, she hung up on me!"

"Rude in the *extreme*!" another woman said with a sniff. "I thought Fran was brought up in polite society! You were only trying to help her see the error of her ways."

"I've concluded she's beyond help, honestly," said Gladys. "I refuse to have this neighborhood taken over by trashy people!"

"Who are the trashy people?" Susan asked, as she laid down two sevens and picked up the thick discard pile, pulled out a seven to place with her other sevens and proceeded to lay down as many of the other cards as she could.

She's winning at this table, Gladys noted. "The trashy people are the Negroes that Jessa Olsen, Fran Carlson, and the Acrees have taken up with!"

"Is that the family with the talented little boy?" Susan asked. "I heard his grandfather taught him how to play the fiddle and that they're going to perform in the park."

"They're the ones, all right. I can't tell you how many times that ugly old truck has parked in front of the Carlsons' house!"

"Not only do they come into our part of town," Ellen added, "but yesterday I saw Fran driving that Negro woman, the boy's mother, out of town!"

"What business can she have had, doing that?" asked Gladys.

"I was wondering the exact same thing," Ellen replied.

"I bet your maid could tell you if you asked her," said Dexter's mother.

"Gladys, please call her in right now—I'm mystified and want an answer!" said Ellen.

Gladys didn't want to, but couldn't hit upon an excuse, so she called, "Rachel, come here, please."

Rachel, already aware that she would be getting a talking-to about how improper it was for her to be mingling with guests, wiped her hands, squared her shoulders, and stepped into the living room. "Yes, ma'am?"

"Rachel, Ellen Riggins saw Fran Carlson driving out of town with that Negro woman from the family that keeps hanging out next door. You wouldn't know what that was about, would you?"

Rachel could see no harm in giving the information, so she said, "Ma'am, I believe they went to the library in Landsdowne to get information about careers for our recent high school graduates."

"Careers? Like what?"

"Teaching and nursing and the like. Margaret already helped Merrybelle's son apply for a truck-driving program, and he starts in September."

"Sounds like something we need for the white high school graduates. Dexter didn't get any counseling at all," Dexter's mother commented before she announced, "I believe I can go out," and laid her last card on the discard pile.

The other women began counting up the points in their hands and subtracting them from the points they had on the board. "We'll have to wait for the other tables to finish their games, so we can swap places," said Gladys, irritated that the substitute player had unsettled the rhythm of the game by showing off and winning so soon. She looked up from counting the points in her own hand to see Rachel still standing at the door. "Rachel, that's all. You can go back to the kitchen, now."

"I think the family with the talented little boy would be

delightful guests," said Dexter's mother. "The little boy's mother was one of the singers in the choir performance. She's a very attractive woman."

There was silence. Finally, Gladys felt pushed by the other guests to defend her home and the neighborhood, so she said, "Susan, we care for our property values in this part of town. We have to! We can't afford to have riff-raff acting like they belong here when they should keep to their own part of town."

"That's the truth," said another woman.

The women at the other two tables had caught a whiff of the conversation and had been listening for some time.

"I just think we're lucky to have people like that in our midst," said Susan.

"And I suppose you think the Negro children should be moving into our schools, too!"

"Well, I can tell you this: I won't rest until I knock some sense into Dexter's head about mistreating the coloreds of this town! I told him it was a disgrace that he was involved with those other boys when the combined choir sang. It was downright un-Christian, that's what it was!"

The other women looked at each other. No one could come up with a retort.

Finally, a woman with school-aged children, Jill, felt compelled to respond. "This town has treated the colored people well—certainly as well as they deserve. That doesn't mean we want to let them sit next to our children in the classroom or eat in the cafeteria!"

The women let out a chorus of agreement:

"Certainly *not*!"

"It's a disgrace. I don't want to even think of it!"

"Dirty, filthy, smelly—they carry all sorts of disease!"

Susan had had enough. "That's an attitude I call uncharitable!"

"Susan Strickland, you may take a relaxed attitude toward

the school crisis, as your son has graduated, but those of us with young children in school have to stand up for our way of life," said Jill. "It's important for people to know their place in society—it makes the wheels go 'round."

"And what are you going to do about it?" replied Susan. "Did you listen to Walter Cronkite last night?"

"We don't need to be told what's best for our own children! Furthermore, I don't believe the Negroes want to be pushed into our schools. They're happy with the way things are. Everyone is better off if we keep the races apart!"

"Have you asked them?" Susan inquired.

"It's always been this way. Putting colored children into the white schools will degrade the quality—it wouldn't be good for anybody! I've been very pleased so far with the education my two kids have gotten."

"What about the quality of education at Overbrook? Just imagine if you were colored and had to send your children there. Would you be happy with that?"

Stunned silence.

Finally, the woman Susan had addressed stammered, "I take—I take offense at being asked to imagine that I was colored! I came here to play cards in what I thought would be polite society" —she looked at Gladys— "*not* to be insulted!"

"I meant no insult," said Susan. "Sometimes it helps to walk in someone's moccasins if we want to know what their life is like."

"I have no plan to imagine myself colored or to walk in anyone's moccasins!" The woman pushed back her chair. "Gladys, I believe I feel a headache coming on. I need to get home and lie down."

Other guests also rose. If one of the card players pulled out, it was their chance to escape the unpleasant situation. Gladys looked from Susan, seated, to the rest of her guests. "Jill, maybe you could just lie down in my guest room while we take a break for coffee and tea, and you'll feel better?"

"Certainly not," she replied. "I'm going home!" She gathered her purse and gloves and headed for the front door. Others followed her, eager to meet outside or on the phone to discuss developments.

As the living room cleared out, Susan said, "Gladys, I'm known for being outspoken, and it seems that I have stepped on a lot of toes. I apologize. I just wish that talented Negro family wanted to come visit me!"

"Susan Strickland, you insulted my friends with your 'holier than thou' attitude, spouting off on a topic you apparently don't have the background to understand!"

"I understand that this is a closed society. People like to pretend they are living in the Old South, glorifying a past they should be ashamed of! This keeping to *one's place in society* business has got a stranglehold on people's hearts, and Dexter's been picking this up from his friends. I may not be welcome in this enclave of 'polite society,' but at least I'm not an ostrich, sticking my head in a hole in the ground! Gladys, that's what you and your friends are doing!"

· CHAPTER 31 ·

The community service project got underway Monday morning. The young men straggled up, one by one, and hung around the front of the poor, run-down school, kicking the weeds in the overgrown patch of green in front.

"Best thing for this place would be a bulldozer," said Matt.

"I just want to do what we have to do and get out of here," said Charlie.

Soon, the high school's Negro custodian, Mr. Borsden, pulled up in a ramshackle truck. He got out and called them over to unload the truck.

Charlie looked at Matt. "We ain't putting up with this!"

But Maney set out for the truck, and Matt and Charlie followed.

"How you boys doing?" asked Mr. Borsden.

At first, there was no answer. Then Charlie retorted, "How would it be if you'd just been released from hell and were assigned to the salt mines?"

Borsden considered that for a minute. "Well, now, I guess it'd be a step up in life, don't you think?"

"He's right about that," said Maney.

Sullenly, they unloaded ladders, claw hammers, buckets of nails, rolls of tar paper, and lumber.

The custodian was acquainted with the boys from his years with the school system and treated them kindly. He tolerated it when they slacked off at every opportunity and made intentional mistakes that undermined the project. Pretty soon, they figured out that it only increased their work.

The three young men learned to depend on each other as they clambered around, removing and replacing the rotten timbers. Working day after day in the July sun, they reroofed the entire schoolhouse. The lifting and nail banging developed their muscles, a fact they were secretly proud of, and they began to take pleasure in a job well done. When they finished the metal roofing, they moved on to repair the steps and painted the halls and classrooms with bright colors. They grew proud of the improvement in the school's appearance.

At one o'clock each afternoon, they went to their assigned apprenticeships. They climbed into the bed of Mr. Bordsden's pickup and rode into downtown Radford, where Matt and Maney got out. Mr. Bordsden then drove Charlie out to Ray's garage.

• • • • •

Jack had decided to find out if Matt's high school education had prepared him to read the law texts. He created a cozy spot in his law office with a leather chair and a small table where books could accumulate. He first assigned Matt to read and take notes on a section of the Constitution, and at the conclusion of his own workday, he set aside time to discuss the section Matt had read.

Jack had forgotten how he had loved debating in high school. Matt clearly took after his father, skilled at argument and able to grasp complex concepts, so they sometimes had it back and forth in a fashion that was stimulating for them both. Jack would take one side and Matt would argue the opposite point of view, and then they would swap sides, with Jack subtly inserting arguments that Matt had not made.

Together, they examined landmark decisions in which the

Constitution had been revisited by the Supreme Court. Jack guided Matt through the arguments, and Matt gradually became acquainted with the Supreme Court justices and their positions on decisions. Soon, Jack and Matt were approaching the Bill of Rights and its relevance to the Supreme Court rulings on civil rights, and they took turns arguing the case.

Jack found himself swayed by the arguments of the Warren Court, as reflected in recent events in Radford. Jessa's ardent support of friendship across the race line and Fran's distress over being rebuffed by Margaret seeped into his reading of Chief Justice Earl Warren's ruling about the schools. Maybe the solution could come with breaking down the barriers that kept the races in their place.

Matt quickly countered with the local argument that mixing of the races was against nature. That reminded Jack of what Fran had said to Jessa about *Romeo and Juliet*, and he had to agree with April's objection that the problem wasn't the love—the problem was the senseless hatred that had to have been instilled in the two clans from birth. The more he thought about it, the more he felt that the Supreme Court ruling offered the promise of real change, not just a hurdle imposed on the South. As his conviction grew, his arguments became more heartfelt, and at one point, he caught Matt looking at him in amazement.

"How can you believe that and still live here where the coloreds are kept down?" asked Matt. "If you really believe that, you have to do something about it!"

"I think you're right, Matt."

· · · · ·

John gruffly invited Maney into his cavernous workroom. The air was stale, so they raised the shades and opened the windows together, letting fresh air enter. Maney grabbed a cloth and started wiping dust off the bench surfaces while John began to set out wooden boxes. When he opened the first box, Maney let out a gasp of pleasure at the sight of the gleaming tools, carefully nested into spaces routed out to fit each piece.

"You have that many planes?" asked Maney.

"This is just the first box," replied John.

"They're all different?"

"Jack planes, smoother planes, jointer planes, planes for putting bevels on the edges of woodwork." Maney picked each one up and admired it, resting it in his hand and stroking the smooth handle.

"I have two Number 4s, and I use them for different things—deep cutting or smoothing. Different blade angles. The secret with planes is to keep the blade sharp."

He hauled another box from beneath the bench. It held hammers and mallets. Maney brushed cobwebs off the peg boards on the wall above the bench. The weathering on the backboard faintly revealed the outlines of the tools that had hung there, and he began to match the hammers to their spaces on the wall. Next came the saws—ripping and finish saws, large and small, stored suspended in an upright box. Finally, there was the miter box and miter saw. Maney's eyes lit up. "Wow, we sure could have used that baby when we repaired the stairs!"

John was pleased to see Maney reverently touch the saws and planes. He obviously delighted in the tools, arranging them logically. As they worked together, the sight and feel of his tools rekindled John's love of carpentry, and he began to be eager to have the shop in working order again.

When they unpacked John's brace and bits, Maney was fascinated by the crank-shaped turning device that gripped and rotated the hole-cutting bit. He spun the ratchet with his fingers, noting its function, took up a bit, studied it, and slid the tang into the jaws of the brace. John busied himself with getting another box opened and left Maney to explore the tool. Then he reached under the bench and offered Maney a block of wood and showed him how to clamp it into the bench clamp. "Drill some holes!"

Maney set the tip of the bit against the wood and leaned in as he pressed the smooth head and began to turn the handle. The bit cut into the block of wood like a knife slicing into cheese; crumbles of wood curled their way out of the hole. "Beautiful!"

"That's what I think," agreed John.

The set of bits included one with a broken tip. "What's up with this one? Should I toss it out?"

"Well, now, if I'd thought it should be tossed out, I don't think I'd have saved it. That bit is good metal, and it should be possible to make something out of it. I've got a forge out back."

"You do? Like for horse-shoeing?"

"Never had a horse come by for a shoe, but there're lots of tools you can fashion yourself if you have a forge."

"Like what?"

"Most of my chisels were made from broken rasps and files. Have a look here." John opened a box with a set of curved chisels. "See this angled chisel? That's one I used when I was making bedsteads with roses and such decorations carved on the posts. See how it has two surfaces for the mallet?"

"Carving in the wood? You do that? We have an old bed that has carving all over the headboard. I love looking at it."

"First thing to learn is how to make something sturdy." John searched among the planks that had been stored away and pulled out some light-colored wood. "Know what kind of wood this is?"

Maney picked up the end of the plank, studied the grain, and smelled it. He looked at John with a question in his face. "Some kind of oak?"

"You were right to smell the wood, but the smell should have told you it isn't oak. This is maple, from a tree that used to stand right in front of the post office. Make a nice box."

"I'd like to have a toolbox. Start accumulating my own tools…"

• • • • •

Charlie hung around in the road and smoked a cigarette before he walked across the parking lot to the garage, making a point of showing up late for his first day at Ray Marshall's Garage. He slouched in, leaned against the door jamb, and took out another cigarette.

Ray said, "First rule is, no smoking in the garage."

Charlie glanced in Jacob's direction, but Jacob kept his head down and continued cleaning battery terminals. Charlie returned the cigarette to the pack.

Ray said, "Charlie, why don't you climb in the tow truck, and we'll go get that hulk Dennis Thorp's been after me to renovate—that's the kind of work you're interested in, isn't it?"

Jacob was relieved when the tow truck pulled away. Ray had promised to manage this internship after Jacob explained that he didn't feel he could work with Charlie. Jacob finished the tune-up and backed that car out of the garage to make space for Thorp's old Chevy.

When the tow truck pulled up, all three had to work together to get the truck positioned in the garage. Once it was detached, Ray parked the tow truck out back and walked around to the garage. He stood looking at the rusty hulk and shook his head. "Had a devil of a time just getting it out of that field. She's pretty much a mess. What d'ya think we should tackle first, Jacob?"

Jacob was looking at the old truck with a bemused expression. "This rig's so familiar… I think it must be the Chevy Mom was forced to sell when my father was killed. Thorp tell you what happened to it?"

"It's mostly been sitting abandoned. He said a field fire swept by the truck a few years back—just a grass fire. The truck had an empty fuel tank, which is probably what saved it. Fire ruined the paint job. Those old tires are petrified, but they were good enough to get it here. He didn't think the fire hurt the engine. Said the clutch was going out, anyway."

Jacob reached for a socket wrench and a breaker bar to try the crank shaft. After putting up some resistance, its rust broke loose. "Drive shaft's free." He turned it and listened for valve noises. "Engine turns freely—that's good." He climbed into the driver's seat, set the brake, and pressed the clutch pedal. "Transmission isn't seized."

Charlie peered in the window. "It's missing the gearshift knob. I think I have one at home that will screw on there."

Jacob grunted approvingly. "Let's check the fluids, if there are any." He lifted the hood and discovered a mouse nest on the tangle of cloth-wound wires. A mouse popped out of the mound of soft field grass and headed for the corner of the garage. "Have to replace the electrical harness."

Charlie leaned in, pulled the dip stick, looked at the cloudy oil at its tip, and handed the stick over to Jacob.

"Not bad—bit of water in the oil. We'll drain and refill it." He set a pan under the truck and shimmied under to release the cap. "See if there's any coolant."

Charlie removed the radiator cap and peered in. "Pretty dry."

As Jacob replaced the dip stick, he nudged the radiator hose, and it crumbled in his hand.

Charlie offered, "If I replace those hoses, we can add water to see the leaks."

Jacob went to the back wall and hooked hoses off a peg. Together, they matched the diameters of the upper and lower hoses and began detaching the old ones. At this point, Ray turned to go into the office. He knew Jacob's fascination with the task would keep him working with Charlie. He said, "Got to lock up the office and get on home. It's my daughter's birthday, and we're having family and her friends over to celebrate."

Jacob replied, "We'll just keep working long enough to see how bad the damage is." To Charlie, he said, "While you're mounting those hoses, I'll fetch some water."

Charlie was still struggling to detach the second hose when Jacob returned with a grimy pitcher full of water. He handed Charlie a small screwdriver to pry with. Once Charlie had secured the new hoses, Jacob poured in the water. The radiator didn't have major leaks, although minor spots would benefit from soldering. Jacob marked them with chalk.

"It'll need new belts, too," said Charlie, turning the fan.

"Yeah."

"Is that a good battery over there? We can set it in here to replace this old one."

Charlie wiggled one of the corroded cables from the battery terminals. "I'll need a wrench and maybe a mallet. Got any soda to clean with?"

Jacob handed him a wrench and reached high on a shelf to get the blackened box of baking soda. Charlie soon had the old battery disconnected, so Jacob lifted it out, brushed away mud and mouse nest material, and put the good battery in its place. Charlie dug into his pocket, brought out a pocketknife, and began to scrape the cables' corroded connectors. Jacob nodded.

Leaving Charlie to clamp the terminals, Jacob poured gas into the throat of the carburetor. "I'll feed it some gas and see if it turns over." He placed the gas can on top of the cab, inserted the hose into the engine intake, and pressed the bulb on the output line until it was primed.

He said, "If you sit there and mind the choke, I'll try to crank it."

Charlie slid into the driver's seat, shifted into neutral, and set the choke to retard the spark. He stepped on the clutch and gas pedal and lowered the throttle until he felt a response from the gas pedal. Looking through the dusty windshield at Jacob, he said, "Choke's out."

Jacob positioned the crank and pulled it a half-turn, then spun it again. The second time, Charlie released the choke and turned the ignition. The engine growled and died, but on the next try, it started up, erupted with a cloud of dark smoke and settled into repetitive clacking. Charlie adjusted the choke and pressed the accelerator. Jacob listened. "Hmmmm. Not bad, but there're timing issues. She should improve when we replace the spark plugs."

"Now"—Jacob leaned into the engine, listened, and turned to face Charlie—"hear that low rattle? Could be something minor, like the exhaust valve loose—might have happened when ya'll were pulling it out of the field." He looked to Charlie for confirmation.

Charlie nodded. "We tangled with some barbed wire."

Charlie revved the engine once more and the clacking increased, so he shut it off.

"We have to replace the clutch, but first we'll clean the valve lifters. Valve's out of adjustment."

Jacob scanned the interior. "I just know this is the truck we owned when my poppa was killed. Momma had to sell it, and I was so young, I don't know who we sold it to."

Charlie looked directly at Jacob. "How old were you when your dad died?"

Jacob climbed into the cab beside him. "I was ten—younger than my son is now. It's a bad thing to happen to a family."

"I know."

"How come?"

"Think you're the only one to lose a father? My dad died in a car accident when I was eight. Mother married a man I hate, and I have to live in that house with him picking on me all the time. I was saving to move out, but that rat-fink Dexter has my job at the Esso station."

"That's a shame. My mother never did remarry. Guess there wasn't a man who could see taking over three children. We were lucky to have Aunt Helen and Uncle Adam to help raise us."

"I didn't get the impression that guy Thorp would take good care of a vehicle. He was a real weasel."

"These trucks are tough. I'm hoping we can get this one going."

"When you think we'll be giving her a spin?"

"Need to swap off those tires and check the brakes first, and the electrical system's an accident ready to happen. Get the oil pressure up and replace the fuel line… We can test it out with the old clutch. Shouldn't be too long. We have to get it out anyway to evaluate the transmission. After we finish this job, I think I know a junker car we can get in here that could be fixed up as a hot rod."

· CHAPTER 32 ·

A couple of weeks after the internships began, Charlie arrived at the garage to find Marvin there alone. "Where's the coon?" he asked.

Marvin cringed at the language. "Jacob and Ray had to take the tow truck out."

"So what am I supposed to do? Knock off?"

"Ray wants us to get this Plymouth up on the lift to change the oil."

"Need to tackle the clutch in the project car."

"Well, I can't help you with that, but I want to see how it's done."

For a while, they focused on the Plymouth. While the old oil drained out, Charlie said, "So how d'ya like working for a nigger?"

"I owe a lot to Jacob," said Marvin, making a point to use his name. "You came in here knowing one end of a dip stick from the other, but I didn't know the first thing. I like this work. Jacob never once made me feel stupid about what I didn't know."

"It's the only kind of work that interests me."

"Lucky you got a chance to work here, then."

"You and Jacob, you act just like you're friends."

"You know, that's what I wanted from the first, but there're so many barriers! From talking with Jacob, I've learned a lot about what it's like to be colored in this town. You'd think I'd have known, as it isn't much different in Landsdowne, where I grew up, but I never really thought about it."

"So? What'd he tell you?"

"Told me everyone grows up knowing how to stay out of harm's way by keeping to themselves. Told me they're taught early how to speak to white folks, always 'yessuh and no-suh and pardon-me-suh,' always careful to not look anybody white in the face in a way that might seem like a challenge."

"Sounds right to me."

"They learn early where they can go and where they can't go—the restaurants, the library, the community center, and, of course, the swimming pool. I bet you don't know what he's supposed to do if he's walking down the sidewalk and a white woman's coming from the other direction?"

"Naw. What's he supposed to do?"

"Jacob said he's supposed to keep his eyes down and get off the sidewalk and walk in the gutter until he gets past her."

"Don't see anything the matter with that."

"Well, the fact is, I guess I felt the same way. At least I didn't give it much mind. Let's back this car out of here. When Ray gets back with the tow truck, he'll probably need the lift."

"Pretty basic, seems to me," said Charlie.

"Except that it's totally wrong, all of it!" said Marvin.

Charlie jerked around to face Marvin. "How d'ya mean?"

"There's no logic behind it at all! Just because that's the way the system operates, and you and I were born into the white side of it, doesn't mean it's right!"

"And what the hell's wrong with it?"

"You and I, Charlie, we learned our roles just like Jacob learned his. We were told that the white race was superior."

"Damn right! That's one thing I agree with my stepdad about."

"I thought you told me you thought your stepdad was a fool."

"He knows what side of the bread is buttered, that's all."

"What's that got to do with being colored or white?"

"It's the only durn thing he wants to talk about!"

"What I've discovered is, there's nothing to it—so-called differences between the races—no logic, no facts to support it, nothing!"

"Knew I was coming to work with nigger lovers! You must be the biggest nigger lover of them all!"

"You can leave any time," Marvin said.

"I'm stuck here, you know that!" replied Charlie.

"Remember when those guys came in demanding to see Ray and cussing Jacob out when he said Ray was home sick? Jacob just mumbled something meek, kept his head down, and played the servile colored man to get them off his back? I've seen him have to go into that role time and time again. If someone comes in who knows he is the real mechanic here, he'll talk to them straight up about the repair job and what needs doing. I figure about half the people have learned that Jacob knows his business, but he knows how to keep those other people off his back."

"Makes the world go 'round."

"I guess that's one way to look at it. By the way, after you left on Friday, he was remarking on how fast you pick up the work. Jacob's pleased at how that junker car you're working on is coming along."

"He said that?"

"Sure. Told Ray you have a good feel for the work."

"Praise from a nigger!"

"Ray says Jacob's the best mechanic he's ever known. Praise from Jacob means a lot!"

"I aim to learn enough to get a mechanic job somewhere else. Get out of this town for good!"

"Nothing the matter with that."

"He said the junker's coming along?"

"What he was thinking is that you might want to give it a paint job, same as we did on Thorp's Chevy."

"That'd be great!"

They heard the tow truck turn in the lot, and Marvin pulled the rope to open the garage door. Charlie secured the door in the open position. As soon as the truck halted in front of the garage, Jacob guided Ray to back the towed vehicle through the narrow opening.

"Hey, Charlie!" said Jacob. "You'll love this sedan! A real chance to get a feel for an older Studebaker—they're classy cars!"

"She's a beaut!"

· CHAPTER 33 ·

Jessa grabbed Janie's letter out of the mailbox. It had a fancy border and red airmail stamp on it, and she'd never gotten a letter with an airmail stamp before. She studied the picture on the stamp. Janie had even written *Par Avion* on the envelope. Excited, Jessa peeled the flap of the bulging envelope back and opened the folded pages. Janie began:

Dear Jessa,

Lots has been going on here (more about that below). Your hometown sounds like it has a lot of wonderful things. Thank you for the feathers. I put them in my flute case for good luck.

I'm sorry you weren't able to collect money for the Negro school. I shared your letter with my parents, and they are sympathetic. They said to tell you that you are brave and that there are problems for us everywhere, so don't think Tennessee is the only place where life is mean. I thought that I should tell you how hard it is for us in Portland, so maybe you will understand why we are planning to leave.

Jessa moaned as she sank onto the top step of the front porch, and as she read the letter, she put her arm around Cassie, who leaned against her.

Michael was sitting on the porch swing, reading.

"What's up, Jessa?" he said. "What's so bad?"

"Janie's family is moving. She says there are problems in Portland. I don't know what. Why, why does she have to move?

I don't want Janie to leave." She continued to read, sharing the page so that Michael could read with her.

When we came here from California, we had no idea how difficult life would be. My father was offered a good job, but finding a house to live in has been impossible, and the place we are renting now is the worst, most run-down place we have ever lived. My parents tried to find a house in a good part of town at first, and there was always some reason why it wasn't for sale anymore, or there were problems with the bank, and then the next week the same house was on the market again. Finally, my parents stopped trying in the nicer parts of town and focused on poorer neighborhoods, and when my father talked with people on the phone, it sounded like it would go through, and then when my parents showed up to sign the papers, there was always an excuse why it wasn't for sale. I am sorry to tell you, but Daddy has accepted a job in Chicago because people tell us it is easier there and we don't want to live in this slum where there's lots of real poverty and people are unhappy and fight. We have tried to find our "neighborhood," but it has been hard, and people say we can find a community in Chicago. I hope so, but I hate leaving the school and the classes I was looking forward to taking next year. I will miss being in class with you and getting to play in the orchestra together.

Here are some other things my parents said I should tell you: The restaurants here in Portland won't seat us, so we never eat out anymore. I needed new shoes, so I went with my mother to a department store, and they wouldn't let me try on shoes, or even just ask for a certain size of shoe and pay for it, so we left the store. I had to trace my foot and send the tracing to my aunt in Los Angeles, and she sent me the shoes I have now. So even where they don't have separate white and colored schools, there are problems.

Jessa, you have been a good friend, and we have had lots of fun together. I'm afraid we won't be here when you get back to Portland, because we are moving soon. We can keep in touch by

writing—maybe we can meet together sometime, traveling by bus?
I still look forward to our plan to bike around Europe and stay in
youth hostels like we've talked about doing.

    Love,

    Janie

Jessa held the letter in her lap, buried her face in Cassie's fur, and sobbed. "I had no idea! How could I have been so blind?" She turned to Michael. "I bet you didn't know about it either—how hard it is to be colored in Portland?"

"Yeah, I didn't know about finding a place to live," admitted Michael.

"The part about her aunt in Los Angeles having to send her shoes because she couldn't buy shoes in a downtown department store—did you know about that?"

"No—you're right, I didn't. Let's ask Dad about it."

Jessa and Michael found Ben repairing the screen in the back-porch door. "Hey, Michael and Jessa, you're just in time to give me a hand with this."

They supported the door upright while Ben slid the rods into the hinges. Then Ben glanced at Jessa's face. "Jessa, what's the matter?" He noticed the letter and envelope that she was holding. "A letter from Janie?"

"They're moving," she blurted out. "Portland was not a good place for them to live. Read this…"

Ben read the letter all the way through, then held out his arm to enclose Jessa. "I'm so very sorry, Jessa. I know you'll miss Janie a lot. We were aware there were problems with housing in Portland, but this brings it closer to home. I wish we'd invited Janie's family over for a visit and made more of an effort to get to know them."

"It's all too late—everything's too late, now. *Nothing's* going to work out!"

· CHAPTER 34 ·

Jessa sat on the front porch swing and looked across the street at the familiar homes. She'd be leaving all this again, soon. The end of summer was rapidly approaching, and her confidence was shaken. She'd arrived so full of plans to fix things, but now she was worried that recruiting Eddie to play in the park wasn't safe. She even questioned what her father had been trying to do. If it caused this much trouble for everyone, was it wrong, too? But then she considered the other side: Wasn't it right to fight against the unfairness of the school board? Jessa remembered how depressed her father had been after touring the schools. For so long he had pushed for fairness, but after he got them to hire Mr. Alton, they'd blocked music instruction for the colored kids. Fixing it wasn't as simple as Jessa had thought. Too many things about Radford needed to change, and it wasn't just Radford, because there were also the problems Janie's family had experienced in Portland. Jessa left the porch, followed by Cassie, and moped around the house, finally flinging herself on the couch.

"Karen, I'm so discouraged. Nothing's going right this summer. Did you know that Fran wanted to work with Margaret, but she sent a message that they can get along just fine without her help?"

Karen moved to sit close to Jessa and put her arm around her as Cassie put her head in Jessa's lap. "Sweet, remember how you felt after you heard your parents had been killed? Furious, distrustful of everyone? And how long did that last? My point is, you didn't snap out of it overnight or in a week."

"Oh," said Jessa, as memories flooded back. She rubbed Cassie's head.

"Jessa, something happened when Fran drove Margaret to Landsdowne. I couldn't figure out what, exactly, because Fran broke down and cried when she started to tell me. That's on top of what happened in the park. You know, when you think it'll be safe to trust, as the Negro women in the choir trusted, and the whites turn against you, you just want to withdraw and lick your wounds. I suspect Margaret wants nothing to do with whites right now. Terrible things have been done to that race, Jessa, things we've isolated ourselves from. You and I view an event like what happened in the park and we can think, *Well, isn't it lucky that nobody was hurt*, but Margaret is still seeing those men with sticks running toward her family."

Michael had been standing in the front doorway, letting in flies, listening. The screen door slammed as he came into the room. "You have no idea, either of you, how bad it is. What I learned from Eddie when we were camping out together has been weighing me down ever since. He told me that Jacob's father was lynched!"

Jessa turned to him in horror. "No! That happened around here?" asked Jessa.

"That's what I understand. They had a farm, but after his father was killed, his mother was forced off and the white man took it over."

Karen said, "That's just too horrible. I think if my father had been hanged like that, I could never find it in me to forgive. I would hate all the people who did it."

Jessa covered her ears. "Jacob and Margaret and Aunt Helen—they all must hate white people. I've been so stupid, saying we should just all be friends, like Janie and I are friends. But with that kind of thing in your life, it just seems impossible. And those guys with their sticks—there's something hard and mean in them. Maybe their families were some of the ones that did the lynching! I understand better now. I think what I should do is talk with Mrs. Carlson. I don't think she understands, either."

"We haven't seen much of Fran, lately. I bet she'd appreciate a visit," said Karen. "Jessa, why don't you bike over and take some of the peaches and apples we gathered at the farm."

"Good! I can do that!"

• • • • •

Merrybelle answered the ring. "Miss Olsen! Miss Fran will be so glad to see you!" She led Jessa back to the deck where Fran was sitting. When she saw her, Jessa knew something was the matter, but Fran pretended things were normal, so Jessa played along. She showed the fruit from her grandfather's farm and Fran asked Merrybelle to put it in the refrigerator. Jessa suspected she didn't really feel like making the pies she'd talked about. After discussing inconsequential things, Jessa got to the topic that brought her there.

"Mrs. Carlson, I've been thinking about what you told us about how Margaret felt about the choir performance and after the trip to Landsdowne, how she didn't want you to work with her anymore."

Fran shuddered and covered her face.

"I talked with Karen about it," Jessa went on, "and Michael told us what he learned from Eddie when they were camping out together. He said Jacob's father was lynched, just to get him out of the way so the neighbor could take over his farm. We didn't know about all that, and for us, the threats from the guys at the park don't feel the same as for people who have had to live with tragedies like lynching. Karen helped me understand how Margaret's probably feeling by reminding me of how I felt when I ran away after my parents and grandfather were killed."

"Jessa, I recall hearing people whispering about lynchings when I was a child, and when we were coming back from Lands-downe, Margaret told me about Jacob's father. When I was a child, it was so hush-hush. I think Jack went into law because he wanted to see real justice around here, and he's lost some cases that really tore him up."

Jessa recalled listening to her father and Mr. Carlson dis-cussing the trials. Not all the discontent the two men had shared had centered around her father's unhappiness with the school board.

"Jessa, your parents were killed and you disappeared, and we were so depressed that Jack really wasn't able to function. I kept plugging away, just trying to keep us going. When you were found, I thought life would begin again, but you left for Portland and my life just seemed to get lost."

Jessa said, "I'm so sorry, Mrs. Carlson. If I'd known my parents' plans, I'd never have run away. I didn't mean to hurt anyone!"

"We don't blame you. The Acrees are a wonderful family, and we understand your choice, but since then, things have been unfolding for me, too. I'm trying to come to terms with my own past and the meaninglessness of my life. I've tried to chart a new path, but it's opened my eyes and given me a taste of what the colored community faces."

"What do you mean, Mrs. Carlson?"

"Oh, I've been displaced from the clubs and service groups in town because nobody wants to hear what I have to say to them. The women have been beastly toward me, but that isn't what depresses me. I was most happy when Margaret and I were getting to know one another and working together on the students' applications. She set me straight about my unearned privilege, too. I guess I was depending on Margaret to help me with that, and I had no right. She has her lovely family, and she doesn't need me. I've wanted to drive over there, but I'm afraid she'll turn me away at the door. Merrybelle says to just wait, give her time, but the waiting is killing me!"

"I think she'd treat me the same way. I don't think Mr. Jacob or Eddie would reject us. If only there was a good excuse— maybe to take something there…"

Fran frowned a moment, thinking. "One thing I remember… Margaret said Eddie and her father need music stands. Are there music stands at your family's music store?"

"We stocked the flimsy ones that fold up. I don't like them nearly as well as the solid ones we have at school, but they're lighter and more transportable."

"I'll talk with Jack about buying two of them. He opens the shop up on Saturdays, and people in town have learned they have to be there in the morning if they want anything."

"That will give her a couple more days… Maybe by then she will be seeing the world differently."

"I should make some refrigerator cookies, so I can bake some up in a jiffy to take over. We could bake a tray for ourselves right now and refrigerate the rest of the dough. Would you like to make cookies with me?"

"That'd be fun."

They worked elbow-to-elbow, just as Fran had worked so many times with Jessa's mother. The wonderful aroma of cookies baking in the oven lifted Fran's spirits, and she began to joke and horse around with Jessa. By the time Jessa was ready to set off for home with cookies, Fran was energized enough to start planning dinner. As Jessa was saying her good-byes, she noticed Merrybelle standing on tiptoe behind Fran. Merrybelle was smiling, and she winked at Jessa! It was the clearest wink of acknowledged triumph Jessa had ever received, and it thrilled her. She thought about it all the ride home. She and Merrybelle were on the same wavelength!

· · · · ·

While Jessa was away, Michael became restless. He missed Eddie and wanted to go biking with him, using Jessa's bike. The Wilsons didn't have a telephone and depended on communicating through Reverend James or Aunt Helen. Eddie had said he would bike over, but he hadn't.

Placing a marker in the library book, Michael remembered discussing *Beautiful Joe* with Eddie. "April, did Jessa say where she was going? I wondered if she and I could go back to the library and she could check out *Beautiful Joe* for Eddie. He doesn't have access to a library in the summer, and it sounded like their school library collection is pretty paltry. I don't know where he lives, but if we can find out, I could bike over and give it to him."

"They don't have a library in the summer?" asked April.

"Did you see any colored kids in the Radford library any of the times we've been there?"

"What a rotten deal! I couldn't get through the summer without a library!"

"Hey, Jessa's friend Jeff said he delivered newspapers in the Negro part of town. I bet Jeff would know which house is Eddie's."

Michael went into the house. "Mother, do you know where Jessa went?"

"She went to the Carlsons'. She's hoping to comfort Fran over Margaret Wilson's rejection of her help."

"I bet Eddie didn't bike over here like we planned because his mother wouldn't let him!"

"I guess that's a likely explanation."

"Phooey. Maybe Jessa can figure how to get things back the way they were."

"I've no idea when Jessa will get back, but I'd appreciate it if you'd shuck the corn for dinner."

"Sure, but if Jessa gets back in time, I need her to go with me to the Radford library to check out a book Eddie wanted."

"If there isn't time this afternoon, won't tomorrow morning do just as well?"

"I suppose so—it's just that when you get an idea, you want to do it right away."

• • • • •

Jessa sailed up the driveway with the package of cookies. All the way home, she'd thought about Merrybelle's wink—it was such shared collusion. Merrybelle must have been concerned over Fran's depression, and she and Merrybelle were on the same wavelength!

It was now late in the afternoon, and Michael had given up on going to the library, but he still broached the topic. "Jessa, Eddie Wilson and I were planning to go biking together sometime, so could I borrow your bike for that?"

"Sure, but I didn't know you'd heard from him," said Jessa.

"Haven't, but I've got this plan. Your friend Jeff probably knows where the Wilsons live, right? Because he has the paper route?"

"Probably so—I hadn't thought of that."

"I suspect Eddie's mother laid down the law that he can't come here, but I thought that if you checked out a book I know he wants to read, I could bike to his house and take it to him."

"What book?"

"*Beautiful Joe*—we talked about it when he was petting Cassie, and he said he wanted a dog of his own."

"That's a great idea—you can be our scout, Michael. You go there and see the lay of the land—if white people are going to be tolerated. Mrs. Carlson wants to get back in touch with Eddie's mother, but she doesn't know how. She said Eddie and his grandfather need music stands, and she wanted to go to the music shop Saturday morning to buy some for them."

Michael pursed his lips. "You think that's a good idea? Mrs. Carlson's rich, and wouldn't that kinda be like the kings throwing out coins to the people from their carriages? Like charity? I don't think it's the right way to be a friend. Anyway, there're music stands under my bed. I bet passing them along would go over better than new ones—more of a friendly thing to do."

"Yeah, I'd forgotten about those. They both need minor repairs. I bet your father will know how to fix them. I'll call Mrs. Carlson and tell her we have these to share."

· CHAPTER 35 ·

Michael tucked *Beautiful Joe* under his arm and set out on Jessa's bike. Jessa watched him until he turned the corner. She crossed her fingers.

Jeff's directions led Michael into a part of town he hadn't seen before. The street was dusty and rutted, and in place of green lawns, worn paths led through weeds to garden patches, old cars, and clusters of chairs under the shade trees. Dogs came out to bark and then wag their tails at him. On the front porches, in addition to a few chairs or rockers, there was often a washing machine or a refrigerator with its cord passing through a window. The grocery on the corner had a repaired screen door half-promoting Sunbeam bread, and by the door sat bushel baskets full of potatoes, apples, and fresh ears of corn.

Three houses down from the store was the Wilson home. Bright flowers grew in pots, and the porch's western exposure was shaded by a curtain of pole-bean vines growing on strings stretched to the porch's roof. Tomato plants and squash were visible in the garden, where Eddie was wielding a hoe.

"Hey, Eddie!" Michael pedaled up to the edge of the garden.

"Michael! Super!" Eddie exclaimed upon seeing Michael.

From the kitchen window, Margaret watched. When Eddie had begged to visit Michael as he had promised, Jacob had overheard her lecturing him on why he shouldn't have anything to do with that family. "But Jessa gave me the violin, and she let us camp in her tree!" He had run into his room in tears. Following the parenting rules they had agreed on, Jacob didn't interfere with her position in front of Eddie, but he took the matter up with her later.

"Margaret, I can't tell you how to think. That's your business. But I can tell you it's downright mean to keep Eddie from seeing his friend!"

Jacob rarely reproached her, and his remark had stung. That had been right after the fiasco of the choir performance, and Eddie had dragged around listlessly but hadn't raised the issue again. In the meantime, Margaret's conscience had bothered her, but she didn't know how to turn things around. Now, with Michael's visit, an opportunity opened up.

She saw Eddie eyeing her warily and knew he expected her to throw a scene and drive Michael away. Instead, she went onto the front porch and waved. "Hello, Michael! Eddie, now that you have a friend here to visit, why don't you knock off that garden work."

"Michael brought me a library book, Mama," said Eddie.

"Well isn't that nice. What book is this?"

"You remember when I told you Mrs. Dawson read *Beautiful Joe* to us for quiet time? I wanted to read it myself, and Michael brought it for me."

She flipped to the back of the book, which was stamped Radford Public Library. "So Jessa checked it out for you?"

"Jessa checked out books for me and April, too," said Michael.

"That's nice of her to go to the trouble for you, Eddie. You must be very careful and get it back to her in perfect condition."

"Of course, Mama. I'll put it in my room. Can I go biking with Michael?"

"*May* I go?"

"Yes, ma'am. May I go biking?"

"I don't see why not. Just don't go too far away and stay out of trouble. Michael, would your family enjoy some of these green beans?" She began to pick long beans off the plants by the porch.

"Oh, yes! I personally love beans, and so does everyone," said Michael.

"I'll have a bag of beans picked and ready when you come back."

The boys biked off at a leisurely pace, to talk as they rode along.

"Don't know what happened, but Mama seems to have forgotten she didn't want me to see you," said Eddie.

They coasted down a long hill that Eddie liked for biking thrills and then headed for the old mill. They explored the ruins of the grist mill, climbing and jumping between the large stone blocks and admiring the spillway. "We better not go farther than this. We could explore more if Daddy were here, but Mama said stay out of trouble. I want to be careful so we can bike together again."

They went to a farm where Eddie knew the owner and there was a herd of goats. They dismounted and stood by the fence. "Don't goats have strange eyes?" asked Eddie.

"It's like the pupil is a sideways rectangle instead of circular," said Michael. "Really weird and creepy!" There were young kids, some still nursing their mothers. "Look at that goat with two kids nursing on her—she must have to make a lot of milk!"

"These are meat goats, and nobody bothers to milk them, but there's other kinds of goat, smaller, that are for milking like cows."

"Jessa said her grandparents had those kinds of goats when she was little. She remembers the creamy milk."

"We better be getting back home. You've got to go by my house to pick up the bag of beans."

When they stopped by the porch, Margaret said, "Michael, I put beans for your family in this bag. Tell everyone I hope they enjoy them."

"Thank you, ma'am," said Michael, taking the bag. "I'll get them home and string and snap them myself! Bye, Eddie, let's go biking again soon!"

"Thanks for the book, and tell Jessa thanks," Eddie called as Michael started off. "I'm going to read it twice! I'll bike over to your place to return it."

· · · · ·

When Michael neared the house, Jessa and Cassie were waiting at the edge of the yard.

"How'd it go?" asked Jessa.

Michael held up the bag. "Beans! We had a great time, coasting down a long hill and exploring around an old mill."

"What about Eddie's mother? Was she friendly? Do you think she didn't want you there?"

"She was okay. Sounds like Eddie can bike over here when he finishes the book. Eddie's mother sent beans for dinner. Want to help me snap them, Jessa?"

"I'll get a bowl to snap into. Do they need washing?"

"I don't think so. They weren't dragging in the dust or anything. Eddie's mother just stood on the porch and picked these off—there were lots more on the other side. It's a neat way to raise beans and shade the porch too."

Jessa returned from the kitchen, where April was helping with dinner. "I told them to put on a pot of water for the beans, so we have to snap and string these fast."

"Give me a handful," said Ben, joining them.

"Now, tell me what Eddie's mother said," said Jessa.

"Let's see, she remembered my name, and she told Eddie

he could quit working in the garden. She was interested in the book and told Eddie he had to take very good care of it."

"So she didn't seem disapproving?"

"No, she was pleasant. We went biking together to some neat places. I did gather from what Eddie said that she had forbidden him to see me, but the last thing he said when I rode away was that he'd bike over here to return the book."

"Oh, good! I'll call Mrs. Carlson and tell her—seems the ice may have broken!"

· CHAPTER 36 ·

Jessa and Michael pulled out the dusty music stands. One had a bent segment that prevented it from sliding into the top segment, and the other one was a different style that had such loose joints that it kept folding up and wouldn't hold the music.

"I think these both can be fixed. There are some tools in the garage if we need them," said Jessa.

"Let's see what Daddy says," said Michael. "I bet he can get them working good as new."

"Mrs. Carlson's coming over to pick them up at ten o'clock. She sounded nervous on the phone. She's baking more of those cookies like I brought home with me to take them over there warm."

"She makes good cookies. Did you see the recipe? Could we make some like that when we get back to Portland?"

"She didn't look up a recipe, but I bet she would write one out if I asked her to."

The two stands were ready and waiting in a paper bag when the Lincoln pulled in front of the house and Fran ran up to the porch. "Hello, everyone! Jack is keeping the music shop open, and several people were waiting there when I dropped him off. He can walk home when he closes so I have use of the car to visit the Wilsons. I appreciate your getting the music stands ready—here are some more cookies for you. I'm in a hurry to get to Margaret's while the others are still warm." She looked beseechingly at everyone gathered on the porch. "Well, wish me luck!"

Karen said, "Fran, you look lovely in that shade of blue. It was my mother's favorite color—just like the sky. I bet it's going to bring you good luck!"

"Thank you—for everything!"

When Fran pulled up at the Wilsons' home, Margaret was wearing her grimy gardening clothes but had switched to hanging clothes on the clothesline. Sweat beaded on her forehead, and big patches were apparent under her arms as she raised them to attach the clothes pins. Eddie was playing with Sarah and another little girl in their sand pile, and he saw the car first. He looked at his mother, working in her worn dress. "Mama, you have company. I'll finish hanging out the clothes."

Margaret turned to see the black Lincoln. Under her breath, she said, "Wouldn't you know it! Here I am, unpresentable for a tar-boiling, and *who* should come…" She was glad to turn the damp clothes over to Eddie. There was nothing to do but head for the porch.

Fran stood just below the steps, holding her offerings, a tense bundle of nerves. When Margaret searched Fran's face, she read the uncertainty, and her heart melted. "Oh, Fran, I'm so glad you've come!"

The box and sack slipped down to the ground, and the two women fell into each other's arms. The hurt melted away as they hugged.

"Margaret, I've thought so much about what you said in the car. It's true. I and my people have done so much harm. I understand—at least I'm trying to. I still hoped we could work together, for the sake of the young people, the next generation, to try to make a better world with fairer treatment for everyone."

"That's just what I want, too!"

"I knew you had a lot of deadlines coming up with the applications. Am I too late to help?"

"The packets need to go out next week."

"Margaret, I heard through the grapevine that the white high school graduates don't get counseling on career opportunities, either. We could work together on that, next year, so all the young people get the guidance they deserve—if you would like to?"

"Fran, I'd like that! Listen, let me fix you some iced tea and you and Dad sit out here on the porch while I change out of these sweaty clothes so we can work together. We can assemble the packets to go out Monday!"

Margaret rushed into the kitchen where her father was sitting at the table reading the paper. She grabbed his shoulder and bent to whisper in his ear, "Daddy, help me out! That Mrs. Carlson is here. Can you occupy her out on the porch and give me a chance to clean up?"

Margaret pulled a pitcher of tea out of the refrigerator, poured the last of it into two glasses, added mint and lemon, and handed them to her father, who joined Fran on the porch. Margaret grabbed fresh clothes and disappeared into the bathroom to take a hasty sponge bath before pulling on a clean dress and pinning back her hair.

By the time Margaret got to the porch, Fran was describing a trip to Nashville and how much she had enjoyed the orchestra performance. She turned to Margaret. "Let's get to these applications. I could take some of the work home to use my typewriter if that would help." Then Fran noticed the forgotten bag with the music stands and the flat box with cookies making greasy spots on the lid. "Oh, goodness, here're the cookies I brought, and I remembered you said Eddie and Mr. Rayburn needed music stands. These were just gathering dust at the Olsens' house—Ben Acree repaired them. Jessa said she wanted them to be used again."

"Thank you, Fran," said Margaret. "Dad, have a look."

He lifted the stands out of the bag and began assembling them. "Appreciate that you thought of us. Yes, these will do nicely!"

"Dad, if you want a cookie, grab it. I want to hide the rest for dessert tonight—don't want the kids spoiling their appetite! My, these look so good—and they're still warm!" she said, taking one and holding out the box to Fran and her father.

Margaret and Fran each munched on a cookie as they settled down at the kitchen table and spread out the partially completed applications. There were sealed letters of recommendations from teachers, employers, and Reverend James, the school transcripts that had finally become available, and the forms and personal statements the students had labored over. The main job was to pull the parts of each application together, put them into large envelopes, and address them. The two women worked away happily, catching up on personal news. Margaret had heard from Rachel that the women of the combined choir had agreed to get together again, so everything in her life was looking brighter. She even relaxed her concern about the plan for Eddie and her father to play in the park music series.

· CHAPTER 37 ·

Abby was practicing her clarinet when her father got home from the bank. He stood in the richly furnished front hallway and listened to the melody flowing out of her bedroom. Her love of music was something he hadn't expected, and he had to admit that in three years of instruction she was becoming a good musician. He shook his head. Jessa's challenge to the school board had been on his mind all day, and when Mr. Alton's wife had come into the bank, he had watched her from his desk, half tempted to go out and introduce himself and ask if he might meet with Bill Alton before school started. Then Reverend James had come in with money collected from the colored community. Now, the sound of Abby's clarinet nagged him so insistently that he went to the phone and rang up the Altons to settle on a time to visit that evening.

· · · · ·

When Mr. Wexler knocked on the Altons' front door, he was immediately greeted by Bill.

"Won't you please come in, Mr. Wexler. Have a seat."

"Bill, thanks for making time to visit with me. I wanted to sound you out on the music situation in Radford."

"Yes, sir. Well, for me, Radford's been a dream come true. I love working with kids like your daughter, Abby. It's so gratifying to see how she's taken to the clarinet—one of my favorite instruments. She's really blossoming in the chamber music group."

"I have to admit there're two reasons for my visit. Abby's one of them, and the other is Jessamine Olsen. She's made an impassioned plea to the school board for music instruction at Overbrook. Abby and Jessamine are in cahoots, and Abby keeps bugging me to do something to help her friend. Jessamine was planning to raise a collection when the choir performance was disrupted by those hoodlums. Of course, there's no way she could collect enough, but her sincerity is undeniable, and Abby expects me to support her."

"Mr. Wexler, I don't see how, with the schedule I have—"

"Bill, nobody expects you to take up the slack. The school board knows you're already giving up your lunch period to squeeze in a class at noon, and we can't possibly expect you to do more. But the plot thickens… Reverend James came to see me at the bank with a proposal for music instruction for the colored kids. I know there's a lot of talent in the Negro community, as was evident at the choir performance, and he offered his church for classes; they have a piano there. Nothing says this has to be managed by the school board, and I'm not sure the members would go along with anything for Overbrook, but the issue is coming to a head. Reverend James wondered if I could advise him on how best to spend money that his congregation collected to promote the instruction."

Wexler uncrossed his legs and leaned forward. "Bill, I don't mind telling you that it almost broke my heart. I can't help thinking that that money represents a lot of sacrifice on the part of somebody, probably a lot of somebodies. It's a testimony to the value they put on music."

"Mr. Wexler, I have a thought. After Jessa described Eddie Wilson's mastery of the violin, I was intrigued and decided to look up this grandfather. We had a wonderful conversation.

He's never taught music, but he's a certified teacher and would love to get back in the classroom, and he knows more about string instruments that I ever will. He and his grandson played a few pieces. He said he had applied to do substitute teaching at Overbrook, so you must have seen his credentials."

"Jamison didn't comment on that, but he may not have taken it seriously, since the teachers usually cover for one another, and we've never needed to pay for a substitute teacher at Overbrook, that I can recall. But there's another issue. I'm treasurer for the school board, and last night I took a second look at the books. What I found puts the issue of Overbrook in a new light. With the repairs the three young men are scheduled to complete on the school properties, we're saving the money allocated for capital improvement, and there have been generous donations of paint and other materials. It's given us a bit of a cushion, financially."

"How about a part-time position? Mr. Rayburn might be willing to teach music part time. Is there enough money to hire him on that basis? I know he and I could work together, and I'd appreciate his assistance on an informal basis with the string-music instruction."

Mr. Wexler stroked his chin. "There's shaping up to be a half-time salary. I'm sure Mr. Rayburn was paid more in Paducah than he'd get here, full time, but if his interest is in getting back to teaching, the salary may not be critical." Mr. Wexler stroked his chin while he considered the possibility. Finally, he said, "Don't mention this to anyone, Bill. I'll go to bat for it at the next board meeting, and if I can convince them, I think we should be able to swing it financially. It'll take some tall talking, more like arm-twisting, to get the board to come around on this one. I'll tell them that we can pool the contribution from Reverend James and any funds Jessa might be able to collect at the park performance this coming Thursday, and, of course, it depends on whether Mr. Rayburn is willing to go along with it. In any case, I'll get back to you."

. . . . .

School started in just three weeks. Mr. Wexler called the school board chairman for an impromptu meeting of the board to take up the music appointment options.

The chairman reluctantly agreed to a brief meeting.

When the members filed in, the tension in the room was palpable, and Mrs. Brians was positively bristling with hostility. "Jamison, you better have a good reason for calling this meeting. I'm sick and tired of being dragged through this Overbrook issue!"

Her ally on the board, Dave Morton, seconded her sentiment. "I think this meeting is a waste of time. It's too late to change anything."

Mr. Jamison rapped the table to call the meeting to order. "I'll turn the floor over to Dave Wexler so that he can bring you up to date on the board's finances."

Wexler took a folded paper from his jacket pocket, unfolded it carefully, gazed out at the board members, and settled his reading glasses on his nose. "Firstly, we have the remainder in the capital improvement and repair budget, two hundred and fourteen dollars. I remind you that we allocated two hundred and fifty dollars for grounds maintenance, work on playground equipment at Edison, and roof repairs at Overbrook. It's apparent that the three young men will accomplish that work, and the custodian generously donated his time to oversee their effort. There were donations of paint and other materials, so this has been a windfall for the board. You have all toured Overbrook, and the work has begun at Edison. I recall that the response of the board was positive." Wexler scanned the table to register each board member's response. "Then there is a monetary contribution, a new development, and that is what prompted me to ask for another meeting of the board." Wexler registered their interest before continuing.

Mrs. Brians said, "I assume that's the money Miss Olsen was hoping to collect. Is that what you're referring to?"

"No, this is different. Reverend James brought a contribution to me at the bank this week. The colored community has presented us with one hundred thirty dollars, collected specifically for supporting music instruction of the colored students, and he offers to open his church as the site of the instruction." The committee members responded with muted grunts and harumphs.

"Together, these two sources of funds total three hundred and eighty dollars. As you correctly recall, Jessamine Olsen was planning to pass a collection plate after the choir performance, but the disruption prevented her attempt. My daughter, Abby, tells me that she plans to pass the plate when Eddie Wilson and his grandfather perform next week. I don't know how much she will be able to collect, but we can add it to this total, and I pledged to match what the community contributes. As you can see, we are getting close to enough to offer a part-time salary to someone."

"But it's too late to initiate a search for a teacher!" interjected Mr. Morton.

"That was my opinion, also, until I consulted Mr. Alton. On his recommendation, I am proposing that we offer this post to Mr. Rayburn. I understand that Mr. Rayburn is a certified teacher, and he applied to do substitute teaching at Overbrook and submitted his credentials."

Mrs. Brians asked, "And just who is this Mr. Rayburn?"

"He's the grandfather who will perform next Thursday with Jacob Wilson's son, Eddie." Wexler turned to Mr. Jamison. "Dan, do you recall seeing Mr. Rayburn's credentials?"

"I did meet Mr. Rayburn earlier in the summer when he applied for substitute teaching. As I recall, his experience is in high school English and history. I simply thanked him and filed it away because we rarely have need for a substitute teacher in the colored school. He's a graduate of Kentucky State College for Negroes, and he pointed out that he was certified to teach all subjects in primary and secondary education."

"And your general impression of him?" Mrs. Brians pursued.

"He's well-spoken and genial."

Mr. Wexler looked at each member of the board. "I understand the committee's resistance to being pushed by outside forces, but we were elected to be responsive to the community, and we'll have a hard time explaining inaction after they've shown so much support for this."

"I beg to differ with your conclusion. That support doesn't necessarily reflect the community at large. I personally know there will be opposition," Mrs. Brians said.

"This whole business is highly irregular. I second the opinion that this doesn't have the backing of the whole community. In fact, I'll go on record opposing it because of community members I know who will oppose it," said Mr. Morton.

"We're already breaking the bank to pay the colored teachers' salaries, and you propose an expansion that will commit us to future expenditures—it's outrageous!" said Mrs. Brians. "You know that music instruction has additional costs attached to it."

"She's right. Putting a part-time teacher at Overbrook will commit us to more expenditures in the future," said Mr. Morton. He pushed his chair back from the table. "This stretches my credulity, Dave!"

"I guess this is the response I expected, although I wish you had heard the argument Bill Alton made for it. He had me convinced."

"Dave, are you sure this idea came from Bill and not from Mr. Rayburn?" asked Mr. Jamison.

"That's right. It's all pie in the sky unless Rayburn is interested—he hasn't been contacted yet. I just thought that if we moved fast, we could put this money to the use it was intended for."

"I could be persuaded to vote for a beginner's class taught by this Mr. Rayburn at Overbrook. Nothing more," said Mr. Jamison. He turned to Mrs. Brians. "Could you go along with that, Betty?"

"We're pushed into a corner, and you know how well I like that. But assuming that this colored man wants to teach music to the colored children, I won't block it."

Mr. Morton said, "I'm going on record in opposition to this one."

Jamison turned to Wexler. "Dave, it looks like we have a majority in support, so I delegate you to approach Mr. Rayburn. Time is of the essence. Can we all agree to learn the outcome by phone? My schedule's getting very cluttered, and I don't want to have to call you all in again."

• • • • •

Mr. Wexler finished his iced tea and set the glass on the porch boards. He rose, reluctantly, and shook Mr. Rayburn's hand warmly. "Mr. Rayburn, this has been most enjoyable. Please convey my thanks to your daughter for the tea. I'll report to the school board, and we'll have the paperwork ready for your signature. School starts on the seventeenth, so we are pushing the envelope for this session, but we really appreciate your willingness to step in to help the school system out."

"I'll love being back in a classroom, Mr. Wexler. A regular appointment is a lot more satisfactory than substitute teaching," said Mr. Rayburn, "and I'll enjoy coordinating with Mr. Alton."

Mr. Wexler walked to his car and drove away. Mr. Rayburn gathered the glasses and went into the house where Margaret was waiting on pins and needles. "Daddy, what was that all about?" she asked. "What's this paperwork?"

"Margie, remember when I registered to do substitute teaching, to get back in a classroom occasionally? Mr. Wexler seems to have reviewed my credentials. They're looking for a part-time music instructor. Mr. Alton apparently broached the subject of hiring me to the school board. I did get the impression they're being pushed to do this."

"That Jessa Olsen! She tells everyone who'll listen that she wants to get music into Overbrook to fulfill her father's dream! What's it to her? I can't help thinking she's meddling, pushing for a music program at Overbrook."

"Apparently it started with Jessa's proposal, and then several things came together to make the board reconsider. Those young men who attacked us when the choir performed have made a lot of improvements to both Overbrook and the rest of the schools, saving capital improvement funds. The surprise for me, although Mr. Wexler thought I'd know about it, is that Reverend James brought substantial funds collected from the Negro community to the bank. He impressed Mr. Wexler with how much support there is for music at Overbrook. We should ask Brother James about that. Anyway, the school board agrees to hire me to teach one introductory class using flutophones for reading music and including a bit of music theory."

"Dad, I know this school system. You'll be such an asset." Margaret gave him a hug.

"There's another part of this that isn't official. It was Mr. Alton's idea. He's asking for my help with the small groups of advanced string students."

"Dad, that's the white students. Is this going to work?"

"Sure do hope so, Margie. It will be extracurricular. I found Mr. Wexler very pleasant. He has a little girl, well, I guess she must be Eddie's age, who plays clarinet, and he's very proud of her. It reminded me of how proud your mother and I were of you at your first recital, Margie."

· CHAPTER 38 ·

Charlie walked the many blocks home in the late afternoon heat with a skip in his step. His arms were smudged with black grease up to the elbow, and his forefinger was throbbing from the hammer-smack it got at Edison. Still, he stepped along with a jaunty pace and actually caught himself whistling, although he quickly squelched the impulse. However, the closer he got to home, the more he began to brace himself for the encounter over the dinner table. Some nights since he had started the internship, he had ducked out, staying away until bedtime, but he was ravenously hungry tonight.

He crossed the porch in two strides and had grabbed the screen door when his stepfather swung onto the end of the porch to catch up with him.

"Thought you were going to move in with the niggers," said his stepdad.

"I'm hungry. The other guys take lunches, and they share with me, but I'm starved," said Charlie.

Charlie's little brother and sisters started chanting, "Nigger lover, nigger lover!" when he headed for the dinner table.

His mother entered from the kitchen. She was a slightly-built woman with rings under her eyes and deep lines of disappointment creasing her face, but she lit up when she saw Charlie. "Son, I've been worried about you. How's the job at the colored school going? You know I tried to get that sheriff to let you go. He had no right to lock you up!"

"I lived through it, Mom. We're working on Edison's playground equipment now. Sure am hungry," said Charlie.

"Dinner's ready." She put a kettle on the center of the table and returned with a tray of buns. There was mustard, pickle relish, and ketchup. Charlie's nose told him hot dogs were in the kettle, and he knew he was entitled to two, so without waiting for the others, he took a fork and stabbed his allotment.

His father arrived from washing up and sat at the head of the table. "So, you wait for me like one dog waits for another?" Eying Charlie's hands, he said, "Guess I know to wash my hands before eating." Charlie looked at his dirty hands holding the bun. "Better tell us what it's like, doing time in the nigger muck."

As Charlie spread relish on the bun, he mumbled something incoherent, and for a time, his interrogation was interrupted by an altercation among his siblings over who got to wield the fly swatter. Charlie assembled his hot dog and bit into it ravenously.

"Got enough of the stench of Overbrook to last a lifetime, did you?" said his stepdad.

"I suppose so, sir," replied Charlie. "But we've got around another week on the playground equipment at Edison."

"Working at Edison's okay, but I never thought someone from this house would lower himself to fixin' up a colored school."

"That roof was pretty rotten."

"Serves 'em right—don't know why we educate pickaninnies. Why do they need to read?"

Charlie's mother sank into her chair. "Could we have a blessing? Bella, can you go ahead?"

Charlie's younger sister began, "Thank you, God..."

Charlie continued to eat, and his stepfather swatted him on the cheek. "Be respectful!" When the Amens had been said, the nagging continued. "Tell how it's going at Ray's garage—you have to work with that coon?"

"No, sir," Charlie lied. "Mr. Marshall and I went out, and first we dragged in an old truck, and now there's another hulk I'm working on."

"That's all?" asked his stepfather, disappointed.

"Pretty much."

"I want you to know we're not going to let this matter drop. I been talking with friends. We're going to take matters into our own hands—don't like this town laying down like a doormat for the coloreds."

Charlie looked up abruptly from his second hot dog.

"In this town it's the whites who're the problem. They don't respect the color line. Don't see a problem cozying up to niggers. That sheriff's for shit, and from what I hear, the Carlsons are playing up to them, too. They'll get the message, though—folks better keep in their place, all of 'em. This is just a threat…"

"What kind of threat?" asked Charlie.

"Well now, I 'spect you're too busy with your community service and your grease-monkey internship to take any interest in what I'm planning."

"No, tell me—I'm interested," said Charlie. A heavy lump in the pit of his stomach made it hard to swallow. "What you guys got planned?"

"Can't tell you, now that you've gone over to the other side."

Charlie stood and said, "Thank you, Mother, for the dinner."

"Charlie, there're doughnut holes for dessert," said his mother.

"Thanks, I'm full. Need to get cleaned up."

Charlie left them and headed for the bathroom, but his stepfather called after him, "We're going to light up this old town—give the community some entertainment since that's what they want."

Charlie ducked behind the door and grabbed its frame,

shaking his head, again and again, at the thought of the praise that Jacob had given him as he left that afternoon.

· · · · ·

The men gathered in the garage behind Charlie's house.

Charlie's father said, "I tell you, things are getting out of hand, and we just gotta do it. If you think we can't pull it off, we oughta bring in those guys I know from Selway—they know how it's supposed to be done!"

"I don't wanta bring in outsiders," said Rob. "I've got rail-road ties that'll burn like gasoline—extras from a pile I got for making a loading ramp."

"The idea is, get in there, set it good, and get the hell out of there. Don't need but three strong men and a good truck to pull it off. You ever been to a cross burning?"

"Sure, but I was a kid," replied Rob. "I remember there was a good pile of wood at the base of the cross to keep it blazing. They didn't burn it on a white man's property, though."

"I say the sheriff's a good target. He thinks he can lock up my stepson for running around at a picnic when he didn't lift a finger to stop this choir singing, even after they warned him. Wish we had the sheriff they got over at Selway. He won't take any nonsense from the niggers."

"Yeah, the Selway sheriff runs a tight ship."

"Course, we gotta lay the message down real clear for the lawyer and his wife, too. It's going around town they're cozy-ing up to niggers—inviting 'em to dinner, if you can believe that. If we lay it out real clear to the whites, could be we'll still have to drive some niggers out of town, but I'm guessing they'll get the message."

"So how's tomorrow night? I'll drop off a couple railroad ties tomorrow morning before work."

"Sure thing, Rob."

The three men worked surreptitiously for two evenings to construct a large cross and round up kindling, shovels for planting the cross, and ropes to haul it into place.

Meanwhile, Music in the Park fliers for the fiddle performance were posted all over town. The Esso gang was too busy to notice, so it was Charlie's stepfather who finally saw it. He ripped the sheet off the grocery store bulletin board and pocketed it.

He greeted his two friends who had gathered in his garage to plan for the cross burning: "Get this, guys! They're at it again—listen: *This program of fiddle music will feature Mr. Rayburn, a retired teacher who recently joined our community, and Eddie Wilson, age eleven, playing a mix of bluegrass, popular, and classical fiddle music.*"

"Who are they?" asked one of his friends.

"Ever heard of Jacob Wilson?"

"Course. Sheriff locked him up for kidnapping that girl—but he didn't do it after all."

"So this kid's related to Jacob? His son?"

"I figure it has to be. This Mr. Rayburn, I don't know—retired—could be his grandfather."

"So! Seems like niggers didn't learn their lesson! This is our chance to do what the boys failed to do, guys. We'll set 'em so straight they'll never forget it!" said Charlie's stepfather.

"I was liking the idea of the cross burning better," said the other man. "I figured we could get away and nobody would know who did it. There in the park, the boys got caught by the sheriff, and I can't afford to get thrown into jail."

"Coloreds are taking liberties, and we can't just stand by and let them get away with it! If Jacob's son is performing, you can bet they'll show up with their picnic stuff again, in our park! Like it says here: *The community is invited to share this music and picnic in Reubens Park.*"

"Count me out. I'm not going in there waving a stick around like the boys done, looking for someone to bash!" said the second man.

"Well now, that's the issue—I don't favor sticks, either," said Charlie's stepfather. "Seems we've got two problems in this town: the coloreds stepping over lines they used to respect and the whites encouraging them."

"But I just want to scare them—that's why I liked the cross burning. I can't afford a run-in with the law."

"We need to get it across to everyone in this town that people got to stay in their place. I say we go for the performers. Load our shotguns with birdshot. They should be easy to chase away—a granddad and an eleven-year-old boy—we'll scare the living daylights out of the performers! We can be out of there before the sheriff wakes up."

· CHAPTER 39 ·

It was mid-morning. Marvin and Jacob were leaning inside a truck while its engine hung suspended above them from the reinforced rafters. Ted eyed the engine warily when he stuck his head in the repair shop. He ushered John Morgan in, sidling around the inside of the garage to avoid the engine.

"What's up?" asked Marvin.

"Is that thing up there safe?" asked Ted.

"Good enough for government work."

"Marvin, Florence said you'd be here. We want to talk to you and Jacob before Charlie gets here. I brought my friend, John Morgan. Florence says you and John are acquainted."

"Hello, Jacob," said John. "I've heard a lot about you and your family. I'm looking forward to the music."

Jacob nodded.

"Jacob, John thought that since it's your son and father-in-law who'll be playing, you should be in on the plan we've hatched. After that fiasco when the choir sang, we want to be ready for anything," said Ted.

"About the music," Jacob said, "Reverend James came by last night. He again urged us to cancel. He's busy on working this music thing out among our people and said we should stay out of the public eye. Eddie was already in bed, and Brother James whispered so he wouldn't hear, but Eddie woke up or wasn't asleep, and came into the kitchen all in tears. Said he really wanted to play and begged to be allowed to. Grandpa Rayburn said he'd go along with whatever we decided. He said it was our town and we knew it best, but he didn't want to put Eddie in danger."

John grimaced at Ted. "Our town, all right…"

Jacob continued, "Margaret's the tough one—she's the musician, and she feels for Eddie. She was real angry over what happened at the choir performance. Had a big ole storm cloud hanging over her about that. But for some reason, she supports the idea of her father and Eddie playing. Brother James just shook his head at her and said he'd seen people killed for less and he's been losing sleep over this Music in the Park. Said it's a white folks' park and we ought to stay away. Said if colored people acted like they had the right to be in that park, white folks'd be forced to show us who's boss."

Marvin shot a look at Jacob. "You didn't tell me about that, Jacob."

"It was a family decision. Margaret and Eddie won out."

"Now I understand why you've been so preoccupied. Wish I could help. I'd like to get off duty and go to the park myself. The sheriff's deputized several people, including Florence's husband."

"I know the sheriff's plans," said Ted. "John here thinks we need something more. He's thinking along the lines of a human shield around the performers—people seemingly just there to enjoy the music, who won't stand out too obviously like the sheriff and his deputy, but who can be on the lookout to spring into action."

"Florence would like that. She's worried. She said the choir was a great hit, but everything went to hell after the attackers got there," said Marvin.

"We're afraid the local white supremacists will make an appearance, better organized and determined to make their point.

John thinks they may be armed, probably to intimidate, but where there's guns, there's the potential for real harm."

At the mention of guns, Jacob looked up, alarmed. "So this won't be just boys like Charlie with sticks? I don't like this talk of guns."

John studied him. "Jacob, these attackers think they're defending their way of life."

"Ain't nobody challenging their way of life, just playing music! It's more than they deserve, for Eddie to play for them, but he wants to do it. Me, I know you can't trust white men."

John sighed. "If there's a lesson the world should have learned from the Nazis, it's the wrongness of this superior-race business. Unfortunately, Radford whites were fed white supremacy from their cradles. Gotta feel superior to somebody and have an enemy to unite against—if it's not a Negro uprising, it's a communist under every bed. That's how they chased me up into the woods."

"They forced you, a white man, out of town?" asked Jacob.

"You got it," said John grimly. "I cursed them with every tree I felled, every saw cut I made, every peg I drove. I'd tried to be a member of this community, but they drove me out. It took a lot of time before my blood wasn't boiling. I walked a long way to other towns to avoid frequenting their businesses. Nobody mourned me when I disappeared, either."

"Sounds worse than I imagined, John," said Marvin. "No wonder you're skeptical about this town. How many people have you rounded up for the human shield? You got the Carlsons, the Acrees, and Mr. Alton?"

"We've already recruited them, and Reverend James' son. I think we've got enough supporters to pull this off. We just wanted you to be in on the plan, Jacob. Tell your father-in-law to not be surprised if a circle of men rushes up to counter a disturbance. Most of the crowd wants no trouble, as we saw at the women's performance, but the shield will be fast and close, ready to move right in."

Jacob nodded grimly. "I'll tell him. I'm thinking Reverend James was right." He turned to Marvin. "How long you figure it's goin' to take, this understanding between your people and my people?"

"Jacob, I wish I could snap my fingers and make it so."

"Nobody's going to just snap out of this idiocy, Marvin. I see changes coming, but it won't be pretty. People of both races have to keep trying, that's all. Negroes will rise up, it's bound to happen, but I may not live to see it," John said.

"Putting my son and father-in-law in danger has me sore afraid," said Jacob.

· CHAPTER 40 ·

Thursday dawned hot and sultry. Eddie had scarcely slept, and now he jumped up from bed and checked his fiddle anxiously to be sure the strings hadn't snapped, as they had in his dream. He tuned the violin, taking satisfaction in pulling the four strings into harmony. The instrument spoke to him, and it was hard to put it down.

Margaret stuck her head into the bedroom. "Honey, you up already? Let your sister sleep until I get breakfast fixed, you hear?"

Eddie pulled on his clothes, humming the Paganini theme that was running through his head all the time now. They'd play it near the end, after the square-dance music his grandfather had taught him. The odor of bacon reached him. That meant the special breakfast menu of bacon and pancakes, which was usually reserved for holidays or someone's birthday. He was grateful that his mother had supported his wish to play, and now she was marking the day with the special breakfast menu.

Sarah called, "Mama."

Eddie dashed into her room to keep her from distracting their mother from breakfast preparation. "Hey, Sarah! What do you want to wear today? It's going to be hot, and you don't want to dress in your pretty clothes until this evening. We're going back to the park, and Grampa and I are playing."

"Bad men drive everyone away?" asked Sarah.

"No way, Sarah! Just good music for people to clap and dance for—you're my best dancer!"

"You play good, Eddie."

"Come on, put on this shirt and that pair of shorts. That's a girl!"

When she was dressed, they went from her tiny bedroom to the kitchen.

"Eddie, dear, please get the knives and forks out," said Margaret. "I've got a stack of pancakes here that should hold us."

"Yessum," said Eddie.

"Morning, Dad," said Margaret when her father walked in. "Eddie's already tuned his violin, but I didn't want him to start playing before breakfast!"

"Raring to go, Eddie?" he asked.

"Yessir! I want us to play that Paganini," said Eddie.

"Okay, after breakfast, we'll practice some, but then we'll do other things until the performance."

"Why do we have to do other things?"

"Eddie, we'll pretend we're like the great Fritz Kreisler. Kreisler was a popular violinist and composer, and his wife made him practice and practice, even though the music was already in his mind and heart. What he would do, to satisfy her and to keep himself fresh for a performance, was practice all sorts of exercises and other pieces, but whatever he was going to play for the concert, he wouldn't touch. Then, when the concert started, he would play as if he were just discovering the music himself, and he would share the beauty of that discovery with the audience."

"Grampa, too much practice kills the music?"

"Honey, if you know your pieces the way Kreisler knew his, the performance becomes a creation. Kreisler played his heart out for his audiences, and they responded in kind."

"Goodness! Well, everyone sit down for breakfast," said

Margaret. "Sarah, climb up. I'll cut up your pancake. Jake, are you up?"

"Coming," called Jacob.

* * * * *

Across town, Jessa and April were setting the breakfast table.

"Looks stormy—come see these ominous clouds," said Ben.

"Oh, no!" exclaimed Jessa. "It just *can't* rain!" She jumped up from the table and looked out the back door. Cassie followed and stuck her head out, too. "Rats! Big, dark clouds!"

"Maybe it won't rain until later tonight," suggested Michael. "I've been watching the pattern. It starts out looking ominous, then clears off and doesn't cloud over again until around sunset."

"I hope so," said April.

"I'm going to make us sandwiches for the picnic—keep it simple. Cold drinks make more sense than that pitcher of tea," said Karen.

"The tea would have been fine if the men hadn't gotten Cassie so agitated," said April.

"Everyone's picnic was disrupted, more or less, but let's not dwell on that," said Ben.

"Oh, I look forward to tonight but also wish it was already over!" said Jessa.

"Jessa, don't expect too much from the collection plate plans," warned Karen. "I don't know how many people bring money to the park. You might announce that contributions can be made at a later time."

* * * * *

At the park, Mr. Alton's volunteers had pulled a grandstand in front of the gazebo and were putting up crepe paper streamers. People were just beginning to fill in the picnic spots when Eddie and his grandfather arrived to check out where they would perform. When Eddie saw Michael, Jessa, and April, he made a beeline for them. Cassie strained at her leash to greet him, wagging her pom-pom tail.

"Good Cassie, good dog!" Eddie said, hugging her.

"Fine weather, after all," said Michael. "Eddie, we were worried this morning."

"So were we! Looked like rain. Grampa and I are *so* ready!"

"Your family's invited to our house for ice cream after the music! Do you like chocolate-covered ice cream popsicles?"

"Love chocolate anything!"

"Then we'll see you!"

Eddie returned to the grandstand and shared the news about the ice cream with his grandfather.

The number of colored families was considerably smaller than for the combined choir performance, but Margaret had leaned hard on her neighbors and friends to attend. Rachel's and Merrybelle's families were spreading their blankets on the far side of the park, and Reverend James and his wife and their married son's family were there, also. The white families had turned out in force, of course. They greeted each other and caught up on the news of the day as they spread their picnic on the blankets while their children joined friends at the playground.

When the crowd had settled down to their meals, Mr. Alton walked to the front of the platform and stood waiting until he had the attention of the audience. When shushing had silenced the chatter, he announced: "Tonight, we're lucky to showcase some exceptional local talent. Mr. Rayburn recently joined our community from Paducah, Kentucky, where he frequently played for dances. He has shared his musical training with his grandson, Eddie Wilson. They have assembled quite a selection of fiddle music for us. Please join me in welcoming them to our performance series!"

There was polite clapping as Mr. Alton rejoined his wife.

The audience studied the performers curiously. Eddie looked very small standing on the platform beside his grandfather. Both were dressed in a snappy Western fashion, as if for a barn dance.

Eddie and his grandfather bowed and took a step forward. They hushed to hear Eddie's childish voice. "Thank you all for coming. We'll begin with familiar melodies that are good to listen to while having a picnic."

He put the violin under his chin, placed his bow, and nodded to his grandfather. Together, they began "Shenandoah," and the warmth of the music gathered the audience into their spell. They followed it with "Sweet Alice Blue Gown," then "Blackberry Blossom," "St. Annie's Reel," and "Wabash Cannonball." The audience, their colorful blankets distributed in patches across the green lawn, responded to the haunting renditions of familiar melodies with a round of applause for each piece. Cassie wagged her tail every time Eddie announced a piece, and she followed events on the grandstand closely.

Eddie explained that the next selections were for barn dances, and struck up a melody appropriate for a Virginia reel while his grandfather clapped, tapped his foot, and called the dance steps. Eddie's small violin sang out and the audience was amazed at his mastery. They had the audience clapping and children dancing, and kept it up nonstop until they had run through the dance selections. They took a bow to thunderous applause.

Eddie stepped to the front of the platform again to announce: "Now, we'll play classical pieces arranged as duets."

They played Bach's "Sheep May Safely Graze," followed by Beethoven's "Ode to Joy." Then Eddie announced the Paganini, and he and his grandfather began the piece that they had worked so hard to master, the "Witches' Dance."

Margaret saw it first, a disturbance in the bushes to the right of the grandstand. Heart in her mouth, she took off running toward the grandstand. Three men emerged from the bushes carrying shotguns held high over their heads. "Radford white pride! Put niggers in their place!" they yelled.

The human shield surged toward the grandstand, but Cassie sped ahead of them all. From the picnic blanket, she streaked across the grass, lashing her leash through the air as she bounded toward the grandstand, letting out a roar of growls. She intercepted the man who approached the grandstand first and sank her teeth through his cuff deep into his ankle. Charlie's stepfather let out a yelp as Cassie tugged and almost toppled him. Off-balance, he grabbed onto the grandstand, but his gun jammed barrel-first into the ground. It discharged with a deafening roar.

On the other side of the grandstand, another intruder took that as a signal and discharged his gun into the air, just before being tackled by Mr. Alton.

Margaret's scream cut above the gunshots as she vaulted onto the grandstand. She threw herself onto Eddie as John Morgan blocked the third assailant trying to climb onto the stage, kicking the man in the face, and Jack pulled him down. The crowd screamed and babies wailed as acrid blue smoke rose over the confused scene. There were cries of "No!" and "Stop! Stop this."

Pandemonium ruled. The sound of the guns' discharges echoed through the park. Eddie sank into Margaret's arms, and his grandfather bent over both of them. Jacob joined John Morgan on the grandstand, sheltering his family. In front of the bandstand, the assailants still scuffled with members of the human shield, arms flailing and curses flying as Ben Acree, Jack Carlson, and Bill Alton rolled with them in the grass. The sheriff and his deputy rushed through the crowd to the grandstand. They confiscated the guns and removed the shell from the only gun that had not been discharged. Ben forced Charlie's stepfather's arms behind his back. Cassie was still hanging on his ankle, and he loudly cursed her. Jessa ducked his flailing arms to get to Cassie, praising her but finally getting her to release her grip. The sheriff and deputy took over, and soon all three attackers were lined up by their captors.

Pungent smoke still hung in the air when John stepped to the front of the bandstand and motioned to the audience to sit down. It was quite a while before the din died down, but his commanding presence eventually held sway over the panicked audience.

"Ladies and gentlemen, the situation is under control. This concert is going to continue!" John pointed to the intruders. "*You* are going to listen. Sheriff, bring them up here. I want them to sit right here in front. When this concert is over, the law will deal with them!"

As the three men were dragged in front of the grandstand, John again turned his attention to the audience. "Everyone, please be seated. We'll get out of the way and let the musicians complete their performance! I want to hear the Paganini!" He led Margaret and Jacob down the steps at the back of the grandstand, where they stood together at the side. The three attackers were forced to sit in a row in front of the musicians, with their captors seated right behind them.

Eddie looked uncertainly at Grampa Rayburn, who grinned as he lifted his instrument from its case. "The show must go on! Eddie, introduce the Paganini again."

Eddie stepped to the front of the grandstand. At one side, he could see his mother being comforted by his father. Jessa and Michael were holding Cassie tightly. He loved that dog! He made the announcement, tucked the violin under his chin, raised his bow, and nodded to his grandfather, who counted a measure barely audibly, and they began to play. The theme began timorously, but as he relaxed, Eddie's command of the lively piece prevailed. Mr. Rayburn accompanied him with a background drawn from the piano score. When it was over, the performers bowed.

The applause was an opportunity for the audience to let off pent-up emotions, and it went on and on. During the extended applause, Fran stood. "Please, as an encore, would you please play 'The Tennessee Waltz'?"

It was Eddie's turn to grin at his grandfather. This had been their ace-in-the-hole—a favorite piece reserved to perform if they got a request. They'd worked out a duet version, with Mr. Rayburn doing a rich background and then switching to play an octave above as Eddie played the melody. It was a smashing success. Again, the audience applauded hard and long.

All this time, Jessa had been waiting for her chance. She climbed the steps onto the grandstand on trembling legs. She looked at the performers and then out at the sea of familiar faces. She found her voice: "I'm so thankful no one was injured. I'm grateful to Eddie Wilson and his grandfather, Mr. Rayburn, for sharing their love of music. Eddie and his grandfather have only been playing violin together since last November. I think everyone can appreciate what an accomplishment this is. They show us all how much music can add to everyone's lives."

She continued, "Here in Radford, music can enrich our lives in many ways. Probably most of you heard the combined choir sing, at least up until the performance was interrupted..." Jessa paused, and there were a few *booooo*'s from the audience.

"I want us to have many more opportunities to sing and listen to music together. Mr. Alton has been teaching music in the white schools for three years now, but we still need to add music to the colored school curriculum. For that good cause, I'm asking you to please contribute to a fund for Overbrook. To start that process, we will be passing collection plates tonight." Jessa nodded to April, Michael, and Jeff, who stood and held up the plates. "And if you want to donate but didn't bring money today," Jessa continued, "the box for donations will be located at the sheriff's office." Jessa made this last point up on the spot and hoped it would be okay. "Oh, yes—just so you know, one of the community leaders has generously offered to match any money you donate. Thank you all for your support of music in Radford."

There was another round of applause as April, Michael, and Jeff began to pass the platters.

Mr. Wexler had been standing by the gazebo, and now he mounted the stairs and faced the audience. "Everyone, I am here as a resident of Radford and also as a representative of the school board. I have an important announcement to make. Miss Jessamine Olsen approached the school board earlier in the summer with a proposal for adding music to the Overbrook curriculum, but at that time, as reported in the *Post*, our budget couldn't cover the expense. Apparently, her idea gained traction among the Negro population of Radford, and they collected money to underwrite the purchase of instruments and music to initiate music instruction as an afterschool program at the AME Church, staffed by volunteers from the community. As I'm sure you all know, there is a rich musical tradition in the colored community, as evidenced by the choir performance and today's exceptional music. I want to welcome Reverend James here so you can acknowledge the support from the colored community. It is my pleasure to announce that in the time since the school board had to turn Jessamine Olsen down about hiring a teacher for Overbrook, the community service performed by the young men who interrupted the choir performance saved us from having to pay for the repairs from our own funds. That, including the outpouring of support from the colored community, has generated sufficient funds to allow us to hire a part-time teacher, and we have offered the job to Mr. Rayburn."

Clapping began at the rear, and soon applause spread throughout the audience. Reverend James, Mr. Wexler, and Mr. Rayburn acknowledged the crowd's approval.

Wexler continued, "Your contributions will be greatly appreciated, as we are counting on your additional support to accomplish this. Mr. Alton, will you join us here on the stage?"

Bill Alton climbed onto the platform, to more applause.

"Hello, everyone. Thank you for coming to the summer music program. I just want to say I've loved getting together with you all on these summer evenings and working with the young people of Radford. I also appreciate the strong support of their families. I'm sure the future of music in Radford is bright, and I want to credit Jessamine Olsen's father, Paul Olsen. I valued his friendship, and as many of you know, he was a member of the school board who worked very hard to get music in the schools." He held out his arm. "Jessa, come here." He welcomed Jessa to the line-up, and she held out her hand and drew Eddie to the front. She managed to smile through her tears.

· · · · ·

Ted's assistant from the *Radford Post* toted a large camera and tripod to the front to get pictures of the three assailants sitting on the ground and the group of men on the bandstand with Jessa. The deputy then produced three sets of handcuffs, and he, Don, and the fire chief began handcuffing the men. Charlie's stepfather staggered along, cursing and limping, so the sheriff pulled up his pant leg to examine the bites Cassie had sunk into his ankle.

"Jessa, these are deep bite marks. I hope your dog has had her rabies shots," said the sheriff.

"Yes, sir, and she's wearing her tags," assured Jessa.

"Good."

"So no one was hurt by the gunshots?" asked Ted.

"Nobody was hurt—this one," the sheriff indicated the shotgun with its barrel busted, "discharged into the ground. I think the pellets of the other one must have landed over in the playground, so nobody was affected."

Charlie's stepfather leered at Eddie and Mr. Rayburn as they joined Margaret and Jacob. He sneered, "Stinkin' coons! All ya'll oughta get out of town!"

John made a move to hit him, but the sheriff stopped him. "Gotta let the law take over now, John. Lead him off."

Jacob leaned against the platform, covering his face, as the sheriff and his deputies led the three men away.

Jack's white shirt was streaked with grass stains and blood. He joined Eddie's family beside the gazebo, shook hands with Reverend James, and said, "Jacob, Margaret, I'm so very sorry this happened!" He addressed the musicians. "Eddie, Mr. Rayburn, the music was wonderful, and the news about your appointment is, too."

Ted and his assistant pushed in to get statements and pose the musicians with their fiddles for photographs. Ted said, "Jessamine, bring that dog here." Cassie approached Eddie eagerly, and the assistant took a picture of Cassie with Eddie, for which she obligingly licked Eddie's face. "Seems like that dog knew what was going on—had you met her before, Eddie?"

"Cassie's my friend," Eddie said, stroking her. "She went camping with us."

"Us?" asked Ted.

"Me and Michael, we took her with us camping."

Jessa said, "Eddie, I'm so glad you weren't hurt. You played beautifully! Mr. Rayburn, I wish my parents could have heard the two of you! And, Mr. Morgan, you saved the day. It was wonderful the way you pulled everything back together!"

Reverend James' son escorted his wife up, Ray Marshall joined them, and Aunt Helen arrived carrying Sarah. Sarah's face was streaked with tears. "Eddie, Eddie," she said, holding out her arms as she was lifted down so that her brother and grandfather could hug her. Helen went to Margaret, who was talking with the minister.

Helen gave Margaret a hug. "Honey, I know how you feel."

Margaret was saying to the minister, "You were right, Brother James. This time we were lucky, but I know now that you were right. I should have listened! It was pride, that's what it was. Pride comes before a fall!"

Fran approached the family. "Margaret, I'm so sorry this happened. The music was wonderful, and there's so much to be proud of!" said Fran.

"Thank you, ma'am," Eddie said, but Margaret moved away and pointedly turned her back when Fran and Karen proposed that they all go to Jessa's house for chocolate-dipped ice cream popsicles. Eddie begged, but Margaret adamantly refused. "We need to get home to our own place. We've had enough of being on display for white people!" Mr. Rayburn shrugged at Jacob, who stood near Margaret. When Fran moved again to touch her, Margaret shifted away. "Guess it was my mistake, to think the races could get along."

"No," wailed Jessa, watching the interaction. "It wasn't a mistake!" She approached the two women. "The races *can* get along. It's just some people that haven't figured it out yet!"

Margaret wheeled around to face Jessa. "Aren't you the smart one! Going to fix things up for us just great, are you? Meddling in other people's lives! Just look what you've done!"

Jessa crumpled onto the ground as the family moved away. "Why, why does everything always go badly?" she sobbed. "I *so* wanted this to be wonderful. I wanted people to see how good it could be!"

Back at the picnic blanket, Jeff and Michael were counting the money. They had twenty-seven dollars in bills and a whole lot of change. "Pretty good haul on such short notice," said Ben.

Jessa hardly acknowledged them. Margaret's searing admonishment echoed in her ears. She kept replaying the scene she had witnessed: Margaret hovering around her father and Eddie and pointedly turning her back on Fran.

They packed up and set out for home. Cassie walked beside Jessa, frequently nudging her, trying to elicit a response, but Jessa was lost in thought. She wished for the thousandth time for the guidance of her parents. She knew Daddy and Mommie would have been pleased with the music—surely they were looking down from Heaven! And the plan for Overbrook had worked out, after all. But the good music, which everyone was enjoying, had failed to bring everyone together. She should be happy because the plan for getting music at Overbrook would go forward, but Margaret—beautiful Margaret—had turned against her, and the bridges she believed could be crossed had become threats to those who ventured to cross them. Her heart ached for Fran, who was crying when Jack led her away.

Michael said, "Jessa, I know Eddie really wanted the ice cream. This is rock bottom."

April said, "It's a shame! We'd planned such a nice party."

Karen and Ben walked along silently. Finally, Karen said, "We should be thankful it wasn't worse. A shotgun at close range could easily have killed someone. I don't think anything like that was intended, but accidents happen—with loaded guns. What a tragedy *that* would have been! When I could see that nobody on the platform had been hit, I worried for *Cassie* because she was right there in front of the platform, and with all that smoke, I couldn't see her."

Michael said, "I saw the sheriff confiscate all the guns. That one that went off next to Cassie was busted apart at the end of the barrel. Whoever owns them is going to have to deal with him—that's what the sheriff said!"

"What about the music?" burst out Jessa. "Music was supposed to draw people together! Music was supposed to heal! Mr. Morgan made them listen, but did you hear what that guy said to Jacob?"

"Aw, come on, Jessa—it's a percentage thing. Some of the audience was on your side," said Michael.

"I think people were angry. Those guys were acting alone, and lots of people disapproved," said April.

"They didn't like it because it offended them," said Ben dryly. "Their delicate Southern psyches..."

"It was inconvenient for the audience, but potentially deadly for the musicians," said Karen.

"Oh, it's horrible! Did you see Eddie's mother? She wouldn't let Mrs. Carlson touch her—wouldn't have anything to do with anyone who's white. She told me I shouldn't get involved in other people's lives."

"There were warning signs, Jessa, and Florence tried to get me to discourage you, but I knew how much it meant to you. I bear some of the responsibility," said Karen.

"I'm afraid this will force the town to go back to strict segregation as the safest course," said Ben.

"Eddie really wanted the ice cream, but it was his mother who wouldn't go along with it," repeated Michael.

"I'm afraid she's given up on trusting whites—all of us," said Jessa.

Karen said, "Jessa, it did put Eddie and his grandfather in jeopardy, and it was partly to serve your own goals. You need to accept that this was exploitation, however good your intentions. These wounds will take time to heal."

Jessa scrunched up her shoulders and grimaced. "I wanted so much to carry on for Daddy! At least I thought that was what I was trying to do, but I bet he wouldn't have pushed people the way I did. I keep messing things up, starting with Jacob and now Margaret and Eddie. I want to leave—we might as well leave tomorrow! All I can do is make trouble, and nothing's going to change here—ever!"

"But didn't you hear about the music program plans?" asked Michael. "Mr. Rayburn seemed pleased by that."

"But what about Margaret?" asked Jessa. "She's rejecting everyone, and Mrs. Carlson's torn up about it."

"Give her time," said Ben.

· CHAPTER 41 ·

Jessa, April, and Michael went to the sheriff's headquarters to get the donation money. Jessa had decided to turn the money over to Mr. Wexler, as she had done immediately with the funds gathered at the concert. She didn't want to face Mr. Jamison or that horrible Mrs. Brians again.

"I'll organize the coins and you count the dollars," said Michael. They poured the box's contents out on Florence's desktop and had to chase a few nickels and pennies that rolled under the desk and across the floor, but Michael was soon making stacks of dimes and quarters to go into the sleeves they'd gotten at the bank while April and Jessa unfolded bills and laid them in stacks. There was a lot more money than had been collected at the park.

"That money came from the whole community," said Florence. "People came in here who had never set foot in the sheriff's office before. Came asking for the donation box for music. I had the impression the kids who are studying music with Mr. Alton were behind some of it."

Jessa sighed. "I see now how stupid I was. It's impossible for me to collect enough money."

Michael butted in. "What I keep trying to tell you is that this phony separate-but-equal business is not going to last. It's the law of the land for schools to be desegregated, and I can't understand why Tennessee thinks it can be different."

Florence gazed at Michael. "Good for you, Michael. I predict you're going to do great things in your life—you and your friend Eddie Wilson. We need more of that spirit here in Radford! And, Jessa, I think we're already seeing changes. Maybe, with Mr. Alton staying around and keeping up Music in the Park, more and more people will come around to a more generous way of thinking."

"But to not have music in the colored school is downright wrong, and it's totally unfair!" said Jessa. "I thought it would be so easy. All I would have to do was explain that music belongs with education. For some kids, it might be the most important part, the reason for sticking around for all the other parts—like having a good dessert to look forward to."

"We have a grand total of eighty-six dollars and sixty-five cents," Michael announced. "I think that's pretty good."

"That's more than I expected would be in that box, and I've been watching people come in to add what they could—mothers brought their children to put their allowance in," said Florence. "Let me see if I can't make one last donation for the good cause." She pulled up her heavy purse and took out a dollar bill. That will bring the grand total to eighty-seven dollars and sixty-five cents. It's like counting backwards. I like numbers that are consecutive!"

"Thank you, Mrs. Florence," said Jessa. "And thanks for putting the box out and keeping it here. This adds to what we collected at the park and the other funds that Mr. Wexler has. The school board will be able to add this to support Mr. Rayburn's appointment—and don't forget, Mr. Wexler will match it."

· CHAPTER 42 ·

It was time to get excited about the start of the school year. The Acrees had scheduled train reservations so that they would have a week to settle in before they all plunged into the new school year in Portland. As the time in Radford drew to a close, Jessa felt sad to leave her Radford friends, and unhappy that she couldn't look forward to seeing Janie when she got back to Portland. Still, the start of school was always exciting. She consoled herself that Radford was going to be better off now that Mr. Rayburn was working with Mr. Alton. Cassie leaned against her as she sat on the top step of the porch.

"We made mistakes, but our hearts were in the right place, is what Grandma would have said," she told Cassie as a tear rolled onto the dog's furry head.

Jessa thought about the wink that Merrybelle had given her and got the warm feeling all over again. Then she thought of the way Margaret had rejected Fran Carlson, and she grimaced. "I do believe in friendships," she whispered to Cassie.

· · · · ·

Karen phoned Helen Wilson. "The Carlsons are planning a going-away party at their home this coming Wednesday evening, Helen, and I hope you are free to come. We want to invite all the people who are close to Jessa. I wondered if you could help me with approaching Margaret and Jacob and their family?" She listened… "Yes, I know, but Margaret has been stonewalling Fran. It won't be the same if they don't attend. Margaret's feelings are perfectly understandable, and I know it may not come off, but we'd really appreciate it if you could talk with her. The party won't be the same if she and the family aren't there."

Helen said Margaret had been generally unapproachable. She blamed herself for allowing her family to be targeted and had withdrawn into a shell. However, Helen agreed it would be a shame to keep Eddie from a party, so she'd try to reason with her.

The plans moved forward, including invitations to Jessa's school friends and their families, John, the Wexlers and Reverend James and his wife and Merrybelle and Rachel and their families. Tables and folding chairs were borrowed from the Methodist church. Fran oversaw all the arrangements, all the while carrying a nagging thought that they had heard nothing from Margaret and Jacob…

When the Carlson lawn began to accumulate signs of the impending celebration, Gladys Blakeley began to watch. Rachel had requested her day off, and given no reason, so Gladys had no one to ask about what was going on. As she watched, her curiosity grew. *Now what could those Carlsons be planning? I know—it must be that the Northerners are leaving! Good riddance!* She began making phone calls and finally chased down the information she sought. "Well, if it takes a shindig to get them out of here, so be it!" Satisfied, she went back to her soap operas.

After dinner, Gladys watched as guests began to arrive. There was quite a variety of vehicles. The Wexler's Chrysler pulled up, followed by Reverend James and his wife. Ray Marshall and his wife and family joined the assembled party, the Altons and the sheriff and his wife arrived, and then, dressed in their best, were Merrybelle and Rachel and their families!

Watching from her window, Gladys' heart was pounding so hard she felt faint. Her voice stuck in her throat as she called her husband away from the TV. "Harold...Harold, I just don't believe my eyes! Look what's going on over there!"

"Is it a wedding reception?" asked Harold.

"Look, just look at the *people,* Harold! There's a mixing of races, the likes of which I've never seen! Can you believe it?"

"If you hadn't broke off with Fran Carlson, we probably would have been invited, Gladys. We used to be closer to the Carlsons. I don't know what happened..."

"But, Harold, what does it mean for property values?"

"I don't see how one mixed-race yard party is going to cut into property values, Gladys."

"Well, *I* care about propriety, Harold! Those maids are prancing around like royalty!"

The chamber musicians were setting up their stands and tuning their instruments.

"Looks to me like they're going to have a good time over there," said Harold.

"Oh, Harold, you're no help," said Gladys.

Aunt Helen pulled up next. Florence met her at the truck and took the cake so Helen could carry a creamy mixture for one of the ice cream makers. They walked to the dessert table together, conversing in an animated manner.

Jessa and April had been put in charge of the churning of the ice cream, so they had recruited help. Michael and his father and April were each assigned one of the churns. It was easy at first but addition of salt and ice by Jessa was needed as the churning progressed. Jessa glanced over at Fran, who was covering the dessert table with a cloth and bouquet of flowers. As she smoothed the cloth, she looked anxiously at the arriving guests, scanning the parking cars for Jacob's truck. Jessa knew what she was thinking, and squeezed her eyes shut tightly as she repeatedly murmured, "I hope, I hope, I hope…"

The observations from the neighboring house continued:

"Harold, this is the living end!" said Gladys.

"Gladys, you're just miffed because you weren't invited," said Harold.

Soon, the student musicians began playing.

"Look, Harold, can you believe it? Dave Wexler's daughter's one of the musicians!"

"There's something the matter with that?"

"This is a scene from Hell!"

"I'll take that as a good sign."

The last vehicle to arrive was Jacob's black truck. Eddie bounded out, followed by Sarah and Margaret. Jacob took his wife's hand, and they walked up the long green lawn to join the festivities. When Fran saw them, tears filled her eyes. She'd almost given up hope when there'd been no news from Helen. She took off running down the lawn, and Jacob stepped aside as Fran fell into Margaret's arms. Jessa and April watched from the porch, where they were churning ice cream; Gladys was now watching from her doorway.

"I don't believe it," said April.

"Oh, it's wonderful! *Wishes do come true!*" said Jessa.